False

Magic

J M Brown

ISBN-10: 0983870519
ISBN-13: 978-0-9838705-1-7
Cover art by Spittfish Designs: http://spittyfish.wordpress.com/

graMix publishing
http://www.gramix.com

DEDICATION

Tina Andriamamenosoa.

Tamiko Moore.

Teresa Smith.

Karen Zhang.

And always, to H.T.T.M.

Also in respectful memory of Michael Stern Hart (March 8, 1947 - September 6, 2011), inventor of the eBook and founder of Project Gutenberg.

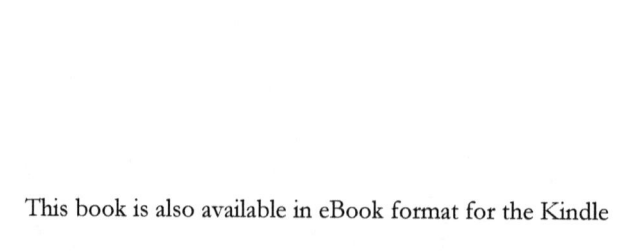
This book is also available in eBook format for the Kindle

CONTENTS

graMix Publications
2

ACKNOWLEDGMENTS

I gratefully acknowledge the many helpful critiques from my generous beta-readers:

Karen Bradwell

Tim B. and Kris M.

Clayton Fan

Ally Medvec

Teresa Moore

Kate S.

Jennifer Sutton

Also in grateful recognition of the support and friendship of:

C. Dimmick

Brian Ampolsk

1 AMOR OMNES, FIDE NEMO
BRENDA

"There is not nearly enough love in this world, but there is far too much trust."

I was just a little girl when my daddy told me that.

"Whenever someone asks you to trust them, they're either a used car salesman, a politician, or some other kind of con man," he said.

"Most people say that you can't have love without trust, but that is wrong, and I'll tell you why.

"I used to have a dog named Ralph, a beautiful golden-haired shepherd-collie mix, and he was my best friend for many years. I loved him. But he got older, and he got sick. He developed arthritis in his hip and couldn't run or jump like he used to. When he would lift his leg to pee, he would sometimes fall over because it hurt too much to keep his leg lifted. He would look embarrassed when he'd lose his balance like that. Some people say that dogs don't have the same feelings that humans do, but if you've ever lived with a dog, and looked him in the eye, you'd know that's wrong too. He got worse. Near the end, he hurt all the time, and sometimes he cried, or seemed to. The vet couldn't do anything for him. I couldn't do anything for him. I couldn't even explain to him why I couldn't make him better. His last night, I fixed him a big steak for dinner and sat with him while he chewed the bone, eventually crushing it in his jaws. I slept on the floor next to him that night. In the morning, we went for our last ride in the car together, down to the animal shelter.

"He must have sensed something was wrong when we entered the little room in the back because he growled at the vet. The vet had a rope with a noose on one end. He slipped this around Ralph's neck, and wound the slack of the rope around his snout a couple of times. 'They bite, sometimes,' the vet

1

said. I could tell Ralph was frightened, so, against the vet's advice, I removed the rope, and lifted the Ralph onto the table myself, laid him down and held him. With hair clippers, the vet shaved a patch of fur from his foreleg to expose the vein. Ralph struggled a little bit at that but I calmed him and held him tighter. 'Don't let him bite you,' the vet reminded me.

"I put my hand over his snout. I knew he could easily bite me, and I knew how strong his jaws were, but my hand was better than the noose. Now, the question is, did I trust him not to bite me?"

That was just what I was wondering too.

"No. I didn't 'trust' him. He was a dog. It would be natural for him to bite when he felt the sting of the needle. I *expected* him to bite me.

"*Let him bite*, I thought. If biting my hand made him feel easier then let him bite it clean off. He was my friend. I loved him."

My dad paused his story there.

"So, daddy," I asked, "did he bite you?"

Dad smiled and looked me straight in the eye. "What do you think, Brenda?" he asked.

"The vet eased the needle into the vein and pushed the plunger in slowly. The prick of the needle startled Ralph, but he relaxed in my arms right away, and slumped down. He blinked once, and then closed his eyes. I could feel all his muscles relax more and more until he was completely limp. It took less than ten seconds. I was a grown man by then, but when I got back in my car, I cried like a little boy.

"No, Ralph didn't bite me. Of course he didn't. He was my friend, but I was his friend too. He trusted me."

I've never forgotten my dad's story. There is nothing simple about simple friendship.

Today, everyone thinks I am such a nice person, but really, I'm not.

I am someone who never forgives an injury or forgets a slight. I know this is probably a character flaw, but in my defense, I never forget a kindness either. And while I may not repay every injury done to me, I always repay every kindness.

I believe children feel things much more intensely than adults. For a little kid, every small misfortune is an inconsolable tragedy.

I was in first grade, and somehow, I had lost the lunch my dad had packed. I probably left it on the school bus. Everyone else had their lunch, but I was empty-handed. I was ashamed that I'd lost it, and I was feeling alone and abandoned. My stomach was growling and I remember the tightness in my chest, my face hot with embarrassment, and the moistness in the corner of my eyes. But just before I burst out sobbing, Amy put her hand on my shoulder and said, "It's ok, Brenda. We can share my lunch! You like peanut butter! We have a cookie, too!"

She gave me half her peanut butter and jelly sandwich, half of the slices of the orange her mom had peeled and packed for her, and broke her cookie in half, giving me the bigger half. We shared the same straw in her juice-box.

We'd been casual friends in pre-school and kindergarten, but for the first time, I understood what it was like to have someone I could count on, a real friend. Nothing in the years since has convinced me otherwise. I know this doesn't sound like a big deal. Amy just shared what she had because she thought it was the right thing to do. It was just one lunch box. I'm sure it didn't mean anything to her at the time. But to a six year old Brenda on the verge of bitter tears, it meant absolutely everything. None of my other friends offered to share; Amy was my life-saver when I needed one.

Amy would never do anything to hurt me.

The cookie was oatmeal-raisin.

2. LOST
AMY

I was looking all over for Brenda.

Of all the things I hated about this school, the uniforms were at the top of my list. White blouse and stupid striped school tie under a dark blazer with a plaid skirt and long socks that made me look like some cloyingly cute Japanese schoolgirl with a blonde wig in some kind of teen porn movie... Well, at least my skirt was a little longer. By early September there was already a fall nip in the air and if the winters in Baltimore were anything like the winters back home in St. Louis... I was dreading the wind swirling up under the outfit. At least Catonsville was a boarding school, so I wouldn't have to appear in public wearing the damn thing.

Still, nobody else was complaining. It wouldn't do to whine too much. My folks had sacrificed a lot to get me in the same school as Brenda, and it really was a good school. Or so they said. Brenda had her heart set on Catonsville for years, it seemed, and she had made it a part of our Plan. We'd been here most of the summer already, since as new students, we had to start near the end of July. The skirt was not too bad when it was hot, but...

I still hadn't decided if the fact that there were no boys was a good thing or not. They might be jerks most of the time but not having them around at all was just plain weird, and getting weirder as the weeks passed by.

Brenda's aunt was supposed to come pick us up to stay with her for the weekend, and maybe take us shopping, so I was looking all over campus for her. That was another thing that was embarrassing. Neither Brenda's family nor mine had ever had much money, and even now, we were both on tight allowances, but after every visit with Aunt Diane, we would find twenty bucks or so had magically appeared in our purse or pocket. Brenda's aunt was a big-name doctor at Johns Hopkins and she and her husband didn't have kids of their own, so they were always spoiling us.

I crossed the quad to the library, passing a couple of seniors with their luggage, moving in. They looked so much older to me. Seniors had a dress code, but except for special events, they didn't have to wear the uniforms. They smiled at me as they passed. Probably laughing at my silly skirt.

Bitches.

The school library worked on the honor system - we scanned our card and books ourselves and did our own checkout. Brenda said this was more about the school saving money on a librarian's salary than it was about demonstrating trust in the students. Brenda had said she planned to stop here, but I didn't see her, so I sat down across from Cleo to wait. She gave me a smile and returned to her reading. The words on the spine of her book were "Malleus Maleficarum."

Catonsville International Academy made all the girls work as part of the curriculum. Brenda and I didn't know any better when we arrived, and we got stuck in the laundry room two evenings a week, but Cleo worked as the library aide. She was there nearly any time she wasn't in class, and seemed to know the library even better than Professor Ross, our English teacher. Everybody knew that Cleo was our go-to girl whenever we wanted to find anything, whether it was a book or something on the web. Since I was trying to find my BFF, I asked her.

"Have you seen Brenda?"

Cleo looked up and smiled again. "She was sitting in your chair two minutes ago, waiting for you. She went to go pee. She'll be back in another minute."

I looked around. The library was empty except for the two of us and a couple of older girls, surfing on their tablets at the far end of the room. I took a deep breath.

"Cleo, can I ask you something?"

"Sure, Amy," her voice dropped to a fake conspiratorial whisper, "sounds serious."

"Well," I said, "I guess. I worry about Brenda a little. If she is really comfortable here."

"Is this about race?" It was a little scary how quick Cleo was to catch on. I nodded. "Do you mind me asking you?"

"No, Amy, not at all. But you and Brenda have been buddies since pre-school. Why can't you talk to her directly?"

"I *did* ask her. She says I'm being silly, but I'm not sure she's being honest with me, or with herself, maybe."

"And you think that because Brenda and I are both black, she might be more forthright with me?" Cleo's face adopted an expression of indignation. I knew she was just teasing me, but my ears burned all the same. I took another deep breath.

"All through grade school," I said, "since at least first grade, I was the minority, one of the few white girls. Lots of times, I was the only white kid. I was fine with that. It's the way school has always been. It's always seemed normal to me. But when I got here, it was just plain freaky to be surrounded by all these other white faces, and I found myself looking around for the normal dark faces, and they're missing, and it's been very... discomforting for me. Now I'm thinking the shock must be greater for her. Am I crazy?"

"Crazy? Well, maybe not for that reason." Cleo chuckled. "Look, I can tell you not to worry about it, but I know you will. I've watched the two of you together. Your bond is stronger than that of most lovers."

She held up her hand to ward off any protest before continuing. "I know you're both straight. We often say people are 'just' friends, adding the 'just' as if to indicate a kind of love that is somehow 'less'. It's not. True friendship isn't anything 'less'. It can be as fundamental as that of a mother for her child, as fierce as that between a boy and his dog, as powerful as the romance between true lovers, as solid as the bond between soldiers in combat, or as strong as any other kind of love."

Sometimes, when Cleo was serious, she seemed much older than the sixteen years she claimed.

"You may not have noticed it at the time," Cleo continued, "but your bond was one of the things that sustained you both back when you were the freakish color. Now, it can be one of the things to help sustain her, not that I think she needs it. You needn't and really shouldn't do anything different. Just continue being her friend and the rest will take care of itself. Besides; Brenda's cute, she's smart, and she's tough. That, and a little bit of luck, is all that a woman needs to make it in this world. Don't worry about her."

3. INQUISITION
BRENDA

My three inquisitors frowned at me from behind the big desk while I sat alone in the chair in the middle of the room. Their faces told me my fate had already been sealed.

For a moment, I wished Amy was beside me, but I dismissed that idea right away. I sure didn't want her mixed up in this. It was all over for me now, but at least, maybe I could keep Amy out of it.

It had been a long school year and I was weary. My mouth was dry and my heart beat slow and heavy. I wanted to close my eyes and sleep.

I thought back to how excited Amy and I had both been when we started at this school last summer, nearly a year ago now. We'd been through a lot since then. It was already May, with the end of the school year only two weeks away.

We'd had high hopes. We knew we'd be challenged academically like never before, but we were both fine with that. "Only the hard things are worthwhile," my dad used to say. Amy and I had each other and we had The Plan, and for the first time, we had the chance to measure ourselves against some really smart girls. We had our fears, of course, but we thought we had the confidence to match those. I guess I'd misjudged what the challenges would be and how big the obstacles.

A year of hard work, the toughest year of my life, and now, all down the crapper. I'd worked so hard. I'd come so close.

Catonsville was the finest high school in the country, or at least the finest girl's school, and certainly the toughest. My grades had been good, and despite what everyone now thought, my conduct impeccable, but none of that mattered now. We all make plans, but I guess the universe has its own plan and doesn't care about ours. This school had been my dream, but now the universe was slapping me awake.

This crap was going to break my mom's heart. Chuck and Di's too. I wondered if anyone would even believe my side of the story. Not that the truth matters much in this world.

I could feel the rage building inside me. No one was listening to me, and no one cared that I was being treated unfairly.

Any temptation to lie down and take it evaporated right then. If they were going to burn me, I wouldn't make it easy for them. I was tired, but I was going to fight.

The door opened up behind me.

4. NINTH CIRCLE
AMY

"The Way of the Warrior has been misunderstood. It is not a means to kill and destroy others. Those who seek to compete and better one another are making a terrible mistake. To smash, injure, or destroy is the worst thing a human being can do. The real Way of a Warrior is to prevent such slaughter - it is the Art of Peace, the power of love." - Osensei Morihei Ueshiba, Kaiso Aikido

Brenda's parents and mine talked about us a lot. I think it was in the summer just before third grade that they presented us with a choice. They wanted us to take up some after-school activity.

Our moms wanted us to take up ballet, their heads no doubt filled with images of us prancing around in precious pink tutus, but our dads were more practical. They suggested we take Tae Kwon Do at the community center. The picture of us in pink tutus filled Brenda and I with absolute horror, and since Brenda could always be counted on to agree with her dad, we chose to break our mother's hearts instead.

So, our dads signed us up, but for Aikido instead of Tae Kwon Do. I think Harvey was convinced of this when he learned that Aikido had been founded by a pacifist.

Within the heart of each of one of us is a reservoir of rage, added to by each injury or injustice we suffer in life. I think my own reservoir is more like a shallow pool that bubbles up and vents a little steam from time to time. But Brenda's reservoir is more like a deep ocean of molten magma, which, if ever released, could consume the world. And while I may vent a little, I have never known Brenda to unleash her anger, except maybe that one time.

I also believe that these reservoirs are not fed by the hurts and injustices themselves, but by our sensitivity to them. Brenda has always been much more sensitive than I, and she has always had much better control. Only a very few have sensed the potential danger in her. When we went to Riverplace JHS, the gang leaders clearly sensed it, and gave her the proper respect and care in dealing with her. But most people are just blissfully ignorant of what lies behind Brenda's calm and sweet and smiling face.

I've often wondered if her dad had sensed it and if that was why he wanted her to study Aikido. Certainly, Aikido stressed restraint and peace, and it had to have benefited her. We stopped going in seventh grade, it was not part of The Plan, and that is when we both started studying in school with a real purpose. Her rage was an inexhaustible fire that fueled her to work with a fiendish passion that swept me up in her wake. So rage can be a valuable tool, if channeled properly.

We were half way through seventh grade when we started to think about college. I don't remember which of us thought about it first--probably Brenda, and probably *not* our parents. The idea grew on us gradually. We had no idea what it would cost except that it would probably be more than we could afford.

At the time, we didn't even realize that our families were poor.

I remember when we talked about it with one of our guidance counselors, he told us not to worry about it until we got into high school. If we graduated from high school, he told us, then maybe we could get into community college later.

He'd been completely useless.

Brenda and I both figured out that if we did get into college, we would have to do it on our own. Nobody was going to help us.

Seventh and eighth grades were good for us academically. We studied like demons, delighting a few of our teachers, confusing most, and astonishing all of them.

Brenda even started studying Chinese. Three evenings a week, after school, she would ride the bus all the way out to Laoshi Sun's house in Clayton for private lessons. She tried to talk me into joining her, but after the first two sessions, even though Mrs. Sun seemed nice, I decided it was way too hard for me. I wasn't even sure my folks could afford it. I'd just gotten a "C" in Introduction to Chemistry, and knew I had to put in extra effort to pull up my grades. So while she was busy learning how to write characters with a brush, I was trying to learn the difference between ionic and covalent bonds. There were many times when I thought Brenda had taken the easier path.

Ninth grade was hell.

Brenda's aunt wanted her to attend her old high school in Baltimore, but her mom wasn't ready to let go. It took a long time for Aunt Diane to convince Miz Sally that it would be best for Brenda's future, and it had taken just as long to convince my folks to let me go with her. By that time, it was too late to apply. Brenda had picked out Catonsville for us, but we kept that a secret from our folks for as long as we could, while we pretended to check out other schools in the Baltimore area.

So, we wound up going to public school near home for ninth grade. Somehow, we got transferred to Riverplace Junior High School. It was not too far from our homes, but the only part of it that was not in disrepair was the double chain link fencing topped with barbed wire that surrounded it. The gang presence was real, not just a bunch of juvenile gangster-wannabes like before. Armed security guards were posted at every entrance and they had even locked and chained the fire exits. Most of the security guards hung out on the roof, though, smoking dope all day, so we rarely saw them.

There is a line from Dante's inferno that says: "The road to Paradise begins in Hell." At Riverside, if Paradise existed, it was much too far away to see. But we had no illusions about where our high school education was beginning.

We figured out right away that we were probably screwed, but there weren't any realistic options, so we just stuck together and to The Plan tighter than ever. It wasn't just the school facilities that were run down. The teachers and students were united in their goal of just marking time; the other parents were either angry and critical or simply uninvolved.

The administration's only interest in learning was how to prevent it from happening.

Getting good grades should have been easy, but unexpectedly, it was some of the teachers who decided we needed to be taken down a peg and gave us poor grades out of some kind of spite. Brenda played this game better than I did, and she still pulled straight "A's". I counted myself lucky to get no "C's" and a few "A's".

We went out of our way to befriend the leaders of the girl gangs. I helped out by assisting part time in the front office, and made sure to pass on any rumors about shakedowns to the right people, and to see that some truancy reports and disciplinary paperwork somehow got misplaced. Brenda and I both acted tough but we were careful not to participate in any illegal activity, or take sides or look down on anyone. She had an attitude that signaled to everyone that while she would help anybody, she was not to be messed with. My association with her extended that coverage to me and to the handful of other students who really did want to learn what they could.

Four years of Aikido, and our willingness to share what we knew didn't hurt. We sort of gathered up our own tiny gang of studious kids and after a few initial problems, soon had the other gangs guaranteeing our safety.

When we graduated junior high in May, even a couple of the girl gang leaders hugged us and cried to see us leave.

All this while, we were working out our strategy for Baltimore, picking out schools (the one in particular) and sowing the seeds with our parents. Both our families got together for a graduation dinner where Brenda and I sprung our trap. We announced that we'd chosen a short list of schools in Baltimore where we would go. Brenda's aunt Diane had said she would be overjoyed to have us live with her and Charlie in their big house, and that she could almost guarantee us admission and scholarships to Bryn Mawr. But our first choice was Catonsville International Academy, and we laid it on thick praising its virtues. The kicker was when we pointed out how we'd worked together the last few years to pull up our grades, and it would be a shame and a risk to split us up now. We promised that if we could not get admitted to the same school together, and I couldn't get a full scholarship to pay for it, we'd drop the whole idea. My folks and Brenda's mom probably agreed because they figured the odds of us making it all happen in time were unlikely.

They really should have known us better by then.

5. BLOODY DRILL
AMY

Back in June, when we flew out to Baltimore, it was my first time on an airplane. Brenda had flown out a few times before to visit her aunt and uncle, so I had myself a guide through the airports. I'm sure I would have gotten lost and been even more freaked out by the groping at security without her beside me.

Chuck and Di had a big house near Johns Hopkins. They had fixed up one of their guest rooms for us. It was freshly painted, had brand new twin beds, separate new dressers for each of us, a desk big enough for two, and a private bath. They clearly planned to have us living with them, no matter what happened. I expected Brenda to complain about having to share the bedroom that used to be her own when she visited, but she didn't say anything about it.

The very next morning, Aunt Diane drove us out to Catonsville. We were both nervous. The admissions exam was supposed to be as hard as or harder than the college-entrance SAT.

Before we went into the room, Brenda and I huddled together in the hallway.

"You're smart, Amy," She told me. "You'll do fine."

I wasn't so sure, but I answered, "You're the smart one. But we've both studied hard for this. Even if we don't make it, your Aunt Di can get us into Bryn Mawr."

Brenda wrinkled her nose at that. She didn't want to go to the same school as her aunt. She had nothing against it, but she wanted to follow her own stars.

I was thinking about all the practice exams we'd taken back home and I was reminded about something I'd read about the Roman army: "Their drills are like bloodless battles, their battles are like bloody drills." I was about to mention this, but then we were called in, and I didn't get the chance. I kept thinking about it though. We'd done our drills, now we were going into battle, and our future lives really were on the line.

About half way through, my throat got really dry and I started coughing. I'd gone easy on the fluids that morning because I was afraid I'd have to pee

13

and that would be a distraction I didn't need. The math section was much harder than I expected, and math was usually my strength. English was my weakness, but that part seemed easy; much too easy, and that worried me a lot too. I barely managed to suppress the coughing and concentrate, and then the proctor called time.

I felt faint. I hadn't finished. I glanced over at Brenda at the far side of the room. She looked dazed and worn out.

"I didn't finish," I moaned.

The proctor lady gave me a warm smile. "Don't worry about that, dear," she said. "Nobody finishes. It is a four hour exam, but we give you less than three hours to complete it."

That sounded incredibly unfair to me.

Fifteen minutes later, I was called in for my interview.

The headmistress turned out to be the lady who had proctored the exam, Dr. Ruth Davis.

"Are you still worried about not finishing the test?"

"A little bit," I said. "I think I understand your strategy, but I'm not used to leaving something unfinished. I don't think I've ever not finished an exam."

"Everyone has that same complaint," she said. "All our applicants take the same test, and they are all given the same amount of time, and none of them ever finishes it. So, it's a fair test, but it comes as a shock to everyone when the time runs out."

"Yes, ma'am. I guess it was the shock that got to me for a moment."

"As I said, don't worry about it, Miss McDonald. May I call you Amy?"

"Yes, ma'am, 'Amy' is fine."

"We are usually rather formal around here, Amy. If you are admitted, your teachers will always call you 'Miss McDonald' rather than 'Amy' and expect you to call them, 'Dr. Ross, 'Dr. Kramer', or 'Ms. Dunham'. We will always speak to you respectfully, and expect you to do the same to us."

Dr. Davis leaned back in her chair before she continued: "But this is just an informal interview, and I want us to be relaxed."

"I understand," I said. "You don't rely on just our grades and the entrance exam and the application essay, you also want to know if we have a personality that will mesh well with the school."

She smiled at me. "I could not have put it better. I know you are smart enough, and your grades, at least for the last few years, may be good enough, but I don't know yet how well you and our school will fit together. That is obviously one reason for this interview. We usually don't hold the interviews the same day as the exam, but since you are visiting from out of town, I'm happy to schedule it this way."

I nodded my head.

"So," she said, "why are you interested in attending Catonsville International Academy. There are plenty of other good schools. Why us?"

I took a deep breath. I had anticipated this question, and rehearsed my answer. "Brenda and I did our homework. We drew up a list of the best High Schools in the country, and especially those in the Baltimore area. Our aunt, I mean, Brenda's aunt, lives in Baltimore, and that makes it easier to get our parent's approval, having a family member next door, so to speak. Aunt Diane is an alumnus of Bryn Mawr, and would like us to go there, but based on our own research, we think *this* school will help us the most in preparing for college, especially if we earn a good recommendation from Catonsville. As you say, there are plenty of good schools, but we believe Catonsville Academy is the best."

"Mm. You do realize that some of our young ladies started applying to their favorite colleges in their freshman year here? You would be entering as a sophomore. Have you chosen a college yet?"

"No, ma'am. We have not yet picked a college. We have a short list of possibilities, but are not ready to commit to any one of them. We know we're starting late and have major challenges ahead, but that does not scare us."

"Tell me about ninth grade."

I'd expected this question too, and I had my answer ready. "We feel that ninth grade could have prepared us better. We felt it necessary to do most of our studying outside the limited curriculum that was available to us. One of the things we did was download the various syllabi that you post on your website for freshmen so we could study those areas on our own."

"You've done a lot of studying on your own, haven't you?"

"Yes ma'am. We started working our way through the Great Books Program. Also, I recently finished all the theorems and proofs in Euclid, and Brenda has been studying Chinese for the past two and a half years with a private tutor. False modesty aside, I think we are well prepared to work successfully here."

The smallest of smiles twitched at the corner of her mouth, but I saw her suppress it right away.

"Tell me about seventh grade."

This is a question I should have anticipated, but hadn't. I knew I had to be careful not to mention The Plan, so I stayed quiet for as long as I could while I tried to come up with something. "Well, Dr. Davis," I told her, "I guess we just looked around at where we were going, and realized that we had to do better in school if we wanted to do better in life. We made a kind of resolution to work harder at our grades, and we've been able to follow through."

She nodded, slowly, as if she thought there was more to it than that, but she didn't ask a follow-up question, so that danger passed.

"Amy," she said, "you keep saying 'we' instead of 'I', as if you and Miss Dickens were a partnership. Tell me about that, please."

"We have been friends for almost our whole lives. We have similar goals and the same determination to succeed. We have worked together and pushed each other to do well. We're best friends, or business partners, I suppose, in the business of achievement, and that business has been good for us, at least the last few years."

"Amy, suppose we were to admit just one of you, and not the other. What then?"

"Respectfully, Dr. Davis, if you admit me but not Brenda, I would have to decline any offer of admission. Brenda and I have been successful because we have worked hard together. Aunt Diane has said she can get us both into Bryn Mawr, but Catonsville International Academy is definitely our first choice. We are a package deal, ma'am. Please don't take that as a slight against this school, but that is the truth of things."

She nodded again.

"Well," she said, "I always appreciate an honest answer. I've studied your application. I don't have any other questions for you at this time; do you have any for me?"

"No, ma'am," I replied. "I'll just add that we've studied your policies and code of conduct and I can assure you that we would have no trouble agreeing to comply with any part of them."

At the door, we shook hands, but before opening the door, I had to add one more thing.

"Dr. Davis," I said, "Brenda is more reserved and private than I am. There may be some questions she might decline to answer. Please don't be offended if that happens or think she is being disrespectful in any way. She was the driving force in wanting us to come here. Catonsville has been her dream for years. I said we were a package deal, but if you can only admit one of us, please admit her. I can make other arrangements for myself."

She raised her eyebrows at that. "You just told me you wouldn't come unless we admitted your friend. Are you now saying that she would come if we declined to admit you?"

"If it comes to that, I'll convince her to accept. As I said, ma'am, Catonsville is her dream. She will make you proud if you admit her."

I waited with Aunt Di in the lobby while Brenda had her interview. When she emerged, she looked as exhausted as I felt.

Aunt Di then took us to Lexington Market for lunch, but we just wandered around the food stalls, not talking much, neither of us feeling hungry. We knew not to expect an immediate answer from the Academy, but we still had the silly hope they would take one look at us and admit us right away. Of course that didn't happen.

The next day, Di took us to tour Bryn Mawr, but that only made us more depressed. She kept telling us how nice it was, how good it was, and she was probably right, the campus and library were beautiful, but we weren't in any mood to listen.

The day after that, Uncle Charlie was going to take us to the inner harbor to see the National Aquarium, but we just stayed home in front of the TV, watching old movies, eating burnt microwave popcorn, waiting for the phone to ring and feeling miserable.

The following day was a Monday, and we were hoping to hear how we did, but the day just dragged on and on with no word. We were about to sit down for an early dinner when the phone rang with the news. We were invited back for a meeting the next day, both of us. Aunt Diane was smiling when she hung up. "Dr. Davis said you both did well on the exam."

"So, did we get admitted?" We asked, almost in unison.

"We'll find out tomorrow," Aunt Di said. "But if they weren't going to admit you, I don't think she would have said you did 'very well' on that test."

We barely got any sleep and were up early.

Dr. Davis welcomed us into her office together to break the news to us. She peered at us over the rim of her glasses. "I am extremely impressed with how high you both scored on our entrance exam. As you discovered, it is not an easy one," she said. "I was not so pleased with your marks prior to seventh grade, however, and neither was the admissions committee. But, Miss Dickens has had straight A's for the last two years, and Miss McDonald has shown significant and steady improvement, which we value even more.

She continued. "Some of our students think this is a hard school, and it is. But it is not because we make it hard, it only seems that way. Your dramatic improvement in seventh, eighth and ninth grades suggests that you may already understand.

"Native intelligence won't lead to success. I've been teaching for a long time, and every year I'm less sure that above some minimal threshold anyone is more 'intelligent' than anyone else. I am absolutely certain that even if 'intelligence' is something real, it cannot be measured accurately. You will succeed here, and later in life, not because you are any smarter, but because you work harder. We will provide an environment that encourages you to work hard, but we will not push you. You must push yourselves. Your scholastic history suggests that you realized this on your own in seventh grade, at least intuitively, and then made the decision to apply yourselves. It was your recent good grades that persuaded us. We'll give you all the resources and guidance and encouragement you need to push yourselves further and farther, but it will, always, be entirely up to you."

She then handed us each a big envelope, and said: "I am pleased to offer you both admission to Catonsville International Academy. After reviewing your applications and knowing that the two of you insist on being a package deal, this includes contingent scholarship offers for you both as well. We think you have great potential. We don't want to lose you to one of our rivals." She nodded to Aunt Diane, a clear reference to Di's alma mater. "Welcome to your new school and your new home."

Brenda and I both qualified for full scholarships, but she failed the means test because she had that insurance money. However, the Academy had something they called an honorarium, for just such cases. She got listed as an academic scholarship student, and she got a token stipend every month for incidentals, same as me. But while I also got my tuition and room and board and most of my books for free, she had to pay for hers.

6. IMPRESSIONS
AMY

We'd sort of expected to be roomed together, but they split us up. The stated reason was to force us to mingle and make new friends. We were told that even twin sisters weren't allowed to room together. Still, our rooms were right across the hall from each other, so we'd still be able to borrow each other's stuff. My room had a Chinese calendar above the desk and a big poster of the town of Xian, China above one of the beds, so I guessed my roommate was Chinese. But there was no sign of her when I unpacked my suitcase. Brenda's roommate was also missing. We were thinking we might not see them until September when the regular classes started, which would give us each a private room until then.

We were sitting in Brenda's room looking at the schedules we'd been given when a freckle-faced girl with red hair and poked her head in and introduced herself. "Hi," she said. "You're both new. It's Brenda Angela Dickens and... Amy Josephine McDonald, right? I'm Ann Warren."

She quickly sorted out which of us was which and explained that our roommates were already on campus, having just started the day before. They were probably at dinner, which was served early on Sundays, and Ann had in fact been sent to fetch us.

"The dining hall is pretty empty right now," Ann told us. "They told me the total student body for all four grades is going to be a hundred eighty-six this year, and only about forty students are attending summer classes. A lot of them are spending the weekends with nearby friends and family."

I hadn't realized that a weekend off-campus was an option. Judging by the high walls and the guards at the gate, I'd already started thinking of the place as a well-manicured prison.

The dining hall held only little more than a dozen students seated at a few tables. Brenda spotted a couple of Asian girls sitting together and headed straight for them, leaving Ann and I trailing behind. Brenda seated herself across from them and introduced herself without any preliminaries. They seemed a little annoyed by the intrusion, but gave their names. Karen

(Qiǎojiě) Jin was the taller one, and Xuěyàn Jin was the shorter of the two. A little reluctantly, I joined them while Ann stalked off to a different table.

The Asian girls were about to resume their dessert when Brenda said something to them in Chinese. Their astonished expressions resembled what yours would be if your family dog pulled out a chair at Thanksgiving dinner, sat down, and asked you, in perfect English, to please pass the mashed potatoes. Brenda had to say another long sentence before the girls recovered from the shock. The tall one replied cautiously, but when Brenda again responded smoothly, the attitude of our table companions instantly became friendly and excited.

They tried to engage me, but their ching-chong-ding-dong talk was all Greek to me. Brenda said something else, and they all switched back to English. Karen, the tall one, turned out to be Brenda's roommate. She spoke English clearly and perfectly, without any kind of accent that I could hear. Karen said she was "ABC", which I guessed meant "born in the USA", but Xuěyàn was "fresh off the boat". Her parents worked at the Chinese Embassy in DC. Xuěyàn spoke rapid-fire English with a thick accent and mangled the grammar to an incredible degree. Despite getting her verbs, plurals and gender pronouns wrong almost every time, I actually had no problem following her. Xuěyàn was my roommate. Both girls seemed genuinely delighted to meet us. I could tell that Brenda's Mandarin was limited from her occasional pauses while she racked her brain for the right word, and she spoke it slowly, but the fact that she spoke it at all had made a good first impression.

Since they had the same last name, I asked, "Are you sisters?"

They responded together, but Xuěyàn said "No," and Karen said "Yes."

Brenda explained that Chinese who shared the same surname considered themselves to be the same family, even if not actually related. The two Jins exchanged looks that made me suspect Brenda might not be completely right, but they didn't contradict her.

I could see immediately that Karen and Brenda shared a similar sense of humor. As roommates, they would either get along great, or wind up killing each other. There were certainly times when I had fantasized about strangling Brenda.

Xuěyàn revealed that her English name was "Maud" and that she had chosen it from some James Bond movie, but I decided to try to call her "Xuěyàn" so she wouldn't think me a complete barbarian. The girls pointed us to the buffet and then stayed with us at the table while we ate.

At one point, I glanced over at Ann's table. She was sitting with a brown-haired girl with dark eyes that did not look friendly. I knew we'd probably snubbed her by sitting with the Jins, and made a mental note to do something about that later.

Back in the room, Xuěyàn helped me hang up the clothes I'd left strewn on my bed and made sure I had my share of the closet space. I was shocked when she told me she was almost a year older than me - I'd guessed she was a young prodigy, maybe fourteen, but not sixteen. We were both sophomores so we'd be sharing most of the same classes.

Xuěyàn admitted she thought Brenda seemed very nice, but looked a little bit "scary". She said she was glad I was her roommate, and then asked me a lot of questions about "black people". It was obvious she'd garnered more than a few dumb ideas from movies and TV, but her curiosity seemed genuinely innocent and certainly without any hatred.

At breakfast the next morning, I saw Ann sitting with her friends, so I abandoned Brenda and our roommates and went to her. I came straight out with it. "Good morning, Ann," I said. "I just want to apologize for last night."

She smiled at me, but I noticed her brown-haired friend frowned. I continued. "You were nice enough to bring us down for dinner, but then we sat with the Jins. I just wanted you to know we weren't snubbing you. Brenda just thought we should get to know our roommates first since we'll be living with them." I rested my hand lightly on her shoulder and added, "So, anyway, thanks for coming to get us last night; that was very thoughtful."

She was about to reply, when the brown-haired girl pasted an obviously fake smile on her face and said, "Ann knows you weren't trying to be rude. I'm Mary Putnam, by the way."

We shook hands and she said, "You don't have to sit with them," she nodded back towards Brenda and the Jins. "You are welcome to sit with us."

I wondered why I would want to, but I knew how to act nice, so I replied, "I'd love to chat with you later, but I can't right now." I pasted a fake smile on my own face and added, "It's great to meet you though, Mary. And Ann, thanks again for last night. See you later."

My immediate hunch was that this was a race thing with Putnam, but I sensed some deeper agenda on her part.

7. FOUL
AMY

A two-hour team sport class twice a week was required. But during the summer, the only thing they had to offer was soccer. Brenda and I had played in grade school, and while we hadn't been stand-outs, we'd been ok. They put us on separate squads, and we usually played against each other. She was faster than me, but not as good at ball control. We were usually assigned to different positions so we didn't come into contact much.

We were on the field one day, playing hard, really getting into it. Mary Putnam was on my team and she was covering Brenda at the far end of the field. They were both going for the ball, when another girl came up and kicked it away.

Just then, Mary collided with Brenda, knocking her sprawling. I saw it and it was more than just a simple foul. Mary had deliberately bumped hard into Brenda from behind after the ball had been kicked away from their area. I started toward them, but Brenda saw me and made a little gesture with her hand, signaling me to keep away.

I stood where I was, my fists clenched. I could feel the anger heat up the back of my neck.

Brenda got up and brushed herself off, while Putnam apologized. I was too far away to hear the words, and her gestures seemed sincere, but I had seen the hit.

Afterward, walking to our next class, I told Brenda, "That foul wasn't an accident. She went out of her way to hit you in the back. What did she say to you?"

"She said she was sorry; said she just wasn't paying attention."

I arched my eyebrows at her.

"I know," she said. "Her apology was lame. It was a deliberate hit. But I can take a few knocks. There's no need to stoop to her level."

"We're in high school," I said. "We're supposed to have left that childishness behind us by now. What the hell is wrong with that bitch, anyway?"

"That's a silly question," Brenda grunted. "Forget about it."

Not likely, I thought. Mary Putnam was showing herself to be a bully, mean and petty. Her only saving grace was that she wasn't good at being a bully. She was essentially harmless, or so I thought.

I knew Brenda could take care of herself. But I would make sure she wouldn't have to.

8. PERFECT ENGLISH
AMY

Summer classes were generally very small. But there was only one English class and we were all lumped in there together. I'd been concerned about Xuěyàn's English, so I sat next to her in case she needed help, as I was sure that she would. On Thursday, we were assigned an in-class essay, and after I finished mine, I offered to help proofread hers.

"Thank you much please," She said.

Xuěyàn was my roommate, after all, and I figured I ought to put out some effort to help her. I had been wondering how she got into this school with such atrocious English. I even talked to Brenda about it. Xuěyàn had money and connections so I assumed she bought her way in, but Brenda insisted this school wouldn't do that.

"Admissions are purely merit-based," Brenda insisted, but I didn't see how that was possible with Xuěyàn. I was being cynical, and that was usually Brenda's job. Brenda was the one who was always accusing *me* of making excuses for other people, and it felt like we'd reversed our usual roles. Xuěyàn knew her math, but that alone shouldn't have gotten her past the gate. I wondered what her application essay had looked like.

Xuěyàn worked slowly and I kept my eyes on the clock. I worried that she wouldn't be done with enough time for me to fix all the errors I was expecting. She finally passed it to me when there was less than ten minutes left in the class.

Reading her paper, I was stunned. Not a single spelling or grammatical error that I could see, and the organization of the paper was clear and to the point, the thesis logical and well-argued. If I had not seen her writing it, I never would have believed it could have been written by Xuěyàn. The harder I looked, the better her essay looked. It was flawless. Even her penmanship was beautiful.

I handed it back to her. "I think it's perfect," I said.

After class, I was tempted to collar her, shove her up against the wall and demand she reveal by what magic or deviltry she had done it, but I realized what it was.

When she spoke, she spat the words out as fast as if they were bullets from a machine gun, not bothering to aim or think or check her ammo. When she wrote, she carefully planned and thought it all out in her head first. Clearly, she knew the rules of English grammar and spelling, but, at least when talking, ignored them. Getting the words out was her focus then, getting them correct was not even a goal.

Later, I decided that if I could teach her to slow down when she talked, maybe she could teach me how to write better English.

9. ALL BLONDES ARE SLUTS
AMY

Brenda was telling blonde jokes when I sat down for dinner. I could tell Xuěyàn was having trouble deciding when to laugh; it was definitely a learning experience for her and I could see her excitement at sharing this new aspect of American culture. She looked a little worried or maybe embarrassed when I sat down, no doubt wondering if I'd overheard the last joke.

Brenda picked up on it too. "Don't worry about telling these jokes in front of Amy," she said. "She's a blonde herself; she won't understand any of them."

"I've already heard all her jokes," I said. "She never has any new material."

Xuěyàn's eyes darted between Brenda and me, and then asked, "You are both fifteen year. Isn't most girl sixteen year? Why not sixteen?"

"We're *almost* sixteen," I told her. "We've always been younger than most of our classmates. My mom told me it was because the cut-off date to start school was December 1st, and Brenda and I were both born in November."

"Your birth-day date same?"

"No, I'm older. November 5th. Brenda is November 22nd. Most people think she is older than me, though."

"I'm a Sagittarius," Brenda interjected. "But Amy's a Scorpio. That explains why she is such a slut."

I buried my head in my hands. I knew what was coming next.

"Amy's a Scorpio, *and* she's a blonde. All blondes are sluts." She smiled and patted me on the head like a dog.

Xuěyàn looked confused, but Karen laughed.

"Will you stop?" I pleaded. "They don't know us well enough for all of your stupid jokes."

Xuěyàn asked, "What is 'slot'?"

Brenda's eyes lit up at the mispronunciation, but thankfully, she let it pass and answered, "Someone who is crazy about boys."

Karen provided an apparently more detailed definition, in Mandarin. Judging by the expression of horror on poor Xuěyàn's face, I felt confident

Karen's explanation was much more elaborate, more graphic, and exaggerated.

Xuěyàn's voice confirmed this when she whispered to me, "You have done sex thing with boy?"

"No, I have not!"

"Maybe not," Brenda said. "But you've been to second base so many times you might as well have..."

"No, no, no! I haven't done that either!"

Xuěyàn's voice was still hushed. "What is second base?"

Brenda explained in Chinese, illustrating further by sticking her hand inside her blouse.

Xuěyàn's eyes got as big as saucers and she stared at me.

"Bitch be crackin', she gotta..." I started to say, but a sharp glance from Brenda made me back up and remember my language. We'd both sworn off that kind of talk years ago, but it was still easy to forget sometimes.

I took a deep breath, but I was still hot.

"Look," I said, "All I ever did was kiss Tommy Chavez in the coat closet in the sixth grade, and this bitch won't let me forget it. I haven't done more than kiss one boy! Most other girls have done much more than me!"

I shouldn't have to defend myself, but my ears were burning. I pulled my blazer tighter. Brenda's grin got bigger and even more stupid-looking.

Slowly, like air escaping from a tire valve, Xuěyàn let out an audible sigh of relief to know her roommate was not a total prostitute.

Probably.

Of course, Brenda wasn't done.

"Amy is just so excited that her birthday is less than two months away," she said, pausing to sip her tea.

We all looked at her, waiting for her next line. We did not have to wait long.

"In Missouri, the age of consent was seventeen," she said. "But in Maryland it's only sixteen."

I punched her in the arm.

"You hit like a girl," she said, still grinning.

I tried to ignore her.

We talked a bit about our families back home and that was interesting.

Karen had been talking about her dad and suddenly seemed to realize she was monopolizing the table conversation. She was sitting directly across

27

from Brenda, so she asked, "What does your father do, Brenda? I don't remember if you've said."

"He sings in a choir," she said. I took another bite of my Jell-O to keep from saying anything.

"A choir? Does that pay very much?" Karen asked.

"No, not really."

"But I guess he has a good singing voice?"

"He has the voice of an angel," Brenda replied.

I thought about kicking her under the table, but I didn't.

Later, I had to explain a lot of things to Xuěyàn. Brenda's twisted sense of humor for one thing. The western Zodiac signs for another, what baseball had to do with sex, and why Brenda and I were friends. The last was the most difficult.

10. CANDY
AMY

We'd been at school for only a few days when we noticed someone new at dinner. She had a ruddy dark-brown complexion and fine features with a narrow Somali or Ethiopian nose and slightly curly black hair down to just past her ears. She looked like a younger version of the super-model Iman, sitting alone with a book.

On an impulse, I left my seat. The new girl looked up when I approached her; her expression completely neutral at first, but she quickly smiled. I stuck out my hand.

"Hi," I said. "I'm Amy McDonald. I'm new. A sophomore."

She took my hand and said, "Cleo Smith, also sophomore."

I asked, "Would you like to join us?"

She hesitated, then her smile got bigger and she said, "Sure."

Karen knew her from the previous year and the two of them were already on good terms, if not actual friends. "So, Cleo, why'd you join us?" Karen asked. "You usually like to sit alone."

"Well," she replied, "Amy invited me over, and I thought I should get acquainted, since three of you are new."

"Cleo is the number one research aide here," Karen said. "She has practically memorized every book in the library. If you need to find anything, ask her first."

Cleo nodded at the compliment but held up her hands in modest protest.

"Brenda and I are from St. Louis," I told her. "Where are you from? Is your family local?"

"I'm originally from Sudan," she said. "I was a refugee, an orphan from the civil war there. The Smiths adopted me when I was little. We lived in Virginia, but since they were killed, my guardians have kept me in boarding schools."

We all stared at her. To lose two sets of parents was unbelievably bad luck. I couldn't even imagine what she must have gone through. I put my hand over hers and said, "I'm sorry."

"That's ok," She said. She waved her hand in the air as if she were brushing away a fly. "Stuff happens. Other people have much bigger problems than me. I have a decent trust fund so I don't have to worry about money for a while."

Brenda nodded, reached over, and gave Cleo's other hand a brief squeeze.

"So, Cleo," I asked, "why are you here for the summer session? You're not new, so you're not here for the orientation, right?"

"That's right," she replied. "As I said, my guardians keep me in boarding school so I can be 'supervised' until I'm twenty-one. I actually like it. I have some projects I can work on, and the school is giving me advanced credit for helping Dr. Ross reorganize the library."

Cleo then asked, "How are you feeling now, Karen? I haven't talked to you since you come back."

"I'm ok. Just making sure I'm caught up. Taking care of all those incompletes I have."

I'm sure I looked confused by that, so Karen added an explanation.

"I caught mono last year and had to drop out in March. I missed the last two months of school. My grades were good enough that they promoted me to sophomore, but I had to agree to start this year early and complete some assignments. I didn't like the idea of summer school, but I got to admit, it's probably a good thing. I think it'll help me get back in the groove and back into school mode. When I was sick, I basically did nothing. It got boring very fast."

Karen gave me a critical eye. "Are you sure you don't want to take Chinese with the rest of us, Amy?"

"I'm sure. I have enough trouble with Spanish, and I'd be out of place in a class where you all are already fluent."

"Ah," Karen said, "but you're wrong. I can speak ok, but I'm basically illiterate in Chinese. So, we'd be in the same boat there. Besides, the summer sessions aren't graded. Or, at least the grades don't count. The purpose of the summer session is not just orientation, or make-up, or review, but evaluation. It's only six weeks. You can try it and then drop it in the fall, no harm done."

"Cleo's very good with languages," she added.

"Well, anyone can learn another language," Cleo countered, "It's not a big deal. Even in remote villages in Africa, it's common for even uneducated people to speak two or three languages, sometimes more."

I must've allowed my skepticism to show, because she looked directly at me.

"In this country," she continued, "I've noticed that people who are trying to learn a new language usually fight it. They focus on the differences and they look at those differences as obstacles. The key is to focus on the similarities and embrace the differences. It's like learning anything else; it all comes down to motivation and desire. I love languages the way some people love video games. Every new one is another fresh opportunity to see what's cool about that particular language, and every language has its own unique and, to my mind, very cool things that make it interesting and different. Besides, if you're learning languages, you'll find that the third comes easier than the second and the fourth is easier than the third, and so on. Picking up languages is not as hard as a lot of people think."

Brenda butted in. "Pay attention, Amy. You might learn something from this one."

She turned to Cleo, adding, "Amy had Spanish the last two years, and it's been tough for her. I tried to get her to study Mandarin with me, but she didn't believe me when I told her Chinese was easier than Spanish. No verb tenses to worry about, no plurals, and there's no gender so you don't have to wonder if it's 'la papa' or 'el Papa'. It's like you say, she took one look at Chinese and got frightened off by the obvious differences. If she'd given it half a chance, she could have mastered it, but no, Amy never listens to me. Maybe she'll listen to you."

Brenda turned back to me. "Chinese is easy, Amy. Even little babies learn it."

11. FAILING AMY

In History class, one of our first assignments was to write a paper on the causes of the Mexican-American war.

During the summer session, Dr. Ross taught History as well as English Composition and Literature. We had a textbook, but she didn't teach from that, and she jumped around a lot. She would talk about the Alamo one day, then the Civil War, then jump back to the War of 1812, and then the Mexican-American war again, and try to tie it all together.

Brenda and I worked on our papers together. The notes we'd taken in class were different, but by comparing our notes, we were able to reconstruct what Dr. Ross had told us and made sure we hit every point she made.

We were proud of our papers and stunned when she returned them both with a mark of "D" and a note to see her during office hours.

"She probably thinks we cheated," Brenda told me.

"How could we cheat on a paper? There's no rule against working together, and we wrote our final drafts independently."

"Maybe she thinks we plagiarized our words from somewhere."

I'd been accused of plagiarism before. More than once in Eighth grade, but only one time in Ninth where they probably just didn't care. A lot of people had a hard time believing Brenda could write too. It was easier for them to assume she'd stolen her words than to think she had any skills of her own. She was always having to prove herself and sometimes that took a lot of energy. If, out of weariness, she were ever to admit she'd copied from some place, then she'd have to produce the source, and since her work *was* original, she couldn't do that. The only thing she could do was keep protesting her innocence until her accusers got tired of harassing her and gave up.

When we poked our heads in her office, Dr. Ross said, "Come in, ladies." She seemed almost cheerful and I could feel Brenda's guard go up.

"You want to talk to us together, Dr. Ross?" I asked.

"Yes," she replied, "I think that's best. Your papers both have the same problem."

We sat down and waited for her to speak first.

"Do you know why I gave you a failing grade on this?"

"No," Brenda said. She did *not* say: "No, *ma'am*."

I just shook my head.

I knew I should wait, but the pressure was building up inside of me and I had to speak.

"We didn't cheat or plagiarize anything," I said.

Dr. Ross blinked her eyes and she sat back a little, obviously startled.

It took her a second to recover.

"I didn't think that," she said.

"I don't question your honesty.

"The problem with your papers is that there's just nothing there.

"All you did was re-hash and re-word what I taught in the class. I don't see any independent thought or evidence of outside reading. Nowhere did you argue with any of my opinions, and it's hard for me to believe you agree with me on every issue."

Well, shit.

Every time before whenever we'd read beyond the textbook, we'd been slapped down if we admitted to it. And we long ago learned that disagreeing with a teacher was not going to win good grades. Now Dr. Ross was trying to tell us that everything we had learned the hard way about school in the past was upside-down.

"Ma'am," Brenda said, "We are not used to contradicting a teacher."

"Get used to it here." Dr. Ross smiled.

"We are not training you to recite facts and opinions," she continued, "We are trying to train you to think critically and originally. For example, one of the other students, Miss Putnam, devoted her entire paper to trying to prove that the root cause of the Mexican-American war was the invention of the cotton gin. She was very convincing. I never mentioned the cotton gin in class.

"And you, Miss Dickens, I remembered you mentioning having read Ulysses S Grant's Memoirs. I half expected you to talk about the opposition to the war and mention how people like young Lt. Grant and young Abe Lincoln considered it an unjust war against a weaker neighbor, and why opinions like theirs were ignored."

She paused to let us think for a couple of seconds.

"Don't be afraid to be controversial. Don't be afraid to be the devil's advocate. The slave states were the ones who pushed for that war the hardest.

You could have argued that winning the war allowed slavery to last longer and boost the whole national economy for a few more years.

"I gave you a 'D' rather than an 'F' because you did have all your facts right, and I think you obviously did understand the material I taught. But that is not enough at this school, and it certainly won't be enough in the real world later."

I felt myself take in a deep breath.

"Fortunately," Ross added, "Your marks in the summer session won't count in calculating your final standing for the year. Accept this grade as a wake-up call, as something you needed to get your attention. I'm sure Dr. Davis gave you her favorite speech when you were admitted; how this school is hard because the students make it hard. You need to stretch yourselves and never seek the easy path. I expect more from you."

At dinner that evening, after telling this story, Cleo said, "I warned you."

"So did I," Karen added, "They are serious about wanting you to challenge them."

"About challenging yourself," Cleo said.

"This is one of the main lessons of the summer orientation," Karen said, "I told you it wasn't enough to just repeat what's in the lectures. The classroom is just a starting point. They expect you to go beyond that."

I vaguely remembered both Karen and Cleo saying something like that to us, but I suppose either Brenda didn't believe them or I wasn't paying attention.

12. THE JEFFERSONS
AMY

We'd just started second grade.

There were three other girls, the Jeffersons, two sisters and a cousin, who were the school bullies. They were always bumping into me, talking about me behind my back, but loud enough so that I could hear, and always calling me names and making faces at me. I didn't understand why they didn't like me, everybody else liked me, but they didn't. I felt more confused than hurt, I think. They were older than me, too. They were in the third or even the fourth grade. Why were they even bothering with a second-grader? That didn't make any sense to me.

One day, in the hallway, one of them just slammed me up against the wall, hard. I don't know why. She put her face up close to mine and said, "What are you looking at, you fugly dumb blonde bitch?" I remember thinking; I'm not bothering you. And what does *fugly* mean? But before I could say anything, she punched me right in the face with her fist. My head bounced off the brick wall behind me and I slid to the ground, dropping my book bag and covering my face. The shock and surprise overwhelmed any pain at first. But immediately, there were more punches and kicks and yelling words that I don't really remember. I was huddled in a ball wondering why this was happening to me and that's when it began to really, really hurt. Somebody was screaming or crying and I was astonished when I realized it was me.

Then, it was the bullies who screamed. I was curled up and didn't see much, but very soon, one of the Jefferson girls was screaming, one was crying, and one was running away. Brenda had come upon the scene and charged in. The Jefferson girls were all bigger than her, but three Jeffersons were no match for one furious Brenda.

Brenda stayed with me in the nurse's office until she was physically dragged away by the security guard and one of the teachers. I had a bloody nose, a black eye, a big bump on my head and a lot of bruises. I hurt all over and I couldn't stop sobbing.

Later, in the principal's office, Brenda held my hand while my mom held me on her lap and wiped my tears. Both of Brenda's parents were there too. I got suspended for two days for fighting. I thought that was so unfair, since I wasn't fighting; I was getting beat up and I didn't understand why the principal didn't know the difference. But he made me apologize for fighting anyway. He said that if I didn't apologize, I would be expelled, and my dad told me to apologize, so I did, even though I didn't think I should.

Brenda was told to do the same, but she refused.

Brenda loved her daddy more than anything in the world, but she stood up to him and lectured him. "I won't apologize! I'm not sorry!" She said, stamping her little foot. "I didn't do anything wrong! They were bullies! They were wrong! You told me I should stand up to bullies, and I did." Everyone tried to get her to just say the words, they even made me ask her to say she was sorry, and I did, but she was stubborn, nothing would get her to say she was wrong when she was sure she was right.

In the end, she wasn't expelled; she was just suspended for two weeks. I think my parents agreed not to sue. They kept me home as sick for that same time, and let the two of us be together, even though I found out later that our two families had a big long discussion about that. The bruises healed, the Jeffersons were transferred to a different school, and I gained a true friend. A courageous friend.

What made Brenda courageous, and I understood this even then as a child, was not her fighting at three to one odds. That was more foolhardy than brave. She was courageous for refusing to apologize and for standing up for the truth and her own sharp sense of justice, even when pressured by the father whose every other word she worshipped.

Brenda's dad took away her TV privileges for two weeks for disobeying him by not apologizing, but that didn't shake her resolve. It was only many years later that we found out Harvey had called Aunt Diane that very night to boast to his sister about how proud he was of his little girl.

13. HOOD RATS

Mary Putnam loved her school. Catonsville International Academy had been her dream for as long as she could remember.

Dickens and McDonald didn't belong here. They were crude and rough. They may have done well with a few tests and grades, but they couldn't fool Mary.

Mary didn't have anything against them personally. She would never actually use the term "hood rats", but that was what they were. They literally were "from the hood", and it showed in everything they did. Their speech, their manners, or their lack thereof, all broadcast their origins to anyone who was paying attention.

By itself, that would have been ok, but they were becoming popular. The two Jins hung out with them, and Cleo Smith was becoming part of their clique too. That was the danger that they posed. Their association with others risked bringing those others down to their level, and eventually, bringing down the entire school.

It had been a mistake to bump into Dickens on the soccer field so blatantly.

Mary knew how stupid it was. Mary was a decent girl trying to frighten a black girl who was used to rough play. She had hoped to draw Brenda into taking a swing at her, but Brenda had kept a lid on the violence that was no doubt basic to her nature. Dickens couldn't keep that act up forever, though. Sooner or later, she'd show her true self and then everyone would know she didn't fit in. Mary was perfectly willing to take a few punches for the good of the school. She wouldn't fight back, she'd let Dickens do all the fighting. She did worry a little about whether or not Brenda carried a knife.

This could still work. All Mary had to do was watch and wait and do a thousand little things to get under Brenda's skin. Like straws piled on a camel's back, eventually one would break the back of Brenda's "nice" act. Dickens and McDonald had both admitted that this was their first decent school; the first decent place they'd been, and they were still feeling their way around.

Class was not just a word, it was something real, and those two didn't have it. They'd been raised in the slums for nearly sixteen years; it was crazy to think they could transform themselves overnight into normal girls. It wasn't even their fault, really. Not that fault had anything to do with it. They didn't belong here and they had to go. They couldn't really be happy here anyway--they'd be happier and better off at some other school where they didn't have to pretend so hard, someplace where they could fit in easier.

Mary had other strategies at her disposal.

Amy and Brenda's "closeness" was not natural. Everyone noticed it. Mary didn't have anything against lesbians--Mary wasn't prejudiced. The school had no policy about girl-on-girl love, but they did have a "no sex on campus" rule that had to apply to girl-girl as well as boy-girl. The school may not have a policy of discriminating against gays, but it didn't want to get a reputation as a lesbian school either. Mary didn't even have to catch them in the act, if the rumors were strong enough.

It didn't matter at all if they actually were gay or not.

Dickens and McDonald had been getting good grades so far on their tests and papers, but with regular classes starting in a couple of weeks, they would be competing in a bigger pool against some tougher fish. The novelty of them would wear off quickly, and the teachers would start giving them grades that were more accurate, and lower. That would take some of the wind out of their sails. A few words in the ears of the right teachers would help the process along. People were easily influenced and easily led, and teachers were no exception to that rule.

Those two were careless, too. Mary had already overheard them use the words "bitch" and "slut" freely and both those words were not only forbidden at the school, but if true, could impact their reputations as well. Reputations were especially important at the Academy, and especially fragile. That was another thing the two of them could not be expected to understand.

Who knows what else the pair might do. Mary had heard Amy mention how they had been friends with actual criminal gangs at their last school. Any hint of that here would get them booted out. Drugs, theft, it might be anything from them. They were no doubt capable of all of it. Their background was probably filled with a long list of sordid experiences.

Dickens and McDonald were going to wind up handing over truck-loads of ammunition against themselves.

It would be almost too easy.

14. LACROSSE
AMY

We had to choose a sport when the fall session started. If we didn't choose, we'd be kept in soccer. That would have been ok, but I'd done that and Brenda and me both thought we should try something different. Brenda decided to take up fencing and tried to get me to sign up too.

"Come on, Amy," she said, "they're always looking for fresh blood..."

But I watched a lacrosse game and that was what appealed to me. It was fast-paced and required some skill, but a player could become competent quickly and maybe expert later. I guess the real reason it appealed to me was that it was something different. I knew Aunt Di played it a little bit at Bryn Mawr, and she had talked it up to me.

Brenda watched me fumble around on the field, and made fun of me afterwards. I was usually fast, but the other girls were *much* faster and at first, I felt like an awkward little kid. I didn't think it would be that much different from soccer, at least the field coverage part, but having to carry a stick while running threw me off completely. Catching the yellow ball with the Crosse stick wasn't a problem for me because in the beginning, I never even got close enough to do it.

The next day, every muscle in my body ached and Brenda gave me grief for that too. But I liked it and decided to stick with it.

As I got better, I found that it was usually relaxing, especially when it was over and after I'd showered and cleaned up. Even running around the field was calming, but for one incident.

The month before, Mary Putnam fouled Brenda on the soccer field. It was clear she didn't like us for some reason. Mary didn't play lacrosse, so I figured I didn't have to worry about any of that crap.

I was wrong.

A bunch of us were scrambling for the ball at the same time when I felt a pain between my shoulder-blades like I'd been shot. I could feel myself go cross-eyed and for a moment, my vision went totally dark. At the same time, somebody's stick got between my legs and I was tripped. I landed face down, and banged my face against my own Crosse when I hit the turf. I lay still. I literally saw stars as my vision returned, and my breathing was ragged. Somebody turned me over, and a minute later, a couple of girls helped me sit up. My back ached, but my breathing returned to normal quick enough.

"Abby should be more careful in the scramble," a voice said.

I heard myself ask, "What happened?"

My voice sounded very high and thin.

" Abby accidently elbowed you in the back and you fell," the other voice said.

"Accidentally?"

"Well, she certainly wouldn't do anything like that on purpose. But she definitely needs to control her moves better. She won't make the school team if she's flailing around like that."

When I stood up, I looked around and saw Abby Parris, one of Mary Putnam's friends standing a little way off. She was looking at me, and smirking.

15. OSTRICHES
AMY

When we were in second grade, our dads took me and Brenda to the petting zoo out by Grant's Farm. They had all the things little girls think are adorable: a miniature pony, pink puppy-sized piglets, fluffy little white lambs, yellow baby chicks and grey ducklings. I remember running around trying to see everything quickly, as if the next animal might disappear before I got to see it.

But when I turned the corner of the barn I came face to face with something monstrous. It towered way over the head of Brenda's dad, on two narrow, naked legs with huge dirty clawed toes. Its long neck resembled a wrinkled, fuzzy snake sprouting from an unruly blob of black feathers, and topped with a tiny big-eyed head that hissed at me. Its long eyelashes struck me as especially hideous. I had never seen an ostrich outside of a picture-book and the reality was both breathtaking and terrifying.

Headmistress Davis had an open lobby outside her office that came into view when I turned the corner of the hallway. I suddenly flashed back to that scene with the ostrich. Sprouting up from a crowd of fawning girls were the heads of four creatures I recognized with a shock of amazement.

Boys!

Inside our school.

Two and a half months cooped up in a completely estrogen-soaked atmosphere, the reminder that boys my same age still existed on the same planet as me was almost a revelation. I stood on my toes to get a better look. They were a fine set of varied specimens, one tall blond guy, one caramel colored African American guy wearing glasses, one short and very fit brown-haired Asian kid, and a tall, tan boy with a mop of jet black hair and his back to me. A new image popped into my head of me standing on a step-stool next to them, running my fingers through their hair, just playing with the different colors and textures.

I couldn't see the last one's face until he turned. His eyes were a startlingly bright blue that seemed to punch through my chest. A part of me knew it was just because I hadn't been around boys for a little while, but another part of me wondered why one boy should have such a strong effect on me.

"So, which one do you want?" Brenda's voice behind me broke the spell.

"What are they doing here?" I asked, ignoring her question.

"They came to see you," she said.

My mouth dropped open, and it took a few seconds to realize she was teasing me.

"They heard what a slut you are, and came to see for themselves," she added, smiling.

I slapped at her, but only connected with her shoulder, which just amused her even more.

"No," I said. "Really. Why are they here?"

"Actually, they came to see me. They know *I'm* a lady."

I wasn't going to get anything out of Brenda except more of her lame jokes, so I rose up on my toes again and craned my neck, trying to get a better look. I was about to move closer when I heard the voice of Dr. Kramer.

"All right, Ladies! Don't block the hallway. You all have classes. Get to them. Now!"

Brenda led me away by the arm while I kept looking backward, trying to get one last look at the ostriches.

At dinner, Professor Davis stood up to make the usual routine announcements. When she finished those, she said, "By now, all of you know we had some young gentlemen visit our school today. I'm sure you are wondering why."

The room got quiet enough for us to hear our own heartbeats.

"As most of you know, our Academy hosts a formal dance in the spring. Gentlemen from a few of the local young men's high schools are invited. We are fortunate to have Ms. Dunham as a member of our faculty. As one of the finest dance teachers in the country, she is a resource of which no other school can boast. We have agreed to allow a few young men from the Elliott Academy take ballroom dance with her, on our campus, after regular hours and perhaps, on a few of the weekends. Some of you will be invited to participate in those classes. While these young men are on our grounds, I expect everyone to be on her best behavior."

She gave us all a very small smile, then added, "Oh, and the dessert tonight is cherry pie."

We learned more about the spring formal when the rules were posted on the boards in the residence halls. First year students would not be eligible to attend the dance. There would not be "dates", as such. A number of boys roughly equal to the number of girls would be invited, and partners would select each other at the dance. There was no mention of dress code; I guessed that would be clarified later. The dance would be held around Easter, still six months away. While on campus, the boys would be tightly restricted to certain areas and denied access to most buildings. Unspoken was the threat of what would happen if there was any "unseemly fraternization".

We also found out that juniors and seniors would be permitted to leave campus to attend proms at some of the boy's schools if they got invited as some guy's real date. Nobody said how they were supposed to meet guys to actually get dates before then.

Brenda and I, and the two Jins, were all sophomores, but except for Karen, this was our first year, and we didn't know if we were considered first year students as far as the dance was concerned. Was "first year" meant to be taken literally, or did it just mean "freshmen?" I wasn't completely sure how I felt about any of this, either. I did want to be invited, but I had to admit it was a little bit scary. I'd never been to a real dance before.

"Aunt Di wants to talk to us," Brenda told me.

"What about?"

"I don't know." She rolled her eyes. "Just put your shoes on and come downstairs."

Me and Brenda sat at the dining room table across from Aunt Di.

"I got a letter from the school," Diane began. "It's about boys being allowed on your campus." She hesitated, then cleared her throat before continuing. "I know you're both intelligent young ladies, but you're old enough now that you need to be extra careful. Especially where boys are concerned. Boys your age are driven more by their hormones than by their good sense."

I stole a quick glance at Brenda. She was blushing as much as I was. Diane didn't seem to notice.

"It's a hard time for girls too. I just want you both to know that I'm here for you. You know you can talk to me about anything and I won't judge you."

She was going to talk about condoms. I just knew it.

This was crazy. There was no way either of us was ready to do anything... We didn't need or want to hear this. Besides, I'd already heard this talk from my own mom.

"And remember, I'm a doctor. I can get you anything you need, if it is a prescription, or anything else."

Yep, this was 'The Condom Talk'. I wished she would hurry up and get this over with.

No such luck.

"If you're not comfortable talking with me, I can set up appointments with some of my friends at the hospital - everything confidential. And don't worry about me telling your parents. I just want you both to be safe. You need to understand all the risks. Your health and safety are the most important things."

I was frozen in my chair. I was afraid to even look at Brenda, but I knew she was frozen in place too.

"And remember," Diane added, "If something does happen - if there is an accident - and you get into trouble, I can make arrangements to help take care of it. I just want you to be safe." She repeated herself.

She was talking about us getting knocked up. Could this possibly get any worse?

"Just one more thing," she said. "My high school was also an all-girls school, and there were a few girls then who were... experimenting. I know some girls are curious sometimes."

Apparently it could get worse.

Much worse.

"Now, I know you're both straight, and I'm not saying you two, either of you, are curious, in that way. Not that there is anything wrong with that, if you are. I just think you are too young to label yourselves. I just want you to know you can come to me if you have any questions about anything or need anything. I just want you both to be safe."

Back upstairs, Brenda and I took a couple of minutes to catch our breath. Brenda was the first to break the ice.

"She probably thinks we're up here 'doing it' right now," She said.

I glared at her. "She can't seriously think we're a couple of fucking Lesbos?"

"Technically, I don't think it's correct to refer to them as 'fucking' Lesbos. There's the issue of having the necessary equipment. Besides, 'lesbians' is the 'proper' term."

"And was she really hinting at arranging an abortion?"

"Oh," Brenda said, "I think it was more than a hint."

"What does your aunt think we are, anyway?"

Brenda shrugged and shook her head. Eventually we decided that Diane didn't know what to think. She hadn't been sixteen herself for a very long time.

She just wanted us to be 'safe'.

16. HARVEY HOSPITAL
AMY

We were only a couple of months into seventh grade when Brenda's mom came to pull her out of school early one day. Her dad had gone into the hospital a couple of days before. It was the second time he'd gone there in as many months. I followed Brenda out and got in the car with her. I didn't have a hall pass, but nobody bothered to stop me. I remember what a mess her mom's hair was. It was usually perfectly coiffed, but not that day.

Harvey looked very tired lying in his hospital bed. There were tubes and wires and lights and machines crowding the tiny room. Brenda immediately went to her dad and laid her head on his chest. "Brenda Angel," he whispered. He put his hand on her shoulder and they stayed like that for a little while.

Suddenly, Brenda jerked up.

"Oh, daddy, I'm sorry. My fat head. Too heavy?"

But Harvey just smiled at her and patted her arm and closed his eyes to rest. I could tell his breathing was rough and slow. Each breath seemed to come farther and farther apart.

Miz Sally kissed his forehead and said, "I'll just check with the nurse, honey. I'll be right back."

She left the room, and I followed her like a lost puppy. I didn't know what to say or do, I didn't like seeing Harvey looking so weak and I hated the way the antiseptic smell stung high up in my nose. I just wandered into a little alcove off the hallway that had a soft drink machine and stared at it for a long time. I wasn't thirsty and I wasn't thinking about anything at all, just staring at the cans behind the glass.

Eventually, I walked back to the room. Just inside the door, I stopped. Brenda was holding her dad's hand in hers and simultaneously punching the call button while whispering, "Daddy?" over and over. One of the machines was emitting a steady, irritating buzz and a light near the door was flashing red.

Miz Sally rushed in, followed by the nurse. While the nurse checked his vitals, Miz Sally caressed Harvey's head, holding back her sobs, and she whimpered, "I thought we'd have more time."

My heart felt like it had sunk into my stomach. It pounded hard, and I fought to fill my own lungs with air. I wanted to run away.

It wasn't until I hugged Brenda from behind that she started crying. Then Miz Sally wrapped her arms around us both and she started crying too, very softly. I tasted salt in the corner of my mouth.

Harvey must have known he was in trouble. He'd taken out a big life insurance policy before he'd gone to the doctor. He had probably shopped around for one he could get without a physical. After he died, the insurance company tried to deny the claim, based on what they called "suspicious timing". Luckily, Brenda's mom was the receptionist for a major law office in St. Louis, and well-liked and respected by everyone there. The president of the law firm made a personal phone call to the president of the life insurance company, and soon after, the policy was paid in full. I never knew how much money it was. Miz Sally still had to keep working for a living, but Brenda would have no worries about tuition, neither at the Academy, nor at any college that she might get admitted to later.

Even after he was gone, Harvey still took care of his little girl.

17. POETRY OF THE FOOT
AMY

"I told you lacrosse would be easier than fencing." I'm sure I sounded very smug because Brenda glared at me.

She was lying on her side on her bed while I sat at her desk. Last week she had been making fun of me, how sore I was after lacrosse, and now it was my turn to get even. "You thought you'd look so cool in your nice white fencing outfit; you thought fencing would be so much more elegant than running around a dirty field outside..."

"I didn't think it would be so much work," she moaned. "My legs are like rubber."

"It's a good thing you're not taking dance class, too. You can barely walk; for sure you wouldn't be able to dance. Of course, that means you won't get the chance to dance with any boys."

"Ms. Dunham says the soreness will pass in a week or so," Brenda said.

A sudden realization made me sit bolt upright.

"You know," I said, "the only girls who are going to be invited to those after-hours classes with the boys will be the girls who are already in Ms. Dunham's regular dance classes."

"And that's not us," she muttered.

"But you *are* in her fencing class," I replied. "Didn't you tell me she complimented you on your footwork?"

Brenda's dark eyes flashed wide open. I could see the gears starting to turn inside her head. They were already spinning inside mine.

Ms. Dunham had office hours the next afternoon, so we went to plead our case together. We made sure our uniforms and hair were immaculate, and we'd worked on the little script we planned to deliver.

Brenda introduced me and then said, "Ms. Dunham, we'd like to apply for the after-hours ballroom dance classes you'll be conducting."

She raised one eyebrow. "Do you have any dance experience?"

I spoke up, "Only a little bit in elementary school, ma'am. Both our mothers always wanted us to take ballet classes, but our fathers made us study Aikido instead." (A little white lie.) "I think we learned a little about

48

movement in four years of Aikido, though, and ballroom dancing is something we've always wanted to study." (A slightly bigger lie.)

Brenda chimed in. "We are both serious students and hard workers, ma'am. We won't disappoint you on that score, if you give us the chance."

"Well," she said, "While I'm sure this isn't just a couple of boy-blind girls acting on impulse," her voice dripped with sarcasm, but she nevertheless smiled. "My list is mostly juniors and seniors. I believe you are both sophomores?"

"Yes, ma'am, we are," I replied. "Of course you know best, ma'am, but shouldn't the sophomore class also be represented? And Brenda and I are both tall for sophomores, and I think most of the boys are also tall. Wouldn't that help with your teaching?"

She looked us over in silence for a while, then said: "I'll consider it. No promises," she warned, "but I'll talk to some of your teachers and review my list of candidates. I've had a lot of young ladies come to me asking the same thing and I need to keep the classes small, so, again; no promises."

Brenda had fencing with her the day after and kept hoping to hear something, but the fencing class was all about fencing, not dancing, and Brenda didn't want to be a pest. We'd figured everyone else would be pestering Ms. Dunham, and we hoped to stand out by playing it cool.

The list was posted the next week and both our names were on it.

I fully expected Brenda to embarrass me at our first dance class. The waiting for her snide comments was excruciating. But the minutes ticked away without a single smart ass crack from her.

Ms. Dunham had us all line up, girls on one side, boys on the other, about three yards apart, and introduce ourselves in turn.

Roberto (Robert, "call me Bobby") Ayala had been the tan, black haired, bright blue eyed ostrich from outside Dr. Davis's office. He was near the far end of the boy's line. After only a glance and a polite smile in my direction, his eyes focused on one of the older girls. Crap, I thought. All that pleading to get here and he's not interested in me. Maybe this was a mistake. Brenda's eyes were roaming over all the boys; I couldn't tell if she had picked out a favorite yet.

I became aware that one of the boys was staring at me. Steve McBride was a tall, sandy haired guy, with an athletic build and a soft and ready smile. Maybe this would work out after all. But Roberto was the one I'd had my heart set on.

Ms. Dunham started out taking the part of the man and picked Sue Spence, a junior, to demonstrate the basic box step with, leading her through the movements, first slow, then in time with the music. She repeated this with each of us girls.

"Now pay attention ladies," she said. "In some ways, our job as the female partner is easy - all we have to do is follow the man's lead. But not every gentleman will be a good or even competent dancer. In that case, just go with the flow. But for now, we'll assume the man always knows what he's doing."

Later, she quoted somebody, saying, "Dancing is wonderful training for girls, it's the first way you learn to guess what a man is going to do before he does it."

She then repeated the process with the boys, but while she had pushed us girls into position, she pulled the boys along, showing them how to lead.

For the guys, she quoted Vince Lombardi, "Football isn't a contact sport; it's a collision sport. Dancing is a contact sport." She added, "Remember, when you hold a lady's hand, you must hold it light, but move with confidence. Signal your intentions clearly and at the right time, don't make her guess what you are going to do."

Two at a time, she paired us up and led us through the steps again. "Footwork is a part of dancing, but the key is not footwork, it is communication with your partner. This you will learn. But do not expect it to come quickly. Like everything else in life, it requires practice."

When my turn came, I was paired up with Steve, the sandy haired guy. My eyes were on a level with his mouth and I could see every twitch of his lips. I could feel his pulse in my hand.

Ms. Dunham grabbed our hands. "No, no, no," she said. "That is not how you hold hands. We'll do turns next time, and this won't work then. Everything I tell you is for a reason." She addressed me directly. "You are not taking his pulse, Miss McDonald; you are not his nurse." I tried not to blush, while she re-arranged our hands and had us go through the motions a little more before separating us.

When I stood back, I saw that he was still watching me. I imagined I could still feel his pulse in my right hand, I could definitely feel the muscles of his arm under my left, and his right hand on my waist. His eyes were brown and soft and seemed to sparkle.

Ms. Dunham moved through each couple, one pair at a time. Then she had us switch partners and the whole room went through the steps together while she watched and made corrections. We switched again and again, until we were back with our original partner. I had danced with Robert, and he seemed nice. Definitely a little bit shy, but he had no trouble making and keeping eye contact. His eyes were certainly very blue. And yet, when I was dancing with him, it was the memory of Steve's pulse that I was focused on. I was anticipating dancing with him again, but just then, Ms. Dunham had us stop. I glanced at the clock; what had seemed like less than twenty minutes had actually been ninety.

She excused the boys and I'm sure all hearts sank a bit as we watched them leave. I hadn't really spoken to any of them.

As soon as they left, we started talking amongst ourselves, but Ms. Dunham put a stop to that. "Before you go, ladies," she said, "I'll mention the one thing nearly all of you were doing wrong. You were anticipating your partner's movements. Don't do that. Let him lead. If he makes a mistake, so be it. Almost the only way you can mess things up is if you try to lead or pull him along. This will become crucial when we try the turns. I told you that the woman has the easiest job, but that is only partly true." She then quoted somebody else: "Remember, Ginger Rogers did everything Fred Astaire did, but she did it backwards and in high heels."

Crap, I thought. I don't have any high heels. And who the hell is Ginger Rogers?

Later, when I mentioned this to Brenda, she admitted that she had a couple pair of heels for church, but they were back in St. Louis, and she didn't even know if they still fit.

"We'll get Aunt Di to take us shopping," she said. "She would love that."

I finally realized that I hadn't paid any attention to Brenda in the class. I asked, "Did you see any guy you liked?"

"Ricky." She said.

"Which one was he?"

"Weren't you paying attention? They all introduced themselves. Ricky Larson. The light-skinned brother with glasses."

I remembered the glasses. "Oh, him. Those glasses didn't do much for him," I said.

"He had warm hands and he knew his steps," Brenda replied, "But yeah, the glasses were a little goofy-looking."

"Maybe," I grinned at her, "When we go shopping for shoes, we can bring him along to shop for glasses."

She ignored my dig. "I don't even know if we'll practice in heels," she said.

"But surely we'll need them for the Spring Dance?" I said.

"We don't know what the dress will be. We might be in flats and uniform. We don't even know if we'll be invited to the Dance. We're just taking lessons now," she said. "And don't call me 'Shirley'."

18. WASH WHITES SEPARATELY
AMY

Brenda and I were sick of working in the laundry room after the first week.

To be fair, the work wasn't really that hard. We were only assistants to the older Hispanic ladies who were paid to do the laundry. We simply put uniforms on hangers, bagged the clean sheets, made sure each item was properly tagged and posted the notices when a job was ready to be picked up. The laundry room itself was hot and humid, and while I got used to it, Brenda found it increasingly harder to deal with. She kept complaining that the humidity was ruining her hair. She always kept it short, in a Halle Berry-style cut, but it still got unmanageable quickly, or so she said. It always looked fine to me.

Finally, she went to Dr. Kramer and asked for a different assignment, but got turned down. If she could find someone to trade with, Dr. Kramer might consider it, but otherwise, Brenda was stuck until next year.

She got more miserable every day, and when we'd get off our shift, she'd stomp back to her room cursing.

It was Karen who proposed the solution. Karen and Xuěyàn had drawn stockroom duty, and this was proving a challenge to Xuěyàn, because her shorter stature made it harder for her to reach the higher shelves. Brenda was taller, and the stockroom would be ideal for her hair; it was cool and dry.

Brenda and I had already been split up by being assigned different rooms. If she went to the stockroom and I stayed in the laundry, we'd be split up again. Karen didn't want to go to the laundry. I think she was afraid some girls would think "Chinese laundry", and she didn't care to deal with their stupid comments. Xuěyàn didn't care; the laundry would be a little cleaner, certainly less dusty than the stockroom.

We all went to see Dr. Kramer together. She seemed sympathetic at first, but then she started asking a few strange questions.

Addressing me and Brenda, she asked, "Weren't you two friends before you came here?"

"Yes," I said. "We've been friends since pre-school." I didn't see how this was relevant.

"So, why do you want to split up now? Have you two been fighting?"

Brenda was sitting at the other side of the room. Even with the Jins sitting between us, I could feel her body stiffen. I knew she was thinking the same thing I was. *What does that have to do with this? And what business would it be of yours if we have been?*

Brenda had pulled up her defenses, so I had to respond for her. I explained about Brenda's hair, Xuěyàn's height, and how this switch made logical sense for everyone. Dr. Kramer frowned and asked Brenda, "Is that true, Miss Dickens?"

Brenda hesitated before responding. I knew she was as offended as I was by the implication that I might not be telling the truth. She needed a moment to choke down her impulse to tell Dr. Kramer to mind her own damn business. But "Amy is right," is all she said.

"Well," Dr. Kramer replied, "I think you're not telling me something, but we can try it, for a while. If there are no problems, then..."

"What the hell was that all about?" I was trying to keep my voice down while we walked back to our rooms.

"You noticed she didn't ask Karen or Xuěyàn any questions?" Brenda asked. "She acted as if they weren't even present."

It was always about us, I thought. So many damn busybodies in this world thought that the friendship between me and Brenda was somehow any of their damn business.

If only they all had just one neck, I could be rid of them all with a single stroke.

19. PROUD FALL
AMY

"The word, 'Stuck-up'. That means 'prideful', yes?"

We were in the middle of tagging jobs behind the laundry counter when Xuěyàn asked this, so her remark seemed to come from nowhere. So many of her questions did.

"Yes," I told her, "it usually means a person who thinks they are better than other people, too superior to talk to ordinary common people. It is not a compliment."

Xuěyàn looked embarrassed by my answer, so I followed up.

"Why? Where did you hear that? Did someone say you were 'stuck-up', Xuěyàn?"

She hesitated, but then, "Not me. They said you."

"Me?"

"And Brenda, too. They said."

"Who is 'they'? Who said that?"

Another hesitation, followed by, "Mary Putnam. She said this word."

I admit that I actually felt hurt. I was the poor newcomer from the wrong side of the tracks. There was no way I was going to be acting stuck up, especially at this school. It was a constant struggle for me to prove I was just as good as anyone else, no way either me or Brenda were stupid enough to think or pretend we were the elites. This was just plain backwards.

Simple spite. That's what it had to be. When you throw a hateful word at somebody, it doesn't need to make logical sense; it just has to be hateful. It's even better if it makes no sense because then it's harder to defend against.

"So," I asked, "why did she say that?"

"I don't know this," Xuěyàn replied.

"Well, what was the context? What was the conversation when this came out?"

"In the hallway, Mary and Ann Warren were talking," Xuěyàn pronounced the latter as 'Ahhn Wrrrr-in'. "You and Brenda they invited to go to movie with them and no, you both said no."

"What? Is that all? We had to study that night. We told her that. Besides, that was the first time they had ever invited us to go anywhere or do anything with them."

"Someone said study was only an excuse to refuse. Someone said you never talked to them because you were 'stuck-up' and snotty."

Xuěyàn's accent got in the way and I actually wasn't sure if she was quoting 'snotty' or 'snooty', but given the context, I guess it didn't matter.

I flashed back to how careful we had been in ninth grade. Riverplace Junior High had been a place where we would have been in serious trouble if there had been any hint of us being 'stuck-up'. At Riverplace we really had been the elite but acting properly humble had been something we knew how to do instinctively. Us? Stuck-up? If we ever had been, it would have been beaten out of us.

Beaten out if we'd been lucky enough to get off so easy.

If anything, it was the sheltered brats at Catonsville who hadn't ever had to learn that lesson. I could feel the heat in my cheeks.

"A lot of the girls here are just spoiled," I said. "They expect everyone to follow them around like puppy dogs, begging for favors and fawning on them like they're ... special. If anyone is stuck-up or proud, it certainly isn't me or Brenda. It's these spoiled rich bitches with their proud noses stuck so high..."

I took a deep breath. I reached out to pat Xuěyàn on the shoulder. She was a naturally sweet girl, and I didn't want her to think I thought she was a bitch, even if she was rich.

"We have a saying that 'pride comes before the fall', meaning that proud people who really are stuck-up should expect a painful fall to be the next thing in their lives."

Xuěyàn was looking past me, so I turned back to the counter. A couple of girls were standing there with shocked looks on their faces. I knew this would go bad for me.

The very next day I learned just how bad when Mary Putnam lost her footing and tumbled down a flight of stairs.

She didn't break anything except her laptop, but she picked up a few bruises, including an ugly one on the side of her face.

The stupid rumors started immediately.

Cleo was the first to share them with me over dinner.

"They say you put a curse on her."

I'm sure my mouth dropped open when I heard that. Brenda laughed.

"Amy couldn't do anything like that," Brenda said, "I'm the one who should know about black magic, not her. Amy's too nice. She doesn't know anything."

She showed her pearly whites in an evil grin and turned around to smile in the direction of Putnam's table. I don't know if Mary or Ann saw her.

"Stop that," I slapped at Brenda, "you'll just encourage this craziness. Don't look over there! Keep quiet!"

"It *is* craziness," I said to Cleo. "Nobody really believes that, right? Curses? Spells? That's bullshit!"

"Just because it's stupid, doesn't mean that nobody will believe it. People believe all kinds of stupid stuff. Did you know that some of these girls actually believe that vampires might be a real thing?"

"Amy doesn't have the teeth for that," Brenda piped in. I gave her a sharp elbow, but it didn't faze her.

"Look," I said, still trying to ignore Brenda and talk to Cleo, "I know I said... was *overheard* saying that 'pride cometh before the fall', but it's just a coincidence. Coincidence is something real, it is a statistical fact, spells and curses are not, they're fantasy. These girls aren't stupid. They must know that."

"Must they?" --Brenda again.

Cleo answered, "I'm sure most do. Maybe all of them. But it only takes one or two to spread a rumor. And that one or two needn't really believe it either. Girls love to gossip, it's in their blood. A good story always trumps the truth and this makes a good story: Young girl with magic powers cast hexes on her enemies. Beware the witch's wrath!"

"It's a good way to ostracize someone," Brenda added. Her joking tone was gone, she was being serious now, and I knew she was right.

I'd never told Brenda about Abby Parris hitting me on the lacrosse field. I'd handled that myself.

Abby probably expected me to avoid her during play after that hit, but of course, I did the opposite. I stayed very close to her every chance I got. When she was looking at me, I would charge at her and at the last minute, run alongside her. When she wasn't looking, I would ease up behind her and then let her suddenly see me right next to her. I could tell that freaked her out. Once or twice, she flailed in my direction with her stick, but now that I knew what to expect from her, I always blocked it, and I never, ever struck back. I would just ignore it. And since I was always on my guard, she never got the chance to use her elbow or anything else again either. She tried a couple of times, but now that I was alert, I could see she was slow and clumsy about it. She reminded me of her buddy Mary Putnam. A wannabe bully, but not very good at it. Whenever I spoke to her, I was especially, exaggeratingly, nice and sweet. After a while that freaked her out more than anything, I think.

Later, I said something to Brenda.

"I think they've given up trying to bully us physically. I think they're trying to play mental games now. A war of wits."

"If so," she replied, "they're not very well armed. Besides, there was only that one physical attack on the soccer field last month. They might still try something like that again."

I still kept quiet about me and Abby on the lacrosse field. No need to worry Brenda more.

She looked at me.

"You didn't really put a curse on that poor girl, did you Amy?"

I took me a few long seconds to catch on that she was teasing me.

I'll give the bitch credit, whenever she did that, I always fell for it until I saw the twinkle in her eye.

I tried to punch her shoulder, but of course, my reaction was predictable, so I missed, and she laughed.

20. PRINCESSES
AMY

When we were little, Brenda and I would often usually over at each other's place on the weekends. After dinner on Saturday, we'd watch DVDs all night until our folks made us turn off the TV and go to bed. We loved all the Pixar and Disney movies, but after we saw The Princess Bride, that became our favorite. It didn't take us long to memorize every line. Even after we outgrew the Disney princess movies, we never got tired of Princess Buttercup and her friends. Our favorite scene was any scene with Andre the Giant in it.

We usually took turns, but I preferred to stay over at Brenda's house. Especially when her Gram was there to cook. Brenda's mom's cooking skills were most charitably described as limited. Brenda's Gram, however, was the best cook in Missouri, or so I thought.

Usually, they took me to their church the next morning. We were not churchgoers in my own family, but my folks never had any objection to this. Brenda's church was loud and cheerful. There was always lots of music and singing, and everyone dressed up super nice, the ladies with colorful dresses and big hats, and after the service, there would be a big supper in the hall behind the church. The ladies would do the cooking, and the older kids would help. I was always made to feel welcome, like I was part of one great big happy family. Afterwards, us kids would do most of the cleanup, and even that was fun. My mom had to go and buy me a nice church dress, so I wouldn't look too out of place. If anyone thought less of me for wearing the same dress every time, they were much too nice to say so.

After Harvey died, they had his funeral in that same church, and Brenda and her mom stopped going. Miz Sally was usually too worn out by the time Sunday rolled around, and Brenda seemed to lose interest. We still had regular sleep-overs on most weekends, and still watched our movies, but we tended to stay more at my apartment than at her house. My mom was a better cook and this also gave Miz Sally some time to relax at home by herself without having to take care of us two brats.

When we watched The Princess Bride after that, we still loved Fezzik, but the scene that now seemed to give Brenda the greatest satisfaction was the one where Inigo Montoya kills Count Rugen. Her grim smile during that scene was almost a snarl.

21. THE RAVEN
AMY

The Academy announced that there would be a small party on Halloween in the dining hall. Halloween fell on a Monday, a school night, so we'd have to finish up by eleven. No outside guests (meaning no boys) would be invited. But we were encouraged to dress "appropriate for the occasion," so I was able to ditch the uniform for one extra day.

Brenda and I hadn't dressed up for Halloween in years. Our dads always used to take us door to door when we were little. My dad never dressed up, but Brenda's dad always got into the spirit of the occasion. Every year, he wore the same costume, that of a giant white rabbit. I once asked him why he was dressed as the Easter Bunny on Halloween, but Harvey just laughed and said he wasn't the Easter Bunny, he was Ralph Ellison. I didn't know who that was, or get the joke, but I've always known her dad was the source of Brenda's twisted and obscure sense of humor.

Uncle Charlie took us to a big costume shop near Maryland General Hospital so we could find outfits for the party. He had a late shift that night down at Mercy Hospital so he took care of us early in the afternoon, while Di stayed back at the house, fixing dinner. I was getting to know Baltimore pretty well by learning where all the hospitals were.

While Aunt Diane was based at Johns Hopkins, Uncle Charlie worked at Mercy and they both had weird schedules and usually not a lot of time together. After a while I figured out that they were using me and Brenda as an excuse to be together more on the weekends. That worked out well for all of us.

I once asked Chuck why Baltimore seemed to have so many hospitals.

"We need them," he told me. "It's because the city doesn't have any grocery stores. But we have lots of cheap fast food joints, and with them, lots of hypertension, diabetes, and general bad health."

In the costume shop, Brenda found a slutty maid's outfit with an incredibly short skirt she wanted me to buy, but I found an inexpensive witch's robe instead. "Equally appropriate for you," she told me. She was having a hard time finding anything she liked. I tried to help her but she wasn't giving me any good feedback on my suggestions. I saw a pink ballerina costume and held it up. "This would at least make your mom happy," I told her. Her sneer told me what she thought of my idea, but an instant later, her eyes lit up and the sneer became a devilish grin. We found a pink one in her size, and she found a high collar Dracula cape of red and black satin and a pair of devil's horns. In the kid's section she found a plastic pitchfork. "I'm ready," she said.

I inventoried her mixed bag. "Brenda," I asked, "What are you thinking?"

She refused to say, but when we got back to the house, she raided Aunt Di's sewing supplies and banished me from our room. She emerged an hour later to go to the laundry room. She had washed the ballerina leotard and went to pull it from the dryer, but she wouldn't let me see it or get back into our room.

Eventually, Di told me to get Brenda to come down for dinner. I knocked on the door and told her it was ready, but she replied, "Ten more minutes! I'll be right down. Don't come in!"

We were sitting at the table when we heard her coming down. The sound of her patent leather flats sounded like hoofs on the stairs. We all gasped in unison when she entered the dining room. She hadn't been washing the pink leotard; she had been dyeing it. It was now a full body suit, blood red. With a swirl, she whipped off the black satin cloak, and spun around to reveal the pointed tail she'd added to her leotard. The horns on her head completed the costume perfectly. She lacked only Satan's goatee.

"Well," she said, in a deep voice, "shall I say grace?"

We were up in our room after dinner, modeling our costumes in the mirror when Di called up to us.

"Girls! We have to go now!"

We glanced at each other, then went to the top of the stairs. Di was below, getting her coat and bag. Brenda asked, "Go where?"

"Sorry," Diane said. "I have an emergency call and have to get to the hospital right away. Don't bother changing, just stuff your bags and come on. If I can, I'll take you back to school after I check on my patient, if not, I'll have to put you in a cab. Come on, we have to go now. I'm sorry."

We raced south. There wasn't much traffic on a Sunday evening, but Brenda noticed we were going the wrong way and asked, "Di, is this the way to Johns Hopkins?"

Di slowed to turn right onto West Fayette Street, then said, "No, my patient is at the VA Medical Center. They should honor my JHU badge and let me park in their staff garage, but keep an eye out for parking in case I have to turn around."

When we were only a block and a half away, I spotted an open public garage and pointed that out. We stopped at North Green Street for the light and I noticed we were right next to Westminster Hall.

I shouted, "Aunt Di! Me and Brenda will get out here! We'll check in at the hospital lobby desk and you can call us or meet us there when you're done."

"What? Why..?" I pointed, and she noticed the people gathered just inside the church's brick and iron fence. It only took her a second to make the connection before she said, "Ok, but don't be too long, and don't go anywhere else."

Brenda did *not* make the connection; I had to practically drag her. "Leave our stuff in the car! Come on! Get out!"

She frowned, but followed me and we got to the sidewalk before the light changed.

"Do you know where we are?" I asked her.

"No...," She answered in a low, suspicious voice, "You tell me."

I pulled her closer to the fence and pointed. It was already dark, but the street lamp shone off the white marble, illuminating the tombstone clearly. She laughed. "I forgot it was here," she said.

There were five people already inside the fence; an older man and his wife both in formal attire like they'd just come from the opera, a younger couple, and a middle aged guy from the church itself. We joined them. Even though I'd left my hat and wig in the car, it was clear that I was a witch, and Brenda was a perfect Lucifer, even without the pitchfork. The older couple smiled at us and stepped aside so we could get close to the tombstone. Some fresh roses lay propped up against it. The base revealed the name: "EDGAR ALLAN POE."

We stood quietly for a good while.

Brenda whispered, "We should have brought him some brandy."

"Cognac, dear," the older lady said. "That was his favorite; he couldn't afford it very often when he was alive."

Her husband added, "And the Man in Black is supposed to bring it on his birthday, not on Halloween. But I'm sure Mr. Poe would have been glad to get the brandy, too."

We all stood a while longer, under a waxing crescent moon, just enjoying the silence and the night. Then the older man gently touched the bronze plaque bearing Poe's likeness, and after his wife did likewise, they turned and left, arm in arm. The young couple repeated the gesture, and then, feeling it might be expected, Brenda and I did the same. When I touched it, I felt an electric spark run up my arm and through my body. It was only my imagination of course, but it felt very real. We didn't speak until we crossed the street and found the hospital entrance.

I made some crack about how easy it had been for Beelzebub to enter consecrated ground, but Brenda replied, "Churches are second home to the Lord of the Flies. Besides, you forget: I'm also an angel."

We sat in the lobby next to the gift shop to wait for Di's call. Our costumes drew more than a few stares. "That was a good idea, Amy," Brenda told me, idly waving her pointed tail in the air. "Tomorrow night there will be a crowd at the tomb and they probably won't let anyone inside the gate. Too many freaks on Halloween."

We had regular classes in the morning, but the 3 pm class was cancelled, as were any evening classes, so we could have our Halloween party.

It wasn't much of a party without any boys, but it was a chance to trade in our damn uniforms and show off our costumes. I had my witch's hat and my scraggly gray wig. People kept asking me where I'd parked my broom. I'd expected Cleo to come dressed as the Queen of Egypt, but she chose to be the Greek goddess Athena, and that costume suited her surprisingly well. Karen came as Annie Oakley. Her holster was empty, and when asked about that, she'd grumble that the sheriff made her check her six-shooter at the jailhouse. Xuěyàn was dressed up as Sacagawea (she said), but with her feather headdress and foam rubber tomahawk, she looked more like a semi-racist cartoon version of Sitting Bull than the Bird Woman of the Lewis and Clark expedition. Then there was Brenda. She had split the back of her cloak so her pointed tail could poke out. Except for her little boobs, she was the very image of the Prince of Darkness.

The hospital gift shop had had some sports items for fans of the Orioles and the Ravens, and there had been a paper-mache Raven wearing a football jersey. It was expensive for what would be a one-night gag, but Brenda had bought it, cut off the jersey, and made me fix the bird to my shoulder to be my familiar. She ended nearly every sentence by croaking out the word, "Nevermore." That got old fast for me, but she kept it up all night.

There was fruit punch and soda, cake and cookies, some little sandwiches (spelled: "Sand-Witches") and other snacks. I looked over the cookies for Brenda's favorite but all they had were chocolate chip and plain sugar cookies. For some reason her favorite was oatmeal-raisin; I don't know why.

We had line dancing, and music, but mostly we just talked and laughed and relaxed.

The award for best costume went to Sue Spence. She was dressed as a silent film star from the 1920's. It was a good costume, but I thought not as good as Brenda's Beelzebub.

Mary Putnam sat at a corner table with two of her posse; Abby Parris and Betty Williams, all of them dressed as angels. They stuck to themselves the whole night. Ann Warren usually sat with them, but I didn't see her.

Near the end of the evening, I could almost swear the punch had been spiked. I was certain I could smell alcohol on a couple of the seniors.

When the party was over, everyone helped clean up. We had signed up to take down the ceiling ribbons so we pulled them down and stuffed them into a couple of trash bags. We were lugging those out the door when we bumped into Abby and Betty.

Immediately, they both shrieked and fell to the floor, going into some kind of fit. They seemed dazed and only semi-conscious and were scratching themselves furiously, alternately moaning and screaming. Betty was tearing at her costume, ripping it to shreds. Brenda and I were right next to them, so we tried to help by restraining them while Karen and others ran for help.

Mary Putnam ran up, looked right at me and asked, "What did you do to them? They weren't bothering you."

I simply froze, open-mouthed, looking up at her. I didn't know how to respond to that. There was no reason to think I would or even could have done anything to hurt anybody.

"Get your hands off them!" Mary shouted, "Leave them alone!"

A crowd gathered and Abby and Betty became calm. Abby seemed to rouse herself as if waking up from a bad dream. She looked up at me holding her and shoved me away. Her eyes were wide and she asked, "What did you do to me?"

The next day, Dr. Kramer was waiting for us just outside our last class.

"Ladies, I need you to come with me, please."

Brenda and I followed behind her as she led the way to her office. I didn't need to glance at Brenda to know what she was thinking. This was about last night and we were going to be blamed somehow.

Seated in the Provost's office, Dr. Kramer just looked at us. It was a bit of a contest to see who would speak first. *How juvenile*, I thought.

Kramer spoke first. "Do you girls have anything to say?"

"About what?" I managed to keep most of the exasperation out of my voice. Brenda just shook her head, very slightly.

"About what happened last night," the Provost said.

I took a deep breath. "All I know is that two of the girls had a fit of some kind and we tried to help them. When they came out of it they seemed to think we did something to hurt them. We did not."

"They think you did."

"They are wrong."

Dr. Kramer tapped her pencil on her desk a few times, probably expecting me to say something else.

We waited her out.

Eventually, "There was a powder found in their clothing. What do you girls know about that?"

I immediately thought 'drugs', and so did Brenda.

"I don't know anything about that," I said.

Brenda spoke up. "What kind of powder?" she asked.

"Are you sure you don't know?"

If I knew, I wouldn't be asking, you dumb bitch.

I kept that thought to myself and said, "No, I don't know."

Dr. Kramer shifted her gaze to stare at Brenda, clearly expecting a direct response from her too.

"I don't know either," Brenda obliged. "Whatever happened had nothing to do with us. We tried to help them."

Dr. Kramer still hadn't answered Brenda's original question, so I repeated it.

"What kind of powder?"

"Well! If you don't know, it really doesn't matter, does it?" The sarcasm in her voice was strong enough it should have peeled off the wallpaper, but all it did was push Brenda close to an explosive response.

Dr. Kramer had no concept of how dangerous it was to insult Brenda to her face so blatantly. She was blissfully ignorant of who and what Brenda represented. Few things could be more reckless than assaulting Brenda's sense of justice with a false accusation.

I reached over to touch Brenda's arm. I expected her to jerk away, but I could feel her muscles relax instead. There would be no explosion. As she had so many times in the past, Brenda just upgraded the rating on her safety valve to handle the increased pressure.

I could never understand how insensitive everyone was to the rage they kept feeding.

"Why did you choose those costumes?" Kramer was talking again.

It took a few seconds for her words to register, not that they seemed to make much sense.

"What do you mean?" I asked.

"Don't act dumb with me, young lady."

Well, it wasn't an act. I really didn't know what she meant.

"I'm sorry, Dr. Kramer," I said, "I don't..."

"Amy really doesn't understand the question," Brenda interjected. "Are you asking if there is some special reason why we chose the costumes we did?"

"That is what I asked."

"Well, ma'am," Brenda replied, "The truth is that we had no specific reason. We went to the costume shop late and there wasn't much available in a reasonable size. Amy's Witch's robe was one-size-fits-all, and I assembled my costume from parts of others. I mean, after all, both Witches and Devils are traditional costumes for Halloween. There's certainly nothing unusual about them."

I nodded my head in agreement. Dr. Kramer looked skeptical.

She asked a different question. "Are either of you two dabbling in the occult?"

Holy shit.

Brenda was not as flabbergasted as I was, but I could tell she was just as disappointed. We may not have seen eye to eye with Dr. Kramer on everything, but we never thought she was stupid. This was the kind of nonsense I might expect from one of the girls, but not from a grown teacher.

"Look," Kramer went on, "I've seen a lot of girls come through here, and from time to time, one or two will start playing with Ouija boards and then start doing other... It starts out as a game, but it can get serious."

Brenda was silently telling me to shut my mouth. It had no doubt dropped open in astonishment.

"I don't know if you girls are church-goers, but if not, you might want to consider it. The school wants its young ladies to develop not just academically and physically, but spiritually and morally as well. Of course, I'm not saying you should attend any *particular* church, but you shouldn't neglect that part of your personal growth."

We both made the expected polite noises and shortly after that, Dr. Kramer released us.

Without actually saying so, she made it abundantly clear that she suspected us of 'something' and was going to be watching us.

Brenda and I huddled in her room later.

"So," I asked, "what's next?"

"You tell me."

"What do you think about this powder?"

"I know why they suspected us. It's an open secret that there is some conflict between you and me and Putnam's 'posse'. We were working in the laundry, we were handling their uniforms. We had means, apparent motive, and opportunity.

"So," I repeated, "what's next?"

"I don't know. But we need to be very careful."

Karen and Cleo both came to us with the rumors. The powder had been itching powder. When I wondered aloud about the likelihood of both girls having a simultaneous allergic reaction to an over-the counter prank powder, Brenda just said, "Yes, it would be an incredible coincidence, wouldn't it?"

22. PILLOW TALK
BRENDA

Amy was nervous about something.

I assumed she was worried about that itching powder crap, so I told her, "Don't sweat this, Amy. It will all blow over."

She looked at me with her face scrunched up in obvious confusion.

"What are you talking about?"

"Aren't you concerned with this stuff about Abby and Betty?"

"Not really. What? You think that'll turn into something serious?"

"Probably not, you just looked worried, Amy."

"I'm fine."

She looked away from me.

"I've been thinking about our dance class."

So that was it.

"You mean about our dance partners; that's what you really mean, right?"

Amy blushed a little, but it faded almost immediately.

"So," I asked, "It is Bobby or Steve?"

She kept me waiting for a few seconds before answering.

"Steve," she said, "Not Bobby."

"I like Ricky," I told her, "keep your hands off him."

We both smiled at that.

"Ricky likes you, too," Amy said. "I think Steve likes me, but I'm not sure."

"Listen to us," I said. "We barely know these guys and already we're planning to get them to be our dates for the Spring Formal. That's six or seven months away. We don't even know if they already have girlfriends."

Amy's eyes widened at that suggestion. She obviously hadn't considered that possibility.

"Do you think they do?"

There was a little tremor in her voice.

"You really like this Steve guy, don't you, Amy?"

"Yeah, I guess I really do."

She paused before adding, "Do you think there is such a thing as love at first sight?"

"Love? Isn't it a little... a lot early to be thinking about that?"

"Brenda, I'm not saying I'm in love. But there's nothing wrong with starting to think about it. We both need to start preparing ourselves for the possibility. The eventuality."

"We need to be careful, you know. We need to remember The Plan."

Amy nodded her head in silent agreement.

"Besides," I continued, "I'm not completely sure I know what love is."

"What do you think it is?"

"Well, I'll tell you. In an abstract sense, it might just be a purely chemical reaction to each other's pheromones. But that's maybe just lust, not love. Maybe it's an intellectual appreciation of someone's virtues..."

"Or some kind of spiritual gift?"

I hadn't known Amy to talk about spiritual stuff before.

"Or," I countered, "It could be an economic calculation of what kind of benefit we can get from the other person, how we can use them, unconsciously maybe. I'd be willing to bet most people never really find out what love is. Maybe nobody does."

"Or maybe it's some other thing. Just hormones?"

"I think we all feel those. What's the chemical? Oxycontin? Maybe we're just machines fueled by our endocrine glands."

Amy didn't respond to that.

"You're really smitten, aren't you, Amy?"

"Maybe."

The answer came slowly from her.

"Maybe love is something different."

"You're just horny," I told her. "Don't let that get you all twisted up. We all have emotions, and those can make us stupid sometimes."

"I'm not going to do anything stupid," Amy said.

23. SWEET SIXTEEN
AMY

"I've decided to go to that fencing tournament," Brenda told me.

"Tournament? What fencing tournament? What do you mean?"

"Amy, I told you about this," she replied. "It's a regular competition against people outside the school. It's Saturday."

"This Saturday? Day after tomorrow? I don't remember you telling me," I replied.

"That's because your head is full of dreams about boys with sandy hair and soft smiles," She chided me. "You've had two dance classes and already your short-term memory is totally shot." She shook her head.

"Wait," I said, "You are actually going to compete against other people, other girls? You've only been fencing for... what? three weeks? I don't care how well you've been doing - are you ready to be in a real competition?"

"Ms. Dunham says it will be good experience. Some of the other competitors will also be novices. You should come along. You can help carry my stuff."

"I'm not your pack mule," I told her. "Besides, I need to finish my reading. I've got a couple of quizzes on Monday."

"Bring your books and tablet with you. You can study there if you get bored. Besides," her eyes twinkled, "It's a mixed open tournament. It's being held at St. John's College in Annapolis. They have college boys."

There wasn't much equipment to help with. She'd ordered her own fencing glove, but it hadn't arrived yet, so except for her own socks and tennis shoes Brenda was still using the school's equipment and uniform.

St. John's did have a nice gymnasium, located right across the street from the Naval Academy. It had an old-time look and feel, but was not run down at all, and the ladies room was clean. The gym had an odd running track like a balcony that wrapped around the mezzanine inside.

There were a few college boys, but not as many as Brenda had led me to expect. There were also some really old guys and some older women, one in her seventies, and a little girl who could not have been more than nine. A number of schools and clubs were represented. The Bryn Mawr sluts had brought their whole team.

I agreed to help keep score. I was nervous about that, but it was easy; the judge simply told me who scored the point and I marked it down. I still managed to make a few mistakes, but they got corrected and nobody got mad at me.

I was able to watch Brenda when she fenced on my strip a couple of times. She got skunked both times, and didn't make it to the second round, but to my untrained eye, she looked good. She scored a couple points on her other three bouts, so when we added up the final results, she didn't place dead last, just next to last. Drenched in sweat, her hair a mess, she looked totally beat, but her eyes were bright and she still had energy. I knew she had enjoyed herself. They had showers in the gym, but nobody had brought a change of clothes, so when we all squeezed into the van, I couldn't resist telling everyone they stank. They all just laughed, but we did drive back with one of the windows half-way down.

I understood that Brenda had dragged me along to try to get me to dump lacrosse and take up fencing with her, but that was not going to happen.

"No thanks." I told her. "The reason you signed up for fencing is because your name is 'Brenda' and because you've watched Mulan and The Princess Bride too many times. I, at least, know the difference between fantasy and reality."

"You know," she replied, "For someone who is always calling me a bitch, you should look in a mirror once in a while."

"No need. I already know I'm beautiful."

I saw her welts and bruises later. For me, however, the trip was still worthwhile. I could tell that she was serious about this fencing crap, and it gave me some ideas about what to get her for her birthday and Christmas, ideas I could share with Aunt Diane.

My own birthday fell on a Saturday this year, and I knew Aunt Diane probably had something planned by the way Brenda was pretending to have forgotten I was sixteen now. Xuěyàn, however, wished me a happy birthday as soon as I woke up, and while I was still in my pajamas, gave me a little box in red wrapping paper. I had told her not to get me anything, but she hadn't listened, of course. Inside was a Chinese seal, carved from emerald jade with the figure of a rat on top and the Chinese name she'd given me engraved intaglio on the bottom. I found out later that she'd had it hand carved in her home town by an artist her family knew and express shipped all the way from Xian, China. I could tell it was special. I hugged her and thanked her as sincerely as I could.

"It's gorgeous," I told her. "Brenda will be very jealous."

Xuěyàn giggled. "I get one for her, also. Do not say to him yet. Two weeks I give for his...her birth-day."

Uncle Charlie picked us up later in his Jaguar, and since it was my birthday, I sat shotgun while Brenda and Di sat in the back. Chuck loved his car and pointed out all the cool features, including the heated leather seats, perfect for winter.

We had dinner at a very nice place on the fifth floor of some nice hotel overlooking the inner harbor. To me, it looked very fancy and I said so.

"I think you'll like it," Chuck told me. "We come here sometimes because it's not too far from Mercy Hospital and it's a great view. Too bad they closed Hausner's restaurant, that was our favorite. You would have like that, too."

I'd never had lobster, and I asked about it in the car, but when I saw the price on the menu, knowing Uncle Charlie was paying, I felt too guilty and went for the crab cakes instead. Brenda was much less shy and she *did* order the lobster, as did both Uncle Charlie and Aunt Di, so I was the only one left out. To top it off, they all told me how good the lobster was and how I should have ordered it. The crab cakes were still ok, though.

We lingered over dinner and it was nice to just relax and admire the view. Aunt Di told me how pretty I looked, and her voice was sincere enough that she made me believe it for a while. Brenda was surprisingly well behaved, not cracking on me a single time, even agreeing that Aunt Di was right, I did look pretty.

The birthday card was for a six-year old child. They had drawn a crude "1" in front of the six to fix it, as a joke - Brenda's idea, no doubt. Inside was a picture of a princess dancing in a ballroom gown in the arms of her prince and the handwritten note: "Coupon: Good for one prom dress or dancing gown, redeemable when needed. Happy 16th Birthday - Your Loving Family in Baltimore - Chuck, Di & Brenda."

I struggled not to cry in the restaurant, and Brenda put her arm around my shoulder until I regained my composure. "Thank you," I whispered, "you've been very good to me."

Uncle Charlie just shrugged and said, "Well, of course. You're family."

Back at the house there were more presents; a beautiful new winter coat from Chuck and Di, and from Brenda, the high heels I'd tried on in the store the day before. "You'll need to start practicing, Amy," she told me. "You know how clumsy you can be."

There was something from my folks, too. It was the broach my mom sometimes wore, one that I'd often admired. It also came with a note.

"Dearest Amy: This is the first piece of jewelry I ever bought for your mom. Now that you are almost grown up, we both agreed that you should have it, so you won't forget us. Remember that we will always be with you even when we're apart. Love, Mom and Dad. Happy Birthday."

Di shoved me into the den so I could call my folks and talk to them in private. I'm different from most girls; I don't like talking on the phone, but we talked for about an hour, maybe the longest phone conversation ever for me. I was surprised that I had that much to say, and even more surprised by how much I liked hearing the sound of their voices.

It was a perfect day.

24. BURN WITCH BURN
BRENDA

Between Abby Parris and Betty Williams, Abby was the bolder of the two. She kept giving us the evil eye whenever she could, while her buddy Betty did everything to avoid all eye contact.

The rumors were that they both still blamed Amy and me for the powder in their uniforms. I could see the logic of that, but they clearly thought we'd done something more than just put itching powder on their clothes. They were reasonably intelligent girls, but apparently vulnerable to suggestions of superstitious nonsense. Maybe they had come up with that idea on their own, but I suspected the suggestion had been planted. Probably by someone they associated with, someone with a strong personality, someone more charismatic.

Someone like Mary Putnam.

A little more than a week later, at dinner, I overheard someone talking about a curse.

Silly me, at first I thought some girl was talking about her period, but as soon as I heard Amy's name mentioned, I knew what it was about.

I glanced over at them just in time to hear Abby say, "Maybe she's a real witch."

I wondered how anyone could be so stupid. Witches? Really?

Amy looked up about that time and followed my gaze. I don't know what she'd overheard up to that point, but she certainly heard the next line from Mary Putnam: "They burn witches, you know."

This bit of info was delivered just a little bit louder than was necessary, to make sure Amy overheard. Before I could stop her, Amy retorted, "Real witches don't fear fire, they spark it."

Betty actually looked a little frightened, but Abby and Mary both smirked.

I elbowed Amy in the ribs. She looked at me with surprise, but when I frowned at her she just nodded. She knew she needed to keep her mouth shut, but she never did the smart thing. I tried to cover her remark.

"Real witches?" I said, "There's no such thing, Amy. Grow up."

Amy nodded her head again. She was at least smart enough to know my comment wasn't directed at her.

Two days later, in the hallway, Mary's book bag burst into flames.

I found out when I bumped into Karen.

"Mary was just standing at the foot of the stairs when somebody spotted smoke from her bag," Karen told me. "She took it off and as soon as she did, there were actual flames. She stepped outside and dumped it in the grass. The backpack burned and one of her books was a little singed. She was lucky. She'd left her tablet up in her room, so all she really lost was the bag itself and a paper notebook."

"How does a book bag catch fire?" I asked.

"Nobody knows."

"And nobody thought to pull the fire alarm?"

"She threw it outside real quick. The provost is investigating."

"Dr. Kramer? Is Mary a smoker? Maybe she had cigarettes and matches, or a lighter in her bag?"

"I don't know, Brenda."

Karen was hesitating. She had something else to say.

"What?" I asked, "What is it?"

"Well, after stomping out the fire, everyone was standing around staring at it, and Mary said, 'I guess I shouldn't have told Amy that they burn witches'."

I should have expected something like this.

I asked, "Did Mary actually accuse Amy of anything?"

"No," Karen said, "at least, not in so many words."

I thanked Karen and went to find Amy.

I found her in the library, talking to Cleo.

I looked around, saw one of the little conference rooms was empty, and pulled Amy up out of her chair and into the room. She started to protest, but she picked up on my manner and went with me quietly. Once I shut the door, I stuck my hands into the pockets of her blazer.

"What the fuck are you doing?" she asked, slapping my hand away.

She froze when I pulled out the disposable lighter, and when I found the hand-rolled joint, she said, "Holy shit!"

Our eyes locked.

"It's not mine, Brenda," she said, "I don't know..."

"I know it's not yours," I cut her off. "It's been planted on you."

Amy's eyes got big as saucers.

"Empty all your pockets," I said.

We went through her book bag too, and we didn't find anything else. A sniff proved the joint was the real thing. I crumpled up the evidence in a couple pieces of paper.

"Go back with Cleo," I told her. "But don't tell her anything. We don't want to drag her into this. I'll get rid of this crap."

Amy went back to a very puzzled Cleo and I made it to the cafeteria. I disposed of the evidence in the trash can by the door. As quick as possible, I returned to the library.

I gave Amy and Cleo an update about the book bag that had caught fire. I was careful not to mention the contraband from Amy's jacket in front of Cleo, and for once, Amy did keep her mouth shut.

We waited.

Dr. Kramer herself showed up instead of sending someone to bring us to her office.

"Miss McDonald," she said, "will you stand up, please."

Amy did as she was asked and didn't even ask why.

Without any preliminaries, Kramer put her hands in Amy's coat pockets. She looked surprised when all she found was a cheap ballpoint pen.

I asked, "What's this about, Dr. Kramer?"

"Never you mind, Miss Dickens." She gave me a hard look before adding, "Will you stand up too, please?"

She didn't find anything on me either and nothing in either of our book bags.

Cleo couldn't keep quiet any longer.

"Dr. Kramer," she said, "Amy and Brenda are too polite, but I believe you are supposed to give a reason when you search a student."

Those were the rules.

We had explicitly given up our rights to privacy when we entered the school, but the school also had obligations when they wanted to conduct a search, and providing a justification was one of those obligations.

Kramer was clearly annoyed, but I always thought everyone was a little afraid of Cleo. Or maybe wary of her money and her lawyers.

"Someone thought they saw you with smoking materials, Miss McDonald. This is a non-smoking campus. And, as you know, it is illegal for anyone under eighteen to possess tobacco. Or anything else."

"We don't smoke," I told her. "We don't smoke, we don't drink, and we don't do drugs. If someone told you otherwise, you should be questioning them and their honesty, not us."

I had raised my voice and when I realized that, I took a deep breath and forced myself to cool down.

"I'm sorry, Dr. Kramer," I added more softly, "but you have been given some bad information."

She gave me a hard look.

I bowed my head slightly, but stood my ground.

"It may be," she said, "that I was misinformed."

That was the closest thing to an apology we were likely to get from her.

Kramer left the room after that.

At least she hadn't brought up witchcraft.

I thought that if Amy had been found with a lighter, that would have gotten her the blame for the burning backpack but cleared her of any of this witchcraft bullshit. Without the lighter, they would think she'd started the fire with magic.

Morons and their bullshit.

I had been very careful to avoid suggesting to Amy that she might actually somehow be responsible for any of this weird stuff. In the first place, I didn't believe she was. I wasn't ready to believe in magic. In the second place, I didn't want *her* to start believing in it. If she thought I was giving it any credence, she might start to buy into it herself. And in the third place, we'd been overheard too many times before, and I didn't want anyone to hear us talking about magic spells and curses. Our enemies would see to it that such talk would only be interpreted the wrong way.

Cleo was looking to me for an explanation, but I just waved her off and took Amy up to her room.

"We shouldn't carry backpacks anymore," I told her.

For a second, Amy looked like the proverbial deer caught in the headlights, but understanding filled her eyes quick enough.

"Yeah," she said, "we don't want anybody slipping anything else into ours."

I added, "It may put other minds at ease, too, if they can see everything we're carrying."

The corners of Amy's mouth turned down. "We've still got pockets in our blazers, so I'm not sure how much that's going to help. But you're right."

She looked around the room as if she expected to find something.

"What we really need," she said, "are a couple of those clear plastic backpacks like the little kids carry. Maybe with a 'Hello Kitty' or Disney princess theme--something as innocent as possible. We should be able to find those. It's going to be a real pain carrying a tablet, a notebook and a couple of books without a bag of some kind."

"You know," she added, "the weird thing is, after her crack about burning witches, I'd just been imagining Mary, tied up and burning at the stake. It was just an idle thought, I wasn't serious."

25. MAGICAL MYSTERY TOUR
AMY

"Get your coats," Cleo told us.

"What do you mean?" I asked.

"You two are coming with me," she said. "We are going for a drive."

"What? A drive?"

"Don't say 'what', just get your coats. We'll be back after lunch."

Cleo's guardians had apparently faxed over the permission form, so we had no trouble signing ourselves out. In the driveway was a huge black limousine. An extremely tall African man with tribal scars on his face, wearing a dark suit that looked very expensive bowed to us and held the door open for us. Cleo called him 'Azim'.

I'd never been in a limo before. It was even nicer inside than Uncle Chuck's Jaguar.

Cleo wouldn't tell us where we were going, but we headed south toward DC. Based on our luxurious ride, I was expecting to pull up to a palace, but instead, we stopped in front of a modest door at the end of a run-down strip mall. The small sign on the door simply read: "Wilson's". The chauffeur helped us out and spoke to Cleo in some foreign language. She responded the same way, and he bowed to her, addressing her as "Kandake". The tiny door opened to steps that led immediately up a narrow passage.

As we climbed, Brenda asked, "What language was that, Arabic?"

"Not Arabic, it's Nobiin," Cleo replied. "It's a Sudanese language."

"He called you 'Kandake', what is that?" I asked.

Cleo turned on the stairway to look at me. "It's just a polite form of address," she said. She waved her hand as if it were nothing.

There was another door at the top of the stairs, and when Cleo opened it, we came face to face with an Egyptian Mummy Sarcophagus.

Cleo tugged on the mummy's false beard and the sarcophagus slid away revealing the entrance to a shop filled with curios. Brenda and I realized where we were at the same time. "It's a magic shop!"

An old guy with a full head of long silver-white hair came from around the counter, and Cleo introduced herself. "Mr. Wilson? I'm Cleo Smith. We spoke on the phone last night. These are my friends, Amy and Brenda."

"Ah, of course. Welcome. And it's just 'Wilson', not '*Mr.* Wilson'. Is it 'Cleo' or 'Cleopatra'?"

"It's just 'Cleo' for me." She answered.

"Ah, so not the Queen of the Nile, but the Muse of History," He said. "Right this way ladies, please."

He led us behind a curtain to a tiny room with a green felt-covered poker table and four chairs and had us all sit.

He was wearing a long-sleeved white dress shirt with fancy ruffles in front, like a man might wear with a tuxedo. He loosened the cuffs and rolled his sleeves up past his elbow leaving his arms bare. He showed us his empty hands, then put his palms together. When he opened them again, he held a deck of cards.

Brenda and I both gasped. There was no way he could have hidden that deck. It was like he'd pulled it right out of thin air. With perfect smoothness, he fanned the whole deck out on the table.

"Please examine the cards, ladies. Don't mark or damage any of them, but otherwise, examine them as much as you please."

It certainly seemed like an ordinary deck of bicycle playing cards, perfectly suitable for playing hearts or solitaire or anything else.

He had us shuffle them, mixing up the order as much as we could. He took the deck back and without doing his own shuffle or any other kind of manipulation (as far as I could see), fanned them out on the table again. They had arranged themselves in perfect order, sorted by suit and value.

Brenda made a little "Oh" sound, but I just stared.

"No matter what you do," he said, "the deck is always stacked against you."

Brenda made a little snorting noise in response to that.

He gave the deck a flick at one end, flipping the whole spread over, face down. I'd seen that before, that was just a simple display of manual dexterity. A moment later, he repeated the process, turning them all back face up.

Now, all the cards were the same. All fifty two cards were the Queen of Hearts.

I was too stunned to say anything, but Brenda... "How did you *do* that?" She asked.

Wilson smiled at us. "I'll teach you," he said.

It was almost a disappointment to learn the trick.

He showed and then taught us a few more illusions.

There were more things with cards, then he pushed a solid rod through a mirror without there being a hole, and he filled the air with snowflakes.

He also pushed a knitting needle through his tongue, then through his hand, and when he pulled it out, there was no mark or hole.

After that, he cleared the table of all props, and showed us his empty hands. He snapped his fingers and his whole hand burst into flames. "This, ladies," he said while the blue flames enveloped his hand, "is sometimes called a 'Hand of Glory', but that is not quite accurate."

With his other, non-burning hand he pulled out a handkerchief and used it to wipe off the fire like you would dry off a wet hand. The flames now gone, he held out his hand. It was unmarked.

He took Brenda aside into the next room, then called the rest of us to watch while he helped Brenda climb into a box and he proceeded to saw her in half. She got into it, moaning and pretend-crying when the saw cut through her, and she later gave her tiny audience a polite bow when she was re-attached and helped out of the box. When I asked her how that trick was done, she stayed in character and acted surprised, saying, "Trick? What trick? That saw blade hurt!"

Cleo asked him if he could cut off the head of a live goose or duck, then re-attach the head and restore it. He said knew that trick, but did not have the necessary props in his shop. Cleo seemed disappointed, but I was not. I had no interest in decapitating an animal, if that was what was actually involved.

We had to promise not to reveal the any of the tricks, and we were eager to agree in exchange for the secrets. I saw Cleo quietly slip him her credit card later. I felt guilty that she was spending money on us, but she obviously didn't mind, so I pretended not to see.

Before we left the shop, Cleo pointed to a can of itching powder on the shelf. I briefly thought about buying a can, but I knew it would be a crazy-bad idea to be found with something like that in our possession.

Her chauffeur then drove us to a fancy French restaurant in the Latham Hotel in Georgetown, and over lunch, Cleo told us what the lesson was that she had wanted us to learn.

"It's all tricks," She said.

"But you saw how convincing even the simplest tricks can be. People want to believe, and they are easy to deceive. Even the most hardened skeptic can be fooled. You two aren't dummies, and yet you were both fooled. If there really was such a thing as true magic, it would be obvious everywhere because its practitioners would be unable to resist using it, and no one would waste their time or cleverness devising these illusions."

"Somebody at school is playing tricks on you," Cleo continued. "I don't know who or why, yet. But the simplest explanation is usually the correct one. I'll figure it out. I just don't want you to worry or start thinking you have been cursed or bewitched or anything crazy like that."

She was making perfect sense, but it still didn't feel quite right.

26. SPARK
AMY

When it was time for Tuesday's dance class, I'd only been sixteen for three days but I felt at least three years older, for some reason. The way Brenda was watching me out of the corner of her eye told me she'd noticed the change too, but she hadn't said anything yet.

We'd tried to get there early, but everyone else beat us to the room. The boys were fully occupied in conversation with the girls. Both Bobby and Steve were talking to Sue Spence, who seemed to have both of them in her orbit. I felt a stab of actual pain in my chest, but when both boys looked at me and smiled, that feeling evaporated. Brenda went straight up to Sue, patted her on the shoulder and told her, "You look nice, Sue. Doesn't she, boys?" With that, she started talking to Steve and Bobby and stole their focus away from Sue, leaving the poor girl wondering how it happened. Brenda's favorite guy Ricky joined them making her the new center of attention. With one hand behind her back, she signaled me to come over, so I did. Brenda made room for me in the little circle, and announced, "Amy just turned sixteen over the weekend, did you guys know that?" Bobby and Ricky immediately congratulated me, but Steve took my hand, held it between both of his and said, "Happy Birthday, Amy. Age usually doesn't mean much, but sixteen is a big milestone." His voice was soft and warm and his sandy brown hair seemed almost to glow when he nodded his head. For the first time, I noticed that his eyes were not just grey, but had a bit of green to them as well.

Ms. Dunham came in just then and separated us up into the usual lines facing each other.

"All right, ladies and gentlemen," she said, "we're going to practice our turns again this evening. And remember to make small-talk with your dance partner. I don't care if you can walk and chew gum at the same time, but you must be able to talk and dance at the same time. Prove to me that you can."

I danced with Bobby first. He seemed a little stand-offish with me, more shy than before. His only comment about my being sixteen now was to ask, "So, does sixteen feel any different?"

It did feel different, but it was still a pretty lame question. I told him it felt a little strange, but 'ok'. Trying to make conversation, I asked him, "Are you and Steve good friends?" As soon as the words came out of my mouth, I knew I shouldn't have asked. He frowned, but said, "We know each other."

We danced in silence after that. Bobby still knew his steps, he moved with confidence, and his eyes were still very blue, but he seemed distracted, his mind obviously elsewhere. He was clearly not thinking about the here and now with his dance partner. I thought back to how I felt when I first saw him, and how the sight of him had stirred something inside me. Those stirrings were gone now, and I felt a little sad.

I moved through a couple of other partners, and wound up with Ricky. He talked a little; certainly *he* could talk and dance at the same time. He pretended to be interested in my background, but that always turned into a question about Brenda. I was tempted to say something to him about his goofy glasses, but I was afraid it might hurt his feelings, and that might hurt Brenda's chances with him.

Eventually, I was paired up with Steve. He took my hand confidently, and slipped his right hand around my waist smoothly. I put my left arm on top of his and it felt like it belonged there.

"I'm sorry I didn't get you a birthday present, Amy. I didn't know."

"You don't have to do that," I told him, but I started wondering what kind of present would be proper for an occasional dance partner. I imagined something extravagant and romantic, like gold jewelry or diamonds, and wondered how I would react if he did something so... wildly inappropriate. It would be crazy at this stage. I shouldn't even be thinking such thoughts.

My eyes were just level with his mouth, and when he spoke, I could see the tip of his tongue moving around inside. When his mouth was closed, I kept imagining how my lips would fit against his, and couldn't help wondering if he kissed me, would his lips be soft or firm?

Every time he raised my hand to signal a turn it would take me by surprise and I'd get flustered. I was able to keep from blushing, but just barely.

Ms. Dunham called a halt to correct something another couple was doing, and Steve and I just stood together, still holding each other in the dance frame. He leaned in, and pulled my waist just a fraction of an inch closer. "You're a beautiful girl, Amy."

I sucked in my breath and felt my cheeks hot and my ears burn.

"I'm sure lots of other guys have told you that, Amy," he added.

No. No guy had ever told me that I was beautiful before.

Ms. Dunham restarted the music and we resumed dancing.

Bobby was paired with Brenda on my immediate left. I noticed that he had overheard Steve's remark and he was frowning. You had your chance, I thought.

The heart goes to those hearts that call to it.

My glance at Bobby and Brenda distracted me and I realized I hadn't thanked Steve for the compliment. I should have thanked him right away, but I'd let the moment pass and I felt awkward about saying something now. I was trying to think of something else to say, but Steve gave me the opening.

"You've done something different with your hair too," he added, "it looks very nice this way, Amy; it frames your face just right."

"Thank you. I ... I just had it trimmed. I shampooed it." I knew it was a stupid reply as soon as I'd said it, but he just smiled.

"So, Amy, do you ever get off-campus?"

I loved the sound of my name from his lips. To me, my name was just a name, just a label, but when he said it, it sounded almost musical. I refocused on his question.

"Brenda's aunt and uncle usually have us over to their house on the weekend."

"Do you ever go anywhere by yourself?"

Just then, Ms. Dunham called time, so I didn't get a chance to answer him. He smiled at me as he left.

Brenda grabbed my arm as we were walking back to our rooms. "Steve is very smooth," she said.

"I *really* like him," I admitted.

"I can see that. You do know what he was hinting at with that 'ever go anywhere by yourself' line, right?"

"Of course I do. He was about to ask me out on a date. Maybe."

"Oh, I'm pretty sure there isn't any 'maybe' about it," she said. "But you don't really know anything about him. Charming and smooth are warning flags, not signs of good intentions."

"Are you jealous?"

"No. Not of him. I just get a bad vibe from him."

"You *are* jealous!"

"I just want you to be careful. Screwing around with boys is not part of The Plan."

I glared at her. "First, I'm old enough to take care of myself, and make my own decisions. Second, a date with a boy doesn't impact The Plan.

Besides, how am I going to learn anything about him or his intentions unless I do spend more time with him, like on a real date. I've never had a real 'adult' date, you know. Finally, if you are interested, you might do well to ask about *my* intentions, not just his."

"Ok," Brenda said. "But you know that the other guys don't really like him. That should tell you something."

"You mean Bobby? He had his chance. What it tells me is that he's just jealous, too."

"Just be careful, Amy."

I expected her to make some slut reference, but she didn't do it this time.

27. COVEN

As soon as Ann got the text from Mary to come to her room, she turned off her computer and went.

Abby and Betty were already there.

"You're late," Mary told Ann. "We were about to get started without you."

"Well I'm here now. What's this all about?"

"It's about the St. Louis girls. We have to decide what to do about them. I'm ready to listen to anyone's ideas."

"I don't understand why we have to do anything. Why do we even care? I mean if they are so bad sooner or later they'll be gone anyway, right?"

"Do you really think they belong here, Ann?"

"No, probably not. I don't think they do."

"Ok, then. Look, Ann, We're not going to get them kicked out. They'll take care of that themselves. All we need to do is make it easy for them to be themselves and help them along."

"What was that business about the itching powder, Mary?"

"It was just a bit of street theatre to see how they would behave. It was a mistake. I admit it."

"And what about that fire in your bookbag? What was that about?"

"That was just a coincidence. I had a lighter in my bag, it must have been defective."

Ann frowned.

"Ann," Mary said, "I didn't deliberately set fire to my own bag. I'm not crazy. It was an accident. But there wasn't any reason not to use it. If some girls are actually dumb enough to believe those hood rats put a curse on me, it's not my responsibility to correct them. Is it?"

Ann thought for a moment before answering."

"No, I guess not. What do you need me to do?"

"Just stick with us and share any ideas you have. You can do that much, right, Ann?"

"I guess so. Sure."

"Ok, then. We're set."

28. THANKSGIVING
BRENDA

I was fencing in the gold medal round at the Olympics.

I caught my opponent's foil in a bind, then disengaged, parried her riposte, and after a quick feint, lunged in for the touch. My point hit her vest in a solid hit and as the buzzer went off, the crowd cheered. I doffed my helmet to give the final salute and take a bow when the whole earth shook, snapping my head back.

It was Amy, shaking me awake, like the proverbial terrier shaking a rat. "Wake up, lazy bitch!"
My eyes strained to focus as I pushed her hands away and I moaned.
"Get up," she said, "you're sixteen now! Pretty soon you'll be sixty and your life will be over. No time to play sleeping beauty, plenty of time to sleep after you're dead."
I rubbed my eyes, but lay where I was. I asked, "What time is..."
"Time to get up! That's what time it is," Amy replied.
As soon as I sat up, I was hit in the face by the clothes she threw at me. "Hurry up and get dressed," she told me. "Oh, and happy birthday!"

She left the room after that and I was tempted to lie back down for just one more minute of sleep, but I groaned instead and sat up. Karen was sound asleep in her own bed, blissfully unaware that Amy had come and already gone. I figured Amy had something planned, so I went into the bathroom to get myself ready. My hair only needed a little work, so I washed my face first. I was just getting started on my hair when Karen barged in and kicked me out so she could use the toilet. She wound up stealing the mirror and sink when she was done, so I just got myself dressed and crossed the hall to Amy and Xuěyàn's room.

My presents were lying out on Amy's bed. A long box, a wide flat box and a much smaller box wrapped in red paper that I guessed was from Xuěyàn.

"Where Qiǎojiě?" Xuěyàn asked. Qiǎojiě was Karen's Chinese name.

I was about to turn around and go get her when she came in, still buttoning her blouse.

Amy handed out the presents, the flat box to Karen, and the small box to Xuěyàn.

"Ok," she said, and then started singing 'Happy Birthday', which the Jins picked up immediately. Against my will, I felt myself blushing and hoping the song would be over quick.

Karen handed me the flat box and smiled while I tore it open. It was a fencing jacket of my own. "You needed this," she told me, "those school jackets looked nasty." I gave her a quick thank you and a hug.

Xuěyàn handed me the small box with both hands and I opened it more delicately. I could not guess what it might be. It was a wooden box with an embroidered silk bag inside, and inside that, a jade seal with the Chinese name Laoshi Sun had given me a few years ago when I started studying with her. Xuěyàn was a little hesitant when I hugged her, but I made it quick to spare her some embarrassment. Amy and Xuěyàn shared a smile that suggested they also shared a secret, but I let that pass.

Of course, I knew what Amy had in the long box, probably. My obvious guess was confirmed when I opened one end and slid out the sword. It was a beautiful electric foil with a maraging steel blade, the first sword I could call my own. It was a left-handed foil, which was just right, since I'd been fencing mostly with my left hand. Apparently, Amy had been paying attention for once.

"Ok," Amy said, "dump your loot in your room. We've got to hurry; they've already started serving breakfast."

When I got back to my room, I noticed Karen's laptop was in screensaver mode and was flashing a new series of family photos I hadn't seen before. One of them surprised me.

"Karen, you were a girl scout?"

"Technically, I still am. My dues are paid up. I just haven't been to any meetings for over a year. I've been way too busy."

"I always wanted to be a girl scout."

"What?" Amy had just come in and overheard me. "You wanted to be a girl scout? Since when?"

Karen asked, "So, why didn't you?"

"It's something I always wanted, but I knew Amy would have hated the uniforms."

"Why didn't you ever say anything?" Amy asked. "I might have been ok with it."

"I did, Amy. I mentioned it many times and you always blew me off."

"No," she said. "I would have remembered something like that."

Of course, that is exactly what Amy would say. She stood with her hands on her hips, almost daring me to contradict her. I just shook my head.

Poor Karen just stood there staring at us, shifting her gaze back and forth between Amy and I. She didn't say anything.

We had an abbreviated class schedule the next day, Wednesday, so we could all leave for home a little early for Thanksgiving. Amy and I were waiting in the parking lot for Uncle Charlie when I noticed a pretty, middle-aged Asian lady, holding a map of the campus and looking confused. On a hunch, I approached her and spoke to her in Mandarin.

"Nǐ hǎo! *May I assist you, madam?*"

She blinked, showing that startled look that was so familiar to me. I confess that I'd developed a perverse pleasure in surprising people and secretly enjoying their reaction. I often imagined how much fun I could have with that if I ever got to visit China.

"*You speak the common speech!*"

"*Not very well, madam. I am only a student. May I assist you?*"

"*I am looking for my daughter,*" she replied. "*She is called Jin Xuěyàn. Her English name is* Maud.*"

I smiled and stuck out my hand. She took it after only a moment's hesitation.

"*We know Xuěyàn very well. I am called* Brenda, *surname* Dickens,*" I waved Amy over. "*This is* Amy; *surname* McDonald, *she shares Xuěyàn's room. Your daughter is a very good student. And she has a very good heart.*"

To Amy, I said, "It's Xuěyàn's mom."

Amy hopped up and ran over, smiling and holding out her hand.

Xuěyàn's mom shook Amy's hand and said to her, "*My daughter has said nice things about you.*"

"*Amy doesn't speak Chinese,*" I told her.

She switched to English. "Ah yes, I forgot. My daughter told me this."

Amy piped up, "I will be happy to take to you find her, Mrs. Jin. She is probably still in our room, packing."

"Go ahead, Amy," I said, "I'll stay here with our bags." I switched back to Mandarin. "*It has been a pleasure to meet you, Madam.*" I couldn't remember

Xuěyàn's mother's proper name, so I kept it generic. I knew better than to repeat Amy's minor 'Mrs. Jin' mistake. Xuěyàn would probably correct her later, or not.

Back at the house, Charlie took a nap on the couch while Amy and I got settled and we all waited for Diane to get home. We had a light dinner, knowing we would stuff ourselves on turkey the next day. For desert, Aunt Di pulled out a birthday cake with sixteen candles and made me blow them out while they all sang that stupid song again. I managed to get all the candles with one breath, but just barely.

There were more presents, of course, all fencing related. My mom had sent me the mask I'd been dying for, Chuck and Di had the rest of the fencing outfit; the knickers, chest and underarm protectors, a stainless steel lame, and a nice big fencing bag to carry it all in. The bag was from Amy's folks. The lame was FIE rated and had the rare zipper in the back, so I would be able to use it whether I fenced right or left handed. I knew Amy had provided them with the list, and she had got everything right, so maybe she really did listen to me sometimes.

It was almost everything I needed and certainly more than I had a right to expect. I know Chuck and Di loved me, but they were sometimes overly generous. I would have to be on my guard that I didn't come to expect stuff and allow myself to get spoiled. I knew Amy often felt guilty when they would get her things, and I understood her feelings very well.

All I needed now was some real fencing shoes and a second sword. Of course, I didn't really *need* those things, but... maybe for Christmas.

Amy had a copy of 'The Princess Bride' and we all watched that after we put away the dishes. Amy and I both laughed at the "I am not left-handed" line, while I fantasized about how I could use the line myself someday. I enjoyed the movie, but for some reason, got a little depressed toward the end. I don't know why.

My mom had tried to cook a turkey once, and the story was still good for laughs at every family gathering, and especially on Thanksgivings. But Aunt Diane had been taught to cook by Gram, and she had done everything perfectly. Not only was the bird done to perfection, but everything came out ready at the same time.

Charlie carved the bird like the skilled surgeon he was and Diane passed the dishes around. She was simply beaming. I looked at her, and she caught herself. "We don't usually have this," she said, "a real family dinner, a real thanksgiving."

She looked at me and Amy.

"We are so happy to have you both here. It reminds me of when I was a little girl."

She shifted her gaze to the overloaded table. "Do you think we have enough food?"

It was not a serious question. By my estimation, we'd be eating leftovers until spring.

I knew that back in St. Louis Amy's folks had invited my mom to eat with them today, but Gram had taken charge and ordered everyone to join her at her church for the Thanksgiving feast they had set up. So, nobody we knew would go hungry today. A lot of diets would be ruined.

29. VOICES
AMY

I didn't recognize the voices for what they were at first. I'm not even sure when it started.

I would hear snatches of words in the dining hall and I can't know if I heard them with my ears or in my head.

In class, there were a couple of times when I heard, or thought I heard, bits of conversation that didn't seem to fit the subject of the class.

I didn't think anything of it at first.

I guess my first real hint that this was something weird was when I was sitting with Cleo in the library and I heard someone speaking in Chinese. I looked around, but the only people in the library that early were me and Cleo.

I said, "What?"

Cleo looked at me funny and said, "Didn't you hear me?"

Cleo had a gift for languages, but I didn't think Chinese was part of her inventory, so I didn't say anything.

I paid attention after that, and it seemed to be happening at least a couple times a week.

I checked the internet and they called it schizophrenia. I figured if I said anything, my next uniform would be a straightjacket and I would like that even less than the damn school skirts.

I gave it a lot of thought.

The voices weren't telling me to do things. They weren't telling me to raise an army and drive the English out of France. Most of the voices sounded like they might be the voices of my classmates. It was just like I was eavesdropping on them. I might not be crazy. I might just be experiencing some freakish super-hearing thing.

I didn't want to worry Brenda with this, and I sure didn't want to tell anyone else.

The incidents became less frequent, or else I was tuning them out or maybe not paying attention after a while.

It was only a little confusing, because I had to be on my toes whenever anybody said anything to me. I had to look around and see who was talking before saying anything.

It was scary at first, but I wasn't really too worried. Whatever it was, I didn't think it was really schizophrenia.

But it was just one more thing to deal with.

30. YELLOW PERIL
BRENDA

I was surprised when it was Xuěyàn who approached me instead of Karen, and that she approached me instead of Amy.

She cornered me in my room after dinner.

"Brenda, may I speak to you?"

"Sure, Xuěyàn. English or Chinese?"

It was a silly question. Xuěyàn never wanted to talk to me in Chinese. I think she had decided that was Karen's job for some reason. I didn't think she was being mean or stuck up about it. I think she just wanted to keep her Chinese conversation to a minimum at the school. I decided she was focused on improving her English rather than helping someone else improve their Chinese, and I had to admit that made perfect sense for her. It was not anything I could criticize her for.

"English, please," she said.

"Sure. What's up?"

Xuěyàn pulled out Karen's chair, sat herself down, smoothed out her skirt and folded her hands in her lap. She sighed and moistened her lips.

"I want to talk about Amy," she said. "I know you say you do not lie to her, but I know you do not tell everything, also."

I could feel myself pull back and I'm sure I raised an eyebrow.

"Please promise to me that you will not tell to Amy this talk."

I didn't know how to respond to that.

"Please promise."

"Well," I answered, "I guess if you think it is that important, then I will. I promise."

Xuěyàn's whole body visibly relaxed.

"I worry about Amy," she said.

"Don't worry about her, Xuěyàn. Amy's tough. She'll get through this, she'll be ok."

Xuěyàn furrowed her brow.

"No," she said. "I don't worry that she will be hurt. I worry that *I* will be hurt. I worry that she will hurt *me*."

I certainly didn't expect to hear that.

"Bad things happen to people when Amy is angry. I don't think she is angry at me, but I live in same place with her and maybe something will happen, maybe there will be a mistake."

I still didn't know what to say. I just let Xuěyàn keep talking.

"Also, maybe some people are her enemies. If they try to hurt her, maybe they will hurt me too. Already I have seen this on the soccer field, girls do not pass me the ball and in class, most other girls avoid me."

"I understand," I said. "Girls blame you for things they think Amy is responsible for. Because you are her roommate, they think you are like... whatever it is that they think Amy is. You feel lonely and blamed for things you have not done."

Xuěyàn reached out and touched my knee. It was an unusual gesture for her. She avoided touching other people, and I always thought, me especially. I didn't think it was a cultural thing, it was just her way.

"Thank you," she said, "that you understand."

"Ok, Xuěyàn. What do we do about it? How can I help?"

"This will hurt you," she warned.

"Don't worry about me. Just tell me what you would like me to do. You have an idea, I think."

She took a deep breath to suck in some courage.

"I'm sorry. I want you to ask to trade rooms with me. That is the number one thing."

"You know the policy. The school deliberately likes to split up friends, just as they didn't want two Chinese girls to share the same room. Besides, Amy and I already asked the provost to let us room together and she refused the request."

"Things have happened since that time. This time it may be different. I'm sorry."

I had to admit she was probably right. Amy and I were like a disease that needed to be contained for the good of the school. Dr. Kramer was very likely to go along with this now.

"I'll have to talk to Karen, you know."

"Brenda. Already Karen and I have talk this. We agree it is best thing for us. She is also worried."

I frowned. Karen could have come to me herself, but chose to have Xuěyàn bring this proposal, their proposal, to me. I understood their position, and couldn't argue with the logic of it, but I still felt hurt and a bit betrayed.

"There is another thing," Xuěyàn continued, "I am sorry, but anymore we do not want to sit near to you in the dining hall."

I let out a low, involuntary moan that surprised me. Xuěyàn's hands flew up to cover her mouth and her eyes looked like they were about to cry.

Just as Xuěyàn had done earlier, I took a deep breath to suck in some courage.

I stood up, stepped over to her, crouched down and hugged her. She didn't try to pull away, but just wept softly. A few seconds later, I was crying too. It had been a long time since I cried but I already sensed that soon enough, I would have a few more reasons to be shedding tears.

Eventually, we dried our faces. She released me from my promise not to tell Amy after I explained that it would be ok. The last thing she said to me was again that she was sorry; the last thing I said to her was that I understood and did not blame either her or Karen.

The first rule of life is self-preservation. It would be wrong to blame someone for just wanting to survive.

I found Amy across the hall in her room. Her reaction when I told her was open-mouthed silence, then she said, "Shit."

"It's back to just us again, Amy," I told her. "We can expect to lose Cleo as a friend too."

"Shit."

"Karen and Xuěyàn are approaching Dr. Kramer right now. Kramer may not feel all that warm and friendly toward us, but I don't think she'll refuse the Jins."

"Shit. We're in deep shit now, sister."

"I know, Amy. But we've survived worse. We just got too relaxed and complacent. Time to re-focus."

Cleo was not at her usual place in the library. She was in her room, alone, so I was able to talk to her freely. I explained the latest event and waited for her reaction. She was quick to pick up on the reason for my little visit.

"You want to know if I'm going to shun you, too."

"It might be the best thing for you to do."

She snorted.

"I'm sure it would be, in the short term. But in the long term, it would mark me as a coward and a weakling. Predators always target the weak members of the herd, and I don't want that to be me. Karen and Xuěyàn are making a mistake."

"I'm not mad at them. Our problems shouldn't be theirs. Besides, they may honestly believe that Amy is a ... a dangerous witch, or something. They may at least have genuine doubts about their safety."

"I know you're defending them because you like the Jins, but they are being cowards."

"No, they are just being prudent. Aren't you the one who's always preaching caution and prudence all the time?"

Cleo just scowled at me.

31. FIRST DATE
AMY

My phone rang just after 10 o'clock. It was Steve.

I took the phone into the bathroom and shut the door. Xuěyàn didn't say anything, but she might have frowned.

"How are you doing tonight, Amy? Did I catch you before you went to bed?" His voice sounded just as warm over the phone as it did in real life.

"No, I'm fine. I mean, I'm not in bed yet. I'm fine. It's nice you called. How are you?"

He laughed softly. "I'm fine too. It's wonderful to hear your voice."

We talked a little bit about my day, but I don't remember any of the actual conversation until he got to the point.

"Amy," he said, "would you like to do something a little bit exciting? A little adventure?"

Of course I would, I thought. But I kept the excitement out of my voice and said, "Like what?"

"Well, nothing too wild. I was thinking you might like to go out for a dinner and a movie tomorrow night. The theater is just four or five blocks away, it should be a nice night; we can walk. It would give us some time to talk without everyone else listening in. We could get to know each other."

I took a deep breath. I could do this. It was a week-day night, so I'd have to sneak out. Brenda wouldn't approve. She might even narc me out.

"Amy?"

"Yes, I'm here. Yes. That's a good idea. I'd love to go." The logistics of the expedition started to fill my head. "Uh, what time?" I asked.

"Well, let me see what's playing and what the show times are, and I can call you in the morning. How's that?"

"That's great!" Wonderful, is what I thought. What was I going to wear?

"Ok, then," he said. "I'll call you in the morning. Have a good night."

"Good night, Steve."

"Sweet dreams, Amy."

I didn't have any dreams, because I too excited to get much sleep.

Sophomores weren't allowed to sign themselves out at night, but one of the juniors owed me a favor and I got her to loan me her ID. The guards never looked at the photo very close; they just looked at the big class letter, 'J' for Junior. So, I didn't need to climb over the wall, I was able to walk right out the front gate around 5:30. I put the drugstore down as my destination, it was only a block away and girls were always going there. The weather had been swinging wildly, some days had been bitter cold, but tonight was only a little cool, almost warm, so I wore only a light coat.

Brenda had done everything she could to dissuade me.

"This isn't part of The Plan," she told me.

"It's just a date," I reminded her. "We can go on dates without hurting The Plan."

"This is moving too fast," she replied. "You should do a double-date or two first. And you definitely should not be sneaking out. You know how dangerous that can be."

"The cinema is only a few blocks away. It's a safe neighborhood, I can take care of myself, and I won't be alone. Steve will be with me."

It's Steve I'm worried about, Brenda was thinking, but she didn't say it out loud.

I rolled my eyes at her.

She took my phone, set the ring to vibrate-only and told me to leave it turned on even in the theater. "I won't call unless absolutely necessary," she said. "But if I do call; answer it."

"Amy, they say that if you give a dog a bad name, he'll live up to it. I know I joke around too much and call you a slut sometimes, but you don't have to live up to that. Don't give in too quick, and don't put too much trust in somebody who hasn't really earned it yet. Remember: love and sex are two different things. They don't always go together."

I was about to snap at her, but she grabbed me, wrapped her arms around me and hugged me tight. "Just be careful, Amy," she whispered.

I guess I was a little early, because I got to the church before Steve. I kept walking back and forth along the edge of the graveyard, afraid he might be waiting at the other end and he might miss me and think I'd stood him up. Eventually he showed. He walked straight up to me and embraced me and right away he kissed me. I was too surprised to resist, enjoy, or even think about it. Just as I was wondering if I should push him away or maybe stick out my tongue a little, he pulled back.

"Amy," he said, "you're cold! Did I keep you waiting?"

"No," I lied, "I just got here a few seconds ago."

He still held me in his arms and rubbed my back to warm me up, his face close to mine. I was wondering if he would kiss me again, and how I should react if he did, when he let me go, and took my hand.

"You're wearing jeans," he said. "You look better in your uniform."

That was the first time anyone complimented me on the damn uniform. "Well," I apologized, "I figured it might be chilly after the movie lets out."

"Come on," he said, "we're running a little late."

He pulled me after him in a brisk walk. It was only two more blocks to the movie theater, and the only time he let go of my hand was to pull out his wallet to pay for the tickets. The coming attractions were still playing, but the movie itself hadn't started. He found us seats in the back. "We can see the whole screen from here," he said. And, I thought, we'll have more privacy, too.

I hadn't paid any attention to what movie was actually playing, but it turned out to be just the latest dumb romantic comedy. I didn't pay much attention to the screen; I was focused on the feel of his hand. Most of the time he kept stroking my hand with his thumb. From time to time, he would turn his head toward mine and I would wonder if he would kiss me again, but he didn't. He adjusted our arms so that his right arm was in my seat, and my left lay over his, our hands still clasped. I shifted around to get more comfortable, and we somehow wound up with our heads resting against each other's. About half way through the feature, he disentangled our arms and put his arm over my shoulder to hug me closer until the credits rolled and the house lights came up.

There was a diner a few doors down, so we went there. It wasn't very crowded and we were able to get a booth in the back.

We had a bad waitress. I hadn't noticed how bad she was until Steve pointed it out to me. First, she brought his tea with a lemon in it after he'd told her no lemon. I hadn't actually heard him say no lemon, but I was distracted, thinking of what we might do next; the waitress had no such excuse. She'd also given us tableware that wasn't really clean but Steve chewed her out for that and we got a new setup.

Steve had already taken Driver's Ed and had his provisional driver's license. He's gotten it only nine months after he got his learner's permit, which he told me was the quickest you could get it in Maryland. He was a junior, almost seventeen, a little more than a year older than me. He talked a lot about what kind of car he was going to get. His parents were planning to get him a BMW sedan, but he wanted something sportier, maybe a Porsche, or something even more exotic.

"What about a truck of some kind?" I asked.

"No. I don't want people to think I'm a redneck."

I wanted to ask how much a Porsche cost, but instead, I asked, "If you got a Porsche, would you get one that's new or used?"

He curled up his lip at that. "A new one of course. I don't want a ride that somebody else has already used."

A new car would be much nicer, I thought. Brenda would not have agreed. We had already figured we were both three years away from our first cars, at best. But we had talked about it. She thought that a used car would be better. Not only would it be cheaper, but the crappier it was, the less we would have to worry about it. It would be less likely to be stolen, we could park more places, and we would be less upset the first time some jerk keyed the paint or dented the fender. We would have more "freedom" with a clunker than some shiny new car that could only break our hearts in a dozen different ways. As usual, her logic was flawless, but some of that was just rationalization. We'd never be able to afford more than a run-down jalopy anyway.

We talked about college plans.

"I'll be going to Yale," he boasted, "My father and grandfather both went there. I've visited a couple of times. The big problem with an old school is that some of the facilities have that old, run-down look. But it's nice enough, I suppose. The prestige is unbeatable, so it's the best."

"What will you be studying?"

"I haven't decided yet. It will be either law or finance, or both. It doesn't really matter too much. College is about making contacts, building networks and getting the diploma."

I thought that the learning opportunity was the big thing, but I also understood that Steve probably knew this subject far better than a naive Midwest girl whose family never went to any college, so I kept my mouth shut.

"My dad has his own network of contacts," Steve continued, "and after graduation I'll get a job at the firm of one of his friends. With that help, I'll be able to get a good job anywhere I want."

In talking about how much money he could make in "the real world", he was throwing around some incredibly big numbers.

"What about you, Amy? Where do you plan to go?"

"Well, Brenda and I haven't started applying anywhere yet."

He frowned.

"You better not wait much longer, you're almost a junior. That's late for the good schools. And frankly, Amy, you always bring up Brenda when I ask about your plans. I'm not interested in her, you know. I'm interested in you." He reached over to touch my hair. I definitely blushed at that.

When we were done with dinner he called for the check. I noticed he wasn't going to leave a tip. I thought you were always supposed to leave a tip, and I asked him about that.

"No, Amy," he informed me, "the tip needs to reflect the quality of service, otherwise you are just encouraging and rewarding bad behavior. It doesn't help her (meaning the waitress) in the long run. She did a lot of things wrong." He gave me a mock stern look. "Besides, you're The Date; you shouldn't be looking at the check. In some more classy restaurants, the lady's menu doesn't even have prices listed."

This was all new to me but it made sense. I knew this was certainly not the first time Steve had taken a girl out, and I was grateful that he knew the proper etiquette for a date.

He helped me on with my coat, and once outside, slipped his arm around my waist.

We walked back by a different route, past some older townhouses. There were lots of trees and few streetlights, so it was a bit dark, but that seemed romantic to me. At one point, he paused beside a narrow driveway between two of the buildings that led to an alleyway.

"So, Amy, are you glad you came out with me tonight?" He asked.

"Yes." I said. I didn't know what else to say.

"Step over here for a minute," he told me, and led me into the driveway where we were out of the light.

He turned us to face each other and he wrapped me in his arms and kissed me.

I felt warm all over. This time he did use his tongue and I tried to return with mine, but I was klutzy about it and we wound up just jabbing our tongues at each other. He pulled back, and for a moment I thought I'd screwed up, but he went back in and this time, when I stuck my tongue out, he actually sucked on it. I know my eyes widened at that, but I tried to act sophisticated and tried to do it to him.

Steve unbuttoned my coat, which took me off-guard a bit, and pulled me into a closer embrace that was warmer against the slight chill. We were kissing and I was getting better at it, I thought. This is what I'd hoped would happen tonight, and my mind was racing ahead to what we might do on future dates.

Both my arms were around his neck and his were around my back. His right hand drifted down to grab my butt and he gave it a little squeeze. I felt my whole body flush and wondered if it was from embarrassment or excitement and if this was the way I was supposed to feel. My ears and cheeks were burning. His hand roamed around to my waist and then under my sweater, up my ribcage to hold my left boob. His fingers moved around the edge of my bra. "This is moving too fast," Brenda had told me earlier. Maybe she was right, but I wasn't going to fuck Steve in an alley, this was just second base, and that was ok on a first date, I thought. Hell, I'm sixteen. Half the girls back at Riverplace had already given up their cherries two years earlier and I hadn't done anything yet, hardly.

I gasped and pulled back a little, but didn't let go.

"Did I scare you?" he whispered.

I breathed deep. "No. No, I'm fine. Just... I needed to catch my breath."

We stayed paused like that for a few moments; my hands still resting on his shoulders, his resting on my waist.

He pulled me in again for another long French kiss. Then I felt his hand at my waistband, starting to creep inside toward my panties, and against my thigh, I could feel his hardness inside his pants. He was no doubt wearing boxers.

Again, I pulled back, but he held me tight.

"I won't hurt you, Amy," he breathed into my ear. "I just want to make you feel good."

I didn't want to, but I had to push him away hard, straining against his arms.

My eyes had adjusted to the dark better, and I could see he was frowning. "Isn't this what you wanted, Amy? You know I care about you and I wouldn't ever hurt you."

"I know," I said. My breathing came harder. "I'm just... I don't know. I'm not ready, maybe. I've been kind of sheltered, I guess. I haven't been on a lot of dates."

He smiled then. "It's ok, Amy. Trust me."

With those words he pulled me back into an even tighter embrace and stuck his tongue in my mouth, so deep it filled my mouth and it was hard to breathe again. I keep gasping for air, I thought, maybe I'm developing asthma or something.

I forced us apart.

"I have to go," I said.

"I thought you liked me, but you don't, do you, Amy?" He sounded sad.

That wasn't it at all. It was me, all me, klutzy and bumbling and stupid, a girl who didn't know how to behave or what to do on a date. I was way out of my depth here.

"I do like you," I replied. "I'm just... not ready. Not here. Not yet."

Steve pulled my coat shut and buttoned one of the buttons.

"It's ok, Amy. I'll walk you back."

We walked back silently, side by side, but not holding hands. When we got a half block from the school, he turned to me.

"Amy, I haven't asked you this before, and you don't have to answer, but... I know you and Brenda are close, but how close are you two, really?"

Shit.

He was thinking me and Brenda were lesbos. That was my fault too.

I was always assuming people would understand that Brenda and I were just friends. I need to make things clear to people, but I just keep assuming they won't assume the wrong thing.

"We're just friends," I said. "We've been friends for a long time, but we're not anything more than that.

"I was just curious," he said. "I'm just not used to being left hanging like that. Good night, Amy."

He gave me a quick kiss, then turned and left. I was so messed up; I forgot to wish him a good night too.

I had no trouble getting back through the gate. I quickly signed the log and scribbled in the check-in time so that it was illegible, the guard didn't bother to read it.

The halls were empty and I was as quiet as I could be climbing the stairs to my room.

When I opened the door, it was not just Xuěyàn, but Karen and Brenda too, all waiting up for me in my room, staring at me.

I stood open-mouthed at the door until Brenda told me to close both and come in.

Brenda's eyes narrowed into suspicious slits almost as narrow as Xuěyàn's and she asked, "Everything go ok?"

For an instant, a flash of anger rose up in me, but the moment passed and I said, "I'm fine. No problems."

She studied my face, then abruptly stood up, grabbed Karen by the arm and pulled her to her feet too. "Ok, then. It's late. We've all got classes in the morning, time to go to bed. Amy, you'll have to tell us everything tomorrow."

As soon as she was gone, I sat on the edge of my bed, still warm from where Brenda had been sitting, and kicked off my shoes. Xuěyàn was watching me. Dr. Kramer had approved the Jin's request to trade rooms so they would be together and me and Brenda would be together, but the move wasn't scheduled until Monday, so Xuěyàn and I were still sharing. She was already in her bed. I knew what she was wondering, but I didn't talk as I pulled out my pajamas and got undressed. Just before I turned out the light, I looked back at her. "No, Xuěyàn. I did not have sex with that boy."

She made some gesture I didn't understand, but smiled, fluffed up her pillow, and squirmed deeper in her bed, no doubt relieved I hadn't become a prostitute.

Yet.

32. STRANGER THAN WE CAN IMAGINE
AMY

"The Universe is not only queerer than we suppose, but queerer than we can suppose." - J. B. S. Haldane, 1927

On Saturday, Brenda was headed to another fencing tournament, all the way up in Towson this time, but I begged off, saying I had to study. She tried to get me to change my mind, but eventually she saw I wasn't going to, and she stopped pestering me.

As soon as the team's minibus pulled away, I ran to the office and signed myself out.

The minute I walked out the gate, I was on the phone to the taxi company, telling them to pick me up at the church two blocks away. They were prompt. The cab pulled up just as I got there. When I gave the address to the driver, he turned around to look at me. "This is going to be expensive," he said.

"I know," I lied as casually as I could, "I've taken this ride before."

Shrugging his shoulders, he flipped on the meter and we headed south. He wasn't kidding about the expense. I watched the meter's digits click higher and higher. I soon realized my wallet was going to be emptied. It wasn't much later that I knew I wouldn't have enough for the return fare. I didn't know how I was going to get back. Use my thumb, maybe. I even began to worry if I'd have enough to pay for just the one-way trip. Eventually we arrived at my destination. I did have enough for the fare, but I had to short-change the driver on the tip. He grunted, but didn't complain, and drove off, leaving me standing alone in front of the door that said simply, "Wilson's".

The door was stiff. I tugged and tugged at it, wondering if maybe I'd made a big mistake about the hours, but then I felt a click and the door opened. I trudged up the stairs, found myself face to face with the mummy sarcophagus, and pulled his beard like I'd seen Cleo do. The mummy slid away like before and I stepped inside.

I called into the room, "Mr. Wilson?"

He appeared from behind one of the many curtains right away.

"Ah, yes. Miss Amy McDonald. Welcome back."

"You remember my name?"

"Memory is a trick like any other. I have a book somewhere around here about how to improve your memory. If I can remember where I put it. And it's 'Wilson' not '*Mr.* Wilson', remember?"

"Yes, sir. Wilson."

"So, Amy, may I call you Amy?"

"Yes, that's fine."

"Excellent. So what can I show you today? Are you interested in anything in particular?"

I took a deep breath.

"Mr... I mean 'Wilson'," I said, "I have to tell you that I don't have any money."

I looked for any reaction, but he seemed unperturbed; as relaxed and friendly as somebody's grandfather. He didn't respond, clearly waiting for me to continue.

"I was hoping, sir, if you have some free time, you would be willing to talk to me about magic in general."

His left eyebrow rose up a tiny bit and his smile disappeared.

"You are having some problems," he whispered. "That is why you are here without your friends."

I nodded my head.

"This way," he said as he raised one of the curtains.

I followed him into another little room holding two plush easy chairs separated by a small tea table and we both sat.

He made a gesture for me to speak first.

"There are some things happening at school that I don't understand," I said. "Weird things. I'm starting to have some crazy ideas about them and wondering who or what is responsible."

He interrupted: "Who says your ideas are crazy?"

"Cleo. Brenda doesn't say anything, but she thinks I'm being silly too. Nobody can explain all the stuff that's going on, and I'm wondering what's real and what isn't. I'm being pressured, or at least herded, I feel, in the direction of having to see a psychiatrist. If that happens, I'll get a label I'll never be able to shake. So before then, I want a different kind of opinion."

"I see..." he said. He sounded exactly like how I imagined a real shrink would sound, but I continued anyway.

"Cleo explained how there is no such thing as real magic. It's all tricks and illusions. She was very convincing."

I was about to go on, but Wilson held up his hand to stop me.

"All magicians, or illusionists if you prefer, got into this business because we were fascinated by the question of what is real and what is not. Especially with regard to what we call 'magic'. Perhaps more than any other group of people, we magicians want magic to be something real. But, also; perhaps more than anyone else, we have the most evidence that it is not. That makes us sad.

"It is our business to see the truth but show the illusion, and we cannot do that unless we understand the difference better than our audience does. Better than anyone does. You came to me hoping that I would be able to tell you that in addition to all the illusions and the tricks, there is also something more. You were right to come to me, because a magician knows. We search for the magical, we hunger for it, but we are always disappointed. So must you be. I will tell you the truth, but it will only make *you* sad."

I shook my head. "No," I told him. "Nothing would make me happier than to know that everything has a rational explanation. That would mean that I'm normal and not some kind of mutant or freak. But I'm not just wishing for empty reassurances. I need the truth, if I can find it."

"Ok," he said. "Tell me everything that's happened."

So I told him my whole story. Sometimes I jumped back to tell him about incidents when Brenda and I were in grade school, but mostly I focused on the weird stuff that was happening to me and people around me now. He listened to everything, interrupting only occasionally to ask me to clarify something.

"Well," he said when I was finished, "that is a remarkable story."
He smiled. "How about some tea?"

Without waiting for an answer, he got up and left me. From somewhere behind another curtain, I could hear running water, clattering cups, the fan of a microwave and then the beeps of the microwave signaling the completion of its cycle. He returned with a tray holding two china tea cups on saucers and a small teapot. As he poured, he said, "I believe your story. But that doesn't mean it is true."

He put the teapot down and waved his finger at me. "Don't be offended. I'm sure you understand that just because someone accurately relates a series of events that they perceived as having happened to them, that does not necessarily mean that their perceptions match the actual facts."

"Still," he added, "While all these events could be faked, I'll say this: It definitely bears close scrutiny.

"Humans are amazing creatures. We are top dog on this planet. We can run down deer in our bare feet, unarmed men have killed grizzly bears and leopards, and we have built tools that let a dozen of us walk on the moon. As for other undocumented abilities, well, those are... undocumented.

"Take a look at Las Vegas. The casinos are the prime example of where we would expect to see paranormal activities at work. It is a place where enormous amounts of money change hands in a potentially anonymous operation, ideally susceptible to manipulation by anyone with special abilities. And yet, every year, the house take mirrors exactly what would be expected by the laws of probability. That fact speaks volumes, doesn't it?

"I want proof before I believe that telepathy, telekinetics, or any paranormal phenomena is real, and I've yet to see it. I'm not ready to say anything is impossible, though. The universe is a peculiar place and we humans have barely scratched the surface of what is yet to be discovered.

"I don't know that I've been much help to you, Amy. But I definitely don't think you are crazy, or a witch."

I sighed. Whether my sigh was one of relief or disappointment, I really don't know.

"Fortunately, for you," He continued, "Miss Smith seems to be an excellent resource for this. She is extremely knowledgeable, sympathetic to you, and a skeptic, which is crucial. She is your best ally here. Your friend Brenda will be your best support, but Cleo is your strongest ally."

"Please, if you talk to Cleo again, don't tell her I was here," I asked.

"I notice you don't ask me not to tell your friend Brenda," he said.

"I'd prefer you don't tell her either."

"But you're not asking me to keep it from your friend."

"Brenda and I never lie to each other. We may keep secrets, sometimes, but we don't ever lie. Not to each other."

Wilson didn't respond right away. I turned to see him bowing his head. "That kind of friendship is very rare, Amy," he said. "I recognized it when I first saw the two of you together. Never let go of it."

He sighed.

"I promise," he added, "I won't tell anyone about our talk without your permission."

When I asked him if he knew of any buses that might take me back, he told me there weren't any and he called me a cab. He picked up on my nervousness.

"You don't have the money to pay for it, do you?"

"Not on me," I admitted. "But they'll wait for me to run in and get some when they drop me off at school, right?"

He pulled out his wallet. I held up my hands to refuse, but he cut me off. "My sainted mother would not forgive me if I were to leave a young lady in any kind of difficulty. You can pay me back later, if your pride insists."

"Thank you, Wilson," I said. I realized then that the courtly gentleman act Wilson affected was mostly not an act at all. "Brenda and I aren't rich like Cleo is," I told him, "but we do have our pride, and we always pay our debts."

Wilson waited outside with me for the taxi to arrive. He held the door for me to get in, but before he shut it, he leaned in a bit.

He asked, "How old do you think Cleo is, really?"

His tone caught me off-guard, but I answered, "She's sixteen, almost seventeen."

He frowned for an instant, then raised both eyebrows, and asked, "Are you sure?"

As soon as I got back, I raided my emergency stash of cash, wrapped the money in a quick thank you note, stuffed it in an envelope addressed to Wilson's shop, slapped my last two stamps on it, and headed down to the mailbox.

Just my luck to run into Brenda on the stairs.

"Oh, Amy!" She said. "Great! Help me with this stuff."

She was loaded down with her big bag of fencing equipment.

"Let me just drop this in the mailbox," I said.

"Who's the letter for?" She asked.

"None of your business."

"Maybe a letter to a sandy-haired boy? You're going to mail it without letting me read it first? Bad girl!"

I pushed past her and made it safely to the mailbox.

Brenda later gave me grief for not helping her, and even more grief for not letting her read my letter.

"It looked like a nice fat letter, too," she said.

I finally had to tell her straight out: "I'm not going to tell you anything about that letter, Brenda."

She pretended to be hurt, but she got the message and didn't ask any more questions about it.

And I'd come up with a new theory about Cleo, too.

Witness Protection Program.

It would explain everything. Witness Protection is a federal program, they gave their enrollees new social security numbers and birth certificates, why not change the birth dates, too? A few years probably wouldn't be very noticeable but should make it much more difficult to find someone. Mob bosses looking for a young twenty-something woman weren't likely to look twice at a high-school girl, right? Especially if she was surrounded by other sixteen-year olds. Some people can pass for someone much younger. I'd thought Xuěyàn was fourteen at first, so why couldn't Cleo be doing something similar?

Maybe she's spent time in prison herself. I could picture her spending a year or so confined to a prison library with nothing to do but read. That would explain how she knew so much. Probably not drugs, but maybe a mob secretary, or maybe human trafficking or even prostitution. Cleo had all but admitted she was no virgin. It could have been anything. Maybe it really had been drugs, or maybe she'd been a hit-girl.

If not prison herself, maybe she was the daughter of some gangster who'd been killed, and she'd turned state's evidence to get revenge on the other gangsters who killed her father.

Stupid ideas.

Probably.

33. GREEN-EYED MONSTER
AMY

"I think you've got your roles mixed up," Brenda told me. "I'm not Othello or Iago and Steve's not Desdemona. I am starting to wonder who *you* are."

Brenda was trying to confuse me, but the facts were plain and simple.

"You don't want me to see Steve, do you?"

She hesitated but said, "I don't think he's good enough for you."

"You're not my mother," I reminded her.

I had a sudden thought.

"You've always been jealous of me."

"Me?" She said, "Jealous of you? What makes you think that?"

"You've never had a real boyfriend," I told her. "The whole reason you keep bringing up Tommy Chavez and calling me a slut is because you're jealous."

"You're right about a couple of things, Amy. Just because I may still be a virgin, that doesn't mean I've never had a boyfriend. I don't tell you everything. Besides, you've never had a 'real' boyfriend either. This business with Steve is too early to deserve a 'boyfriend' label. But I *was* jealous of you and Tommy. I had my eyes on him before you even knew he existed. You stole him from me."

"You were interested in Tommy?"

"You never listen, Amy. And you never remember. I was the one who introduced you to Tommy. Whether or not you recall it, I told you I thought he was cute. Why would I say that if I wasn't interested in him?"

"I don't remember that!"

"That's exactly what I'm saying. You got him interested in you *after* I said I liked him. Next thing I know, you're kissing him in the coat closet. One of us may have been jealous, all right. But I don't think it was me."

Brenda had to be imagining this. She did have a good imagination.

"If you're not jealous of me," I said, "then why don't you want me dating Steve?"

"I keep telling you, Amy. He is not a nice guy. I don't trust him. You shouldn't either."

"You're wrong," I told her. "You don't trust anybody. Besides, if I'm such a bad judge of character, what does that say about us being friends? Was it a mistake for me to think you were a friend? Should I reconsider that too?"

"What specific reason do you have for not trusting Steve, Brenda? Don't give me any crap about just getting a 'bad vibe' from him."

"Ok," she said. "I guess that's fair."

She nodded her head. "I've heard stories from Ricky and Bobby."

I could feel my face crunch into a deep frown. "What kind of stories?"

"Steve has had lots of girlfriends before. He doesn't keep them very long, and he brags about screwing them."

"I don't believe that. That he brags about screwing girls. Did Roberto tell you that? Why would you talk about some other guy's sexploits with Bobby or Ricky? When did you have that conversation?"

"Well, Amy, they didn't come right out and say it like that, but that's what they meant."

"Even if that's true, it just means what I said before; Bobby and Ricky are jealous too."

34. HOLIDAY
BRENDA

Christmas break started the third Saturday in December and classes didn't resume until after the first week in January. It was a long break; maybe to make up for the short break over Thanksgiving.

The problem with living in the suburbs is that the busses don't always go where you need to go. But I was able to check out a route that took me up to Security Square Mall, so I was able to go and do my Christmas shopping by myself.

Amy was always losing gloves, so I got her a pair of those for Christmas. I thought about getting cheap ones, or two identical pair since I knew she'd soon lose one, but instead, I got her just one good pair of nice calfskin gloves.

I didn't forget Cleo either.

She had been very good to us, and always helpful and always cheerful about it.

I'd seen her looking at a picture of a bust of Eratosthenes in a book. She was practically mooning over the guy like some tween girl crushing on a photo of her favorite teen idol. On at least two different occasions, she brought up his name. She spoke about him with real reverence.

I thought that a copy of one of his books would be a nice gift for her, but my research told me that every one of his books had been lost over the centuries. All that remained were a few fragments and excerpts quoted by other ancient mathematicians. Then I found a fairly new book that compiled those fragments into a nearly complete volume of his Geographika, and got that for her. It wasn't cheap, but I sprang for it anyway. I hesitated about talking it over with Amy, but when I did, she insisted on chipping in too. We were able to get it before we left for the holidays.

When we presented it to Cleo, the first thing she said was, "You shouldn't have gotten me anything."

But when she unwrapped it, she sucked in her breath. And when she opened it up and looked at a few of the pages, she made a little sound in her throat that I hadn't heard before. She shut the book and I thought she was going to hug it. She didn't do that, but she laid it gently in her lap and caressed the cover.

"Thank you," she said in a small voice, "This is very thoughtful."

She put her hand to her cheek and I almost thought she was going to cry. I'd never seen Cleo get emotional before.

She started to say something else, but I guessed what it would be and I cut her off.

"Don't get us anything in return, Cleo. Just don't. You've done so much for us; let us do this one little thing for you."

For a second, I thought she was going to argue, but she just nodded her head and continued stroking the book.

"It's just a shame," Amy said, "That none of his books have survived complete."

"Yes," Cleo replied with a sly smile, "it's a shame. But, who knows, extant copies might still re-surface someday."

Christmas wound up being a pretty low-key affair, which suited me just fine.

Chuck and Di had set up a big tree in their living room, something they usually didn't bother with. They knew they couldn't keep us for Christmas, my mom, and Amy's folks wouldn't allow that, but they made us promise to be back in time for 'Greek Christmas' on January 8th. That way we could celebrate with Chuck and Di in Baltimore too.

Amy and I had planned to take the train back to St. Louis. We thought it would be cheaper and would save our folks some money, but our folks said it wasn't *that* much cheaper, and the plane would get us back and forth faster, so we did that.

Once we were back home, Amy and I spent most of our time with our respective families, but we still got together a few times.

We got together Christmas afternoon for dinner and to trade gifts.

Amy got me gloves, too. Two epee gloves, one for each hand. My mom didn't know what else to get me, so she got me socks and underwear and a sweater. Nothing fancy, but all useful and all things I actually needed. She got an identical sweater for Amy.

Amy's parents got me book gift cards, which were also good and practical.

My mom was extra-clingy, which was a new thing from her. I noticed the house was immaculate and assumed she had spent a lot of time cleaning. Burning nervous energy in her empty house, maybe.

Amy rode with me one morning on the bus out to pay my respects to Laoshi Sun. She was happy to see us and fixed us brunch. I hadn't been very original, and had got her gloves for Christmas too. But I'd also brought the essays I had written in Chinese class and showed those to her. I'd gotten good marks on them and thought it would make her happy to know that her teaching had not been wasted. She was initially very happy, but the visit quickly turned into a criticism of my work and an impromptu lesson. She was always very strict with me, but when we left, she hugged me and said, "I am very proud of you, Brenda. Keep working hard. Write to me sometimes."

We'd neglected Amy during the visit, but the Galleria was only a few blocks from Mrs. Sun's house, so we went there to window-shop before catching a bus for home. We were not the only ones window shopping.
There was a young girl pushing a stroller, and Amy recognized her before I did. It was Tonya, who had been a leader of one of the gangs at Riverplace. She recognized us right away.
She had put on some weight, and the baby in the stroller was hers, less than two months old. She seemed tired, but perked up as we talked. We took her to the food court and even though we'd already eaten, we got some food. Tonya even let Amy and I take turns holding her baby and let us feed it the bottle while we talked.
She asked, "Are you still in school?"
"Yeah," I told her, "we're just home for Christmas. We have to go back next week."
"Do you like it?"
"It's a good school. A lot of hard work. No boys, though."
Tonya just smiled at that.
"What are the other girls like there?"
"Mostly normal girls," Amy interjected. "Only a few of them are the rich, snobby bitch type. Some of them are very nice. It's a little weird because Brenda and I are the only ones who don't come from money. But, like I say, some of them are very nice."
"I didn't bother to go back this year," Tonya said. "I was too far along when school started, and then after I had the baby, I didn't have no time for

school no more. It was kind of a surprise. I didn't even know I was carryin' 'till late."

We talked some more but then it started to get awkward so I said, "We better get back, Amy, our folks will get upset if we're too late."

Tonya didn't cry when we said goodbye, but it was a near thing. The last thing she said to us was: "Do good in that school of yours." I had a lot of questions for her, but I didn't want to ask, probably because I didn't want to hear the answers.

Amy and I were pretty quiet on the ride back home.
We weren't Tonya.
But we could have been.

35. RESOLUTIONS
AMY

While I was home for the holidays, my dad asked me if I was going to make any New Year's resolutions.

"Just focus more on my schoolwork," I told him.

But there was more to it than that.

Coming back on the plane, there was a mix-up with our tickets. Brenda and I both got on the same plane, but seats were re-assigned for some reason and I got seated next to some old white guy with bad breath who kept talking to another old guy about trucks and bass boats and fishing. They left me alone, though, so I had time to think.

A new year's resolution was probably a good idea, if I could think of the right one.

Magic.

To someone who hadn't experienced it, the whole idea of magic sounded wonderful and "magical", but to me, it meant nothing but one disaster after another. If what I'd been experiencing was real, and was magic, it was nothing to be happy about. It certainly had done nothing to make my life any easier. Not one positive thing had come from it, but several negative things had.

That would make a good resolution.

No more magic. No more voices.

No more thinking about magic.

No more doing, or thinking about doing anything related to magic or any so-called "powers".

From now on, anytime I thought something paranormal had happened or was maybe about to happen, I would ignore it.

Maybe, if I pretended it didn't exist, it might not exist. If I can make things happen, maybe I can make things 'not-happen' too.

It might go away.

Maybe the voices would stop too.

Greek Christmas at Chuck and Di's house was relaxed too.

They overloaded us with presents, all wrapped up in shiny paper with ribbons and big bows. One of the best presents was luggage, burgundy for me, black for Brenda.

"You need a good set of luggage to travel back and forth between St. Louis and Baltimore," Chuck told us.

We also got new book bags of some rugged canvas.

"I thought you needed something better than those cheap see-through plastic bags I saw you with," Diane said.

Brenda and I thanked her, but we just looked at each other. No point in telling Di why we had the see-through bags.

When we got back to school, we stored our new luggage in our closets and went downstairs to the 24-hour snack bar. It had been pretty much picked over during the holiday. They wouldn't re-stock it for another day or two.

"There's nothing good here," I told Brenda.

She pointed to the soda machine, but I just rolled my eyes at her.

"Sugar and caffeine are not what I need. I'm just tired. The year is barely half over. We've still got five more months of this."

"Don't worry," Brenda reminded me. "It's 2012. The world ends in 347 days. All your troubles will be over then."

I showed her my middle finger.

She focused on my single raised digit and, with a bright smile, said, "Thanks, Amy. You're number one with me, too."

36. DEVIL'S BARGAIN
AMY

I was pretty sure Brenda and I were the only virgins in the whole damn school.

Whenever I thought about it, I felt like my life, and the whole world were passing me by.

It made sense to not play around with boys back at Riverplace; the guys there were all very bad news and the cute ones were exactly the worst of the worst. There had been plenty of baby-mommas to remind us that temptations had consequences. The fact that we were apparently the only ones who understood the severity of those consequences kept us focused. So many of the other girls back home thought getting knocked up was no big deal. Their so-called boyfriends either lacked any sense of responsibility, or lacked whatever it takes to follow through on it. Poor Tonya knew better now, but it was too late for her.

But things were different now, for me.

The quality of the guys had improved, I thought, and besides, I had resources those Riverplace girls didn't. I was better prepared to handle anything that might happen.

I didn't see why I shouldn't learn about sex and explore. That should be part of my education, too, right? As long as I was careful.

It's not like I was going to get married at sixteen and drop out of school.

I could take care of myself. I wasn't planning on sleeping with every guy I met, or even with just any guy. Steve was just one guy. And he seemed like a decent one. He was obviously smart enough to get into that fancy school of his, he knew a lot, and could afford to pamper a girl. It's not like I needed to be pampered. I was no gold-digger out for his money--I'm sure lots of girls were. It's just that being treated to a little bit of luxury was... luxurious. There was nothing wrong with that as long as I didn't let it go to my head.

I was even ok with the fact that Steve probably had some experience already. I didn't believe Brenda's bad-mouthing of him. That was just her trying to keep us apart. Maybe she meant well, maybe she even believed it, but she didn't know him like I did.

There was one way I could shut Brenda up.

I found her in her room working on a history paper.

"Brenda, I want to talk to you about Steve."

She clicked "save" on her laptop and spun around to face me.

"You've thought about what I said about him."

"Yes, Brenda. I have."

"So, do you know what you're going to do?"

"Maybe." I wasn't going to tell her everything, but I wasn't going to lie to her either.

"So?"

"You're worried I'm going to sleep with him."

"No, Amy. I'm really not."

"What? You said..."

"No, I'm not worried that you're going to screw him, I'm worried that you're going to get hurt. Getting screwed is just the... 'wind-up' to getting hurt."

"He's not going to hurt me, and besides..."

Brenda held up her hands to stop me.

"We're getting off-track again," she said. "You came here to tell me something. Let's get back to that."

"I want to make a bargain with you," I told her.

She raised her eyebrows at that.

"You don't want me to fuck him, at least not yet," I said. "Ok, I won't. At least not yet."

"You had just one date with him just before the holiday break. But I know you're still thinking about putting out for him."

"Of course I'm *thinking* about it. Every girl here thinks about sex, and probably everyone will do it eventually, it doesn't mean that they, or I, are going to do it tonight. Even you *think* about it."

The corner of Brenda's lip twisted up for a moment in the briefest of near-smiles.

"And," I conceded, "Maybe I am. But I will promise not to rush into it if you promise not to bad-mouth him again."

She opened her mouth, then closed it again.

After a couple of seconds, she said, "details."

"Ok," I replied. "You have to promise not to criticize him unless it's something you can personally vouch for. If you see something yourself, you can talk about that, but no more repeating rumors or gossip from the other guys."

She frowned, and I continued. "I promise not to sleep with him on our next date. If I do it on a later date, I'll absolutely use protection. I'll be very careful. We don't even know if I'll get a second date, much less a third or a fourth. And, I'll remember The Plan. I'm not going to neglect my studies, or run off and get married or anything dumb like that."

Brenda's frown deepened.

"I might hear something very important," she said. "Something you might call just gossip, but something you might need to know. You want me to keep quiet even when I think it might threaten you?"

"I'll give you one freebie. If you hear something, you can tell me, but you can only do it once. So, be sure your source is reliable and be sure the gossip is really important." I paused. "I'm being very generous, Brenda. I don't really have to make any kind of bargain with you. My love-life isn't covered by The Plan, as long as I'm careful. You don't have any rights to even this much."

"Amy," she said, "do you really understand why I'm so concerned about this?"

"You're trying to be a friend," I answered, "you're just not going about it the right way."

"That's only part of it. The other part is very selfish. If you get messed up, for any reason; and lose your focus, and your work suffers, then I risk being stuck here by myself. Remember what got us here. It's hard to succeed, and much harder to succeed alone. Don't forget, Amy; we're in hostile territory. We need each other."

I had to agree with that.

"Ok," I said. "This bargain doesn't change that. But constantly cracking on my boyfriend or possible-boyfriend hurts me too. This is a fair compromise. Do you agree to it?"

Brenda was quiet for a long time.

"Ok, Amy," she said. "I agree. I'm not so sure it's a good deal for you, but it's a deal."

We didn't sign a piece of paper with our names in blood or anything stupid like that. We didn't even shake hands on it. We never bothered with that crap. One good thing about us: with each other, we always kept our word.

I was sure Brenda would continue to worry despite the assurances I'd just given her. Probably not as much anymore, but she'd still worry.

My life would be a little easier too, not having to listen to her bitching over Steve. I'd be fine. I'd be careful and I wasn't about to ruin my life over some boy, so matter how green his eyes were, how nice his hair or how soft his smile.

I not stupid, I thought to myself.

37. THE MAN IN BLACK
AMY

January 19th fell on a school day and I knew it would be difficult to get downtown. But I knew Cleo was a fan so I went to see her. She was at her usual table in the library, so I pulled up a chair opposite her.

"Cleo, tomorrow is the nineteenth. Do you know whose birthday it is?"

She grinned, a stupid, goofy-looking grin that she might have copied from Brenda.

"Of course I do," she said. "It's Dolly Parton's birthday. A very nice lady."

I didn't expect that answer.

I assumed she was right, but I was clueless how or why she would know such a thing. I recovered easily enough.

"No. Someone earlier."

"Janis Joplin?"

"No, no, no.

Paul Cezanne? Robert E. Lee?"

"Cleo, you're getting to be as bad as Brenda. It's..."

"Edgar Allan Poe," she said.

I just folded my arms and nodded.

"So," she said, "what do you want to do? Get together here in the library over a cask of Amontillado and read his poetry?"

"I don't know what Amontillado is. I was thinking, if we had a ride, we could visit his grave tomorrow night and see if the Poe Toaster shows up."

"And you came to me because I have a car?"

She was definitely teasing me.

I smiled. "Guilty as charged. Also, I know you are a fan of Poe."

She returned my smile. "But you didn't do your homework, Amy. The Poe Toaster is not supposed to show up in the evening, he always showed up before dawn. We'd have to get up very early if we want to see The Man in Black."

I hadn't known that.

"So, what time would we have to be there, you think?"

"Probably by four-thirty in the morning. We'd have to leave the school by four. We'd have to be out of bed by three-thirty. Do you think you can do that?"

Now that she spelled it all out, I wasn't at all sure. I wasn't sure how badly I wanted to go, especially given that the Poe Toaster had been a no-show for the last couple of years.

"What do you think, Cleo? Did *you* want to go? Is this a crazy idea?"

"I tell you what, Amy. If you really want to go, I'll have Azim drive us."

I was starting to feel guilty now.

"This is a big imposition," I said, "I hadn't thought it through. I could get up that early, but now poor Azim has to get up too, maybe this was a stupid suggestion."

"No, Amy, it really isn't. If you are sure you can be ready on time, we can do it. We can get up a group. The car will hold six comfortably, and we can squeeze in a few more, if we're all friendly enough."

"But," I had to ask, "Do *you* want to go, *really?*"

She leaned back.

"Yeah," she said, "I guess I really do. I've never been, and even if the toaster is still a no-show, there will be a small crowd and plenty of imposters. Hell, we could bring the roses and cognac ourselves."

"Where would we get the booze?"

"Azim. He'll take care of everything."

"Ok. I'll talk to Brenda and the Jins and see if they're up for it. But even if they're not, as long as you are, so am I."

"Good. I'll let you handle the guest list, just let me know at dinner tonight how many and I'll call Azim to confirm. I'll call him right now to give him a heads-up. I'll talk to Dr. Davis and clear it with her, she's met Azim and knows how serious and responsible he is, so that will be a big help. We'll be back at school in time for breakfast."

I stood up to leave. I was already excited by this expedition, but not really sure what I hoped for.

"Oh, and Amy, Amontillado is a variety of Sherry, a fortified Spanish wine. 'The Cask of Amontillado' is the title of one of his short stories."

Even though I was still a pariah at school, I talked to a few other girls about going, but the three-thirty AM wake-up call was a deal-killer for everyone but Brenda. I'm not even sure why she was ok with it, the idea of being up that early was clearly a shock to her, and while she was a big literature buff, I didn't think Poe was anything special to her.

Now that Brenda and I were sharing the same room, we didn't have to worry about waking up the Jins when the alarm went off in the wee hours.

We turned in right after dinner. I hadn't realized how noisy the dorm was in the evening until I tried to get to sleep early. No sooner did I fall asleep it seemed, than the alarm went off. 3:30 AM. I checked the weather on my phone; it was barely above freezing outside. I was tempted to call the whole thing off, but it was too late for that, so I shook Brenda awake and got dressed and fixed myself up as quick as I could.

We'd forgotten to say where we would meet Cleo, but she knocked on our door at ten to four. I was all ready, and Brenda was just fixing her hair so we grabbed our heavy coats and followed Cleo downstairs. It was bitterly cold walking to the parking lot, but the sky was clear and the stars were more brilliant than I'd ever remembered seeing them. Cleo's limo was pulled up as close as it could be, engine idling, a cloud of exhaust vapor enveloping the rear of the car. As soon as we approached, Azim got out and held the back door open for us.

"Good morning, ladies." It was the first time I'd heard him speak English. He had an Afro-British accent which combined with his immaculate dark suit made him seem like a high-class English butler.

"I'm sorry to get you up so early, Mr. Azim," I told him.

He smiled briefly and gave us all a slight bow. "It is no trouble at all, miss. Please do not concern yourself."

The inside of the limo was delightfully warm.

Brenda squirmed deep into her seat. "Wake me up when we get there," she said.

But Cleo had other ideas. "You can catch up on your beauty rest on the way back. How about a drink first?"

She slid back a panel to reveal a built-in bar. "Come on," she said, "we need to make a toast before we get there."

Brenda looked surprised, but I just shook my head. "We don't drink," I told Cleo.

"We're not going to take more than a sip. The rest of the bottle is for Edgar. He hasn't had any for quite a while, so he gets the lion's share. But should we do the traditional Cognac, or the Amontillado?"

"Just a sip? I've never had either one," Brenda said. "Which one do you think, Amy?"

"How about one sip of each, just for the taste," Cleo suggested. She opened the Cognac first and poured a splash of it into one of the glasses from the bar and handed it to Brenda who just held it and studied its color. Then Cleo gave me a glass and poured herself an amount that was more than a mere splash.

She held her glass out and me and Brenda copied her gesture.

"To Edgar," Cleo announced, "may he rest in peace, knowing he is remembered with respect and affection."

We clinked our glasses and drank.

It burned only a little, but still brought tears to my eyes. I admit it had a nice aftertaste. I still had a little bit left in my glass, and not knowing how else to dispose of it, drank that down too. Brenda was more alert than me and had spotted the tiny sink in the built in bar and poured her reminder down that. She grinned at me but didn't say anything. Cleo drank all of hers.

"Now," Cleo said, "The Amontillado."

"Ok, but just a tiny splash," I warned, "less than before."

"Coward," Cleo called me, but she only poured me the tiny bit I'd asked for. Brenda was slow to hold out her glass, but she did, and after Cleo poured her own glass, held it out for another toast. She didn't seem to know what to toast to, but Brenda had one.

"To The Man in Black," she said, "may The Poe Toaster re-appear to honor our poet, and may he be absent, nevermore."

We clinked our glasses again and drank. The Amontillado burned more and the odor stung my nose. The taste was so different I couldn't tell if I liked it or not.

While Cleo put our glasses back in the bar, she slid the partition open enough to ask Azim, "Did you get the roses?"

"Yes, Kandake. I have them next to me. One dozen, as you asked."

"Thank you, Azim."

"We are close, Kandake. I can let you out in front of the gate and go park the car, then come back when you call, if you wish."

"Yes, Azim, do that, please."

A few minutes later, he pulled up right in front of the gate, next to a parked police car, put on his flashers and held the door for us to get out. The cold got to me immediately, and I was about to shove my hands in my pocket, but before he disappeared, Azim handed me the roses to carry so I had to take them. I knew I should have brought my gloves.

There was a small crowd, less than a dozen. A few wore a ribbon-badge that read 'Edgar Allan Poe Society of Baltimore.'

Cleo was talking to one of the guys with the badges and she called me over. "Come on, Amy, this way."

She led us past the big tombstone we'd visited on Halloween Eve and around to the side of the church to a smaller maker. It had a carving of a bird on top. The stone read: "Original Burial Place of Edgar Allan Poe from October 9, 1849 until November 17, 1875."

"You girls are here early," the guy with the badge told us.

Cleo set the bottle of cognac up against the stone. "Give me three of the roses," she told me.

"Shouldn't we leave this at his tombstone?" I gestured with my head back to it.

"No, this is the traditional place. We'll put our offering on the side in case the real Poe Toaster shows up."

My frozen fingers fumbled to pick out three good roses and I handed them over. Cleo arranged them in a triangle surrounding the bottle, at which the badge-guy raised a surprised eyebrow.

We stood for a moment admiring our work. There was a fallen leaf lying on the stone. Brenda leaned over and brushed it off. "We're not done yet," Cleo said, leading us back to the big tombstone. There were a few roses already scattered there. Cleo gestured to Brenda for the bottle of Amontillado she was carrying. Brenda handed it over and Cleo put that down in a clear space. She held up three fingers for me, so I selected and handed over three more roses, which she arranged as she had done before. She came over and took another rose from me, broke the stem a little shorter and then, grabbing the lapel of badge-guy stuck the rose behind his badge. She took yet another rose and looking around, found another guy with a Poe Society badge and repeated her operation. I followed her while she distributed two more roses to the other two badge guys. There were still three roses left, making me realize we'd actually had a baker's dozen of the roses. One she stuck in my coat, one in Brenda's and the last in her own.

There was a soft round of applause from the crowd. At first, I assumed it was for Cleo, but then I saw the Man in Black. He was a middle aged white guy with a dark hat pulled low and a white scarf pulled high, carrying a bottle and three roses. One of the badge-guys approached him.

"This way, sir," he told him and led him back to the small marker. The Man in Black also left a folded-up note with his offering. He knelt briefly, then rose, paused, and quickly left the graveyard, disappearing down the street.

There was a trashcan just outside the fence where I was disposing of the rose stems and the paper wrapper when I nearly bumped into a different Man in Black, dressed like the first, also carrying roses and a bottle. I followed and watched him repeat the ritual, but he disappeared down the other street. A larger crowd had gathered by that time, more than twenty, and someone tried to take a picture, but the crowd booed and there were no more photos. Or at least, no more camera flashes.

Brenda came up to me. "There will probably be more imposters," she said.

"The real one might still come."

"How can we tell?" She asked.

One of the Society guys overheard us and said, "We'll know. There is a secret signal the real toaster always gave. These two weren't him."

We waited around some more, but around five-thirty, another of the Society guys told us the genuine Poe Toaster was a no-show again this year.

"The Poe Society should nominate a new one," Brenda told him.

He smiled at her. "It's been debated."

Cleo came over and asked, "Ready to go?"

It had been a good experience, but me and Brenda were both ready. My fingers had been in my pockets since I'd discarded the rose-stems and they had at least warmed up a little.

"Azim is parked over behind Lexington Market," Cleo said. "It's only a couple blocks; the walk will get our circulation back."

We headed east on West Fayette for a block then crossed the street and headed up North Paca. After another block, the parking lot was in sight when a couple of guys stepped out of the shadows in front of us. Me and Brenda recognized the type immediately. Punks out looking for money and trouble. The fat one stepped right up in my face, the other one went for Brenda. They were older than us, nineteen or twenty maybe. They each had a knife. Cleo had been on the phone with Azim and was just putting it away. Brenda and I shoved her behind us.

"Alright bitches, the fuckin' money! Unless you want your pretty face cut!" The one in front of me was holding his knife wrong. He was too close and he held the knife in front of my face, up at my shoulder level. I had raised my hands to signal surrender, so this put his knife less than six inches from my hand. Brenda was facing nearly the identical situation.

I could scarcely believe it. I'd never been threatened with a weapon in my life. I'd never been robbed or mugged. We'd rehearsed this exact scene in Aikido class a hundred times, and been taught that if the real thing ever happened we were to hand over our purses. That is the best way, the proper way to handle a mugging. I was ready to do just that, but of course, I had no purse and no money on me. We hadn't planned to go shopping at 5 o'clock in the morning; we'd left our money back in our rooms.

Brenda's guy slapped her. He didn't slap her hard, just a quick slap to shake her into compliance and make her afraid.

One should never pick a fight with a stranger. It is the height of folly. You cannot know who the stranger is or what she is capable of.

The knife was right in front of my face, very close to my raised hand. Without thinking about what I was doing, I wrapped my hand around the blade and twisted it in the direction against his grip. His fingers unrolled just as they always did with the rubber knife in Aikido class, leaving him empty handed and with me holding the blade. Brenda had done the same thing, simultaneous with me. I don't know which of us was more astonished, our would-be attackers, or ourselves.

For a couple of moments we all stood in stunned silence. I remember most clearly the look of hurt feelings in my attacker's eyes, as if he'd just been the victim of some grievous insult. Visible anger quickly flashed over his face, but before any of us could move, a tall shadow brushed me aside.

There was a very loud sound, like a whip crack, immediately followed by another. Both of our assailants collapsed to the ground. Azim was towering over them, saying something that had to be a string of Nobiian curses. He picked them both up, one in each hand and threw them up against the chain link fence beside the sidewalk and slapped them again. His open palm against their faces sounded another pair of whip cracks. And again, the blows knocked them to the ground. He kicked them both a couple of times, then picked one of them up by the arms and held him in the air.

"So, young gentle-*man*! You threaten these good ladies with a knife? If we were in my country, I would cut off your manhood first, and your hand second!" He propped the one he was holding up against the fence and

132

slapped both of them again. The head of the one on the fence flopped at the end of its neck so violently I thought Azim had snapped the neck. I half-expected the head to pop off. He had to lean down to slap the one on the ground. He took a half-step back, allowing the one against the fence to fall on top of his confederate. Another swift kick for each and Azim turned to us. I noticed his coat had come unbuttoned and under his arm, in a shoulder holster, he was wearing an absolutely enormous gun.

He bowed to us as he buttoned his coat back up. "Please forgive me, ladies, I should not have abandoned you. It will not happen again. Are either of you hurt in any way?"

As he said this, not waiting for us to reply, he very gently pried the knives from our hands and after snapping each one in half, he threw them out in the middle of the street.

Cleo came up then and Azim bowed to her. He spoke to her in their own language, but I recognized the English words "police" and "Catonsville." She replied in the same tongue, then turned to us.

"We're not going to bother calling the cops," she told us, "let's go. The car is just up ahead."

We walked in silence, Azim sometimes glancing behind us. Once in the car, the heat came on quick and it felt oppressive. I was already hot and my hands were shaking, Brenda's too, though not as bad. Cleo seemed perfectly calm. When we stopped at the first traffic light I could see Azim watching us in the rear-view mirror. He slid open the partition.

"Do not be embarrassed by the shaking, miss," he said. "It is caused by your adrenaline. It is normal. It will pass in only a few minutes. You did very well. You have done nothing to be ashamed of."

Back at the school, when we got out of the car, I noticed for the first time how very thick the door and window glass were. This wasn't just a limousine, it was a tank.

Cleo suggested we not say anything to anyone and we were quick to agree to the wisdom of that. We did get back in time for breakfast, but I really wasn't hungry at all. Cleo had to force me to choke down a banana and a half glass of OJ. I couldn't focus in my first two classes, but by the time lunch rolled around; I'd basically recovered and was able to eat. I ate like a pig, I guess to make up for my light breakfast and low blood sugar. By dinner, Brenda and I were both able to tell about the scene in the churchyard, carefully omitting any mention of us tasting alcohol or being accosted by a couple of punks.

Cleo, and no doubt Azim as well, were vampires.

That, at least, was my latest stupid theory. Probably not the evil blood-sucking kind like in the movies, but some other kind of immortal that fed on who knew what. The souls of evil-doers, maybe? Azim looked abnormal. At seven feet tall, thin but inhumanly strong, even if Cleo was human, I wasn't at all so sure about her bodyguard. The gun told me he was more than just her chauffeur. His performance that night told me that while he carried a gun he would rarely need to use it. I wondered if it was loaded with silver bullets to defend against werewolves, the vampire's natural enemy.

I looked up 'Kandake' on the web. It was easy to find. It was an ancient title of the queens of Nubia, who were called the 'Candace' by the Romans. Candace was Cleo's middle name. I'd seen it on her ID card the last time we signed out. Cleo Candace Smith. She was, I supposed, more than just some lost orphan. She was probably some tribal princess, or maybe more. According to the internet, the last recorded 'True' Candace (or Kandake) was 'Lahideamani' in 314 AD.

If Cleo was older than she appeared, I had to wonder, how much older was she?

Or, maybe I really was just crazy.

38. YEAR OF THE DRAGON
BRENDA

Amy and I lingered over dessert. Dinner was some pseudo-Chinese dish in honor of Chinese New Year which fell late in January that year. At least the rice was done properly. Karen was eyeing the food critically, but Xuěyàn had dug in with relish. I suppose she just assumed it was another strange American dish to savor, which I guess it was. Out of the corner of my eye I could tell she was especially puzzled but delighted with the fortune cookie. I knew they didn't have that American invention in China. I assume Karen explained it to her. The Jins finished their whispered conversation and disappeared first, then the rest of the hall eventually cleared out.

"I'm sorry, Brenda," Amy told me. "I know this would have been a little better if you'd been able to share it with our Chinese friends. It's my fault."

"It is not your fault. Stuff happens."

"Your mom used to say everything happens for a reason."

That comment pissed me off. Amy should have known it would.

"I don't believe that. Not in any sense or interpretation of the phrase." I put more of an edge in my voice than was necessary and was instantly sorry, but I let it go.

"Stuff just happens," I reminded her.

"I miss the Jins too," she said, wistfully.

"We'll get through this," I said, "just stick to The Plan." I'm sure I was trying to convince myself as much as Amy.

We were done, so we bussed our table and walked back to our room in silence. Amy had been especially quiet lately, so I just followed her lead and gave her space.

When we opened the door to our room, we got a shock.

All my stuff was gone. Xuěyàn was putting up the poster of her hometown on the wall above my bed, which was covered with her clothes.

"What the fuck?" Amy asked. But my own question was right behind hers.

"What's going on, Xuěyàn?"

"Now you not sleep here," she replied. "You are with Qiǎojiě-Karen again. Like before." She wore a stupid grin; no doubt a copy of the grin Amy was always accusing me of wearing.

I could actually feel my heart stop, then resume beating, pitter-pat.

The door opened again and Karen came in. She gently pushed Amy aside and came up and hugged me.

"We made a mistake," she said. "We were wrong to turn our backs on you. Please forgive us."

I hugged her right back.

"Nothing to forgive," I told her. "Neither I nor Amy resented you for... anything. Putting some distance between us was probably the smart thing." I pulled back from her a bit. "It may still be the smart play. Are you sure you want to do this?"

"We are quite sure," Xuěyàn added. "We were afraid before. I don't like afraid. This is better."

Xuěyàn then hugged Amy. She was a little awkward about it, but she initiated it, something I don't think she'd ever done before.

We all broke apart, then instantly reformed into a kind of four-way football huddle and laughed.

"Xuěyàn has something," Karen said, nodding to her.

"There was big New-Year party today at Chinese Embassy," Xuěyàn said. "Saturday there will be another party because today not everyone is able to be for this one. We will all go. You will be my father's guests."

She looked at Amy.

"Don't worry, every person will speak English."

We spent the rest of the week trying to decide what to wear to Xuěyàn's embassy. When Diane heard about it, she insisted on taking us shopping for dresses Friday night after school.

I was looking for something red, but that has always been Amy's least favorite color. She would have looked good in red, and I would have looked even better. I kept flashing back to my Lucifer outfit, but in the end, we settled on two pink dresses. We got different styles and different shades of pink to match our different complexions. Di had been to embassy parties before, something I hadn't known, and she knew exactly what kind of dresses were appropriate, so we basically let her pick for us. Xuěyàn had told us that the Chinese embassy would be much less formal than the French, for example, but Di reminded us we would be representing our country and needed to make a good impression. In this situation, it was better to be slightly overdressed than underdressed.

Xuěyàn's mom picked us up in her big Buick on Saturday and drove us down to the Embassy in DC. Xuěyàn rode up front with her mom. Her mom was a very nice person, but as a driver, she was beyond terrifying. The painted lines on the road seemed to have no meaning whatsoever for her. In the back seat, Karen and Amy and I double-checked our seatbelts every five minutes and held hands so tight our knuckles turned white. By some stroke of luck we made it there alive, but not looking forward to the return trip. When we got close, Xuěyàn's mom pointed out the other embassies clustered in the same neighborhood. Singapore was next door and Israel across the street. There was an underground parking garage and the guards just waved us in.

Upstairs, Xuěyàn's mom had her stand beside her in the receiving line, and Xuěyàn had us stand beside her. As two of the cultural attaches, Xuěyàn's parents stood just down from the Ambassador and his wife. As expected, I was the main side show exhibit, but that was fine with me. I enjoyed the reactions when they heard this black girl talking like a real person. Whenever I could, I would quote some traditional aphorism or a famous line from one of the classic Chinese novels, and that made me seem much more fluent than I really was. I was having a great time. Unfortunately, most of the guests were not Chinese, so my fun was limited.

One of these guests was introduced to us as Dr. Fernando, representing Guatemala. He was a former Guatemalan ambassador to the US, standing in for the current ambassador who was back home for a while. When Mr. Jin introduced his daughter Xuěyàn, he mentioned that she was a student at Catonsville; Dr. Fernando seemed to get very interested and took a good hard look at me and at Amy. My immediate assumption was not complimentary to him, especially when he stepped aside to greet us specifically.

"Am I correct in assuming you are Brenda and Amy?"

Amy's mouth dropped open and she poked her neck out slightly. She always reminded me of a turtle sticking its head out of its shell whenever she did that. My own reaction in these kinds of situations was to pull back. No one had introduced us to him, and I didn't think he'd overheard any earlier introduction, so I had to ask.

"How do you know that, sir?"

As he shook my hand he answered, "The son of my good friend and neighbor attends school at Ellicott Academy. He is taking dance lessons at your school. I believe you know him."

Amy asked before I could.

"What's his name?"

"Roberto Ayala."

Well, that was certainly a surprise. Amy was stupefied into silence, so I had to pick up the thread.

"Yes, sir, we know him very well. We have both danced with him many times. He is a nice guy." I considered my next line, mindful that Amy was standing next to me. "Bobby is a good dancer, and a gentleman."

That made him smile broadly, and his chest actually puffed out a little bit.

"I am glad to hear you say so," He said. "I have a coffee finca near Antigua. The Ayala family lives next door to me. I have known Roberto since he was a baby."

"A finca is a farm," Amy whispered to me.

He turned to take Amy's hand.

"You are Amy McDonald, am I right?"

She blushed.

"Yes, sir. Bobby mentioned us by name?"

"Yes he did. Our families celebrated Christmas together in Antigua and he talked about his dance classes, and his dance partners, a great deal."

"What did he say?" Amy asked.

"Only good things. He has enormous respect for both of you."

That comment sounded suspicious to me, so I had to ask, "Why is that? Why respect?"

Dr. Fernando lowered his voice and escorted us a few steps away.

"The Ayala family is one of the oldest in Guatemala, and one of the most prestigious. They are a minor branch of the descendants of Bernal Diaz del Castillo, who was with Cortes during the conquest. But nowadays his family is not wealthy by any means. Sending Roberto to school in the U.S. has been a great sacrifice for them. If you will forgive me for mentioning this, he knows you both come from humble means as he does, and like him, you have worked hard to get to where you are. He understands, as I suspect few of your other classmates do, what you have accomplished so far. Of course he respects you."

We were all silent for a moment, while Amy frowned and looked at the tile floor.

I asked, "Didn't Bernal Diaz write that book about the history of the conquest of the Aztecs? Isn't that the guy you mean?"

"*La Historia verdadera de la conquista de la Nueva España*", Amy replied, "The True History. That's him."

"*Hablas español, señorita McDonald?*"

"*Sí, señor, pero mi español es muy pobre.*"

"*No señorita, su acento es perfecto.*"

Amy and Dr. Fernando continued for a while, in Spanish, and I admit it was a little annoying. I was being excluded from the conversation. I was only able to pick out a few words. This, I thought, must be how Amy felt when I spoke Chinese with Karen. After a while, Dr. Fernando switched back to English.

The first thing he did was address me.

"Your friend doesn't believe me when I tell her how good her Spanish is."

"That is one of her biggest problems. Amy is constantly underrating her own abilities. Never thinks she is good enough. I keep telling her not to belittle herself." I gave Amy a sharp glance before adding the reproach, "There are plenty of others around who will do that for her."

We were able to talk more with Dr. Fernando after he made his rounds. He actually seemed to make it a point to talk to us two girls instead of all the big shots who were his real peers.

I asked, "Can you tell us what you do at your embassy, Dr. Fernando?"

"Oh," he said, "I'm not attached to the embassy anymore. I just help out sometimes, when I am in town. I'm an archaeologist, an epigrapher. I'm in D.C. for a conference at the Pre-Colombian Society and was asked to represent my country here tonight."

I thought I knew what an epigrapher was, but I wasn't sure. I was about to ask, but this time, Amy beat me to it.

"What does an epigrapher do, exactly?"

"When we are exploring an archaeological site, we often discover stela or stone panels or stairways inscribed with Mayan hieroglyphics. My job is to decipher them. We can now decipher about ninety percent. When I started, about all we understood were the calendar glyphs, but we've made amazing progress in a very short time. Mostly thanks to a few brilliant insights by some very dedicated people."

"So," Amy asked, "you work in the jungle? Are you a field archaeologist? How dangerous is it?"

"It's not too dangerous. You just need to take basic precautions. At present, I'm working at a site whose Mayan name translates as 'nest of snakes' and it is aptly named. But, while we find snakes everywhere, no one has been bitten in two years, and the most serious injuries we've had are a few malaria and dehydration cases. If you drink enough water and take your malaria pills, and keep your eyes open, you're fine."

"I've always wanted to visit the Mayan ruins," Amy commented.

"If you come, I'll be happy to assist you. I can put you in touch with all the right people. And don't worry; we have a special tourist police force in place just to ensure your safety." He paused before continuing. "You should definitely see Tikal, but there are many other interesting and important ruins worth seeing too."

I decided to re-direct the conversation.

"Bobby has very blue eyes," I said. "Who does he get that from?"

"His mother is from Puerto Rico, and she has blue eyes, though not as blue as his. When he was in primary school, all the children would tease him about it, and all the girls wanted to be his girlfriend."

"I've thought about going to Mexico for the summer to study Spanish," Amy said, "Do they have immersion schools in Guatemala? Could the embassy help me find one?"

"Yes, they have many well-established summer schools in Antigua. Antigua is the old colonial capitol, very picturesque. Also, if you are interested in the archaeology, the town of Flores, near Tikal, has a number of schools. The internet is probably a better resource for finding a school than the embassy."

"So," I asked, "If Bobby was so popular, did he have many girlfriends back home? Do you know?"

"They were always chasing him. He was always popular, but it became annoying to him. He felt they were more interested in the color of his eyes than in him. I don't think he has a regular girlfriend now." His own eyes twinkled as he said this.

Amy asked, "Do you need a passport to visit Guatemala?"

"Yes, you do. Now... Mostly, you need it to get back into the United States."

"Bobby doesn't seem to have any accent," I said, "Did he study English in Guatemala?"

"Of course. Everyone, nearly everyone who attends school, studies English. His mother teaches English in the primary school. Roberto grew up bi-lingual."

I was running out of things to say, I could tell Amy didn't care for the subject of my questions. We had both been subjecting Dr. Fernando to a close examination that bordered on being impolite and I knew better than to ask him his opinion about that 2012 end-of-Mayan-calendar crap.

Just then a string of firecrackers went off in the middle of the room and a dancing dragon puppet entered with a half-dozen little kids underneath it. The band at the far end of the hall played a faster tempo while the dragon danced and snaked through the room and more firecrackers went off. The big French doors opened up and we all moved outside onto the small lawn. Guards kept us back, next to the doors while more fireworks went off on the lawn and the dragon danced under the rain of sparks and falling embers.

Waiters were handing everyone a glass of Chinese wine, and Amy and I both took one to hold, if not to drink. Xuěyàn saw us and came over.

"You have to drink."

"We are both underage," Amy reminded her.

"And we don't drink," I added.

Xuěyàn laughed.

"The embassy is our land. Chinese sovereign territory land. You are in China now. There is no minimum drinking age in China."

Amy was incredulous. "No minimum age? Really?"

"Yes, under eighteen may not buy, but may drink. Also, no drunken teenager in China. Only old people get drunk, so no problem."

Amy and I looked at each other.

"We still don't drink," she said.

"Just take little bit. You do not have to drink the whole thing," Xuěyàn said. She frowned at us. "But you should. It is the polite thing."

Again, Amy and I looked at each other. Then we nodded.

Turning back to Xuěyàn, we raised our glasses simultaneously and then took a long swallow. It had a bitter taste at first, but then some fruity after-taste. I didn't think it was bad, not that I was qualified to pass judgment. Amy's face flushed immediately, but it quickly faded. We didn't take a second sip, but Xuěyàn seemed satisfied that we at least took one healthy draught.

Back inside, the buffet table had been efficiently cleared and filled with red gift bags, each one emblazoned with a gold dragon on the side. A reverse receiving line formed and as we passed, the Ambassador himself handed each of us one of the bags and thanked us for coming. Amy was in front of me and when she was handed her bag, she said, "*xièxie*." As far as I know, her 'thank you' was the first time she'd attempted a Chinese word, and she even got the tones right.

We were too busy clutching each other in terror on the drive back to look in the bags until we were safely in our rooms.

There was a card thanking us for celebrating the new year with the embassy, a small book (in English) on the Chinese calendar, some tourist brochures, a year of the dragon T-shirt (size large), a silk fan, two heavy silk scarves; one red and one black, and a nice dragon-themed fountain pen in a beautiful lacquer gift box. Last, but not least, there was a small bottle of the wine we'd been served at the party. We could pass that on to Chuck and Di. Alcohol was contraband that we'd have to get off-campus as soon as possible.

39. BAD MOUTH
AMY

Thursday was the next dance class.

At the time, I didn't know if it was my imagination or not, but Steve's hands felt warmer than on Tuesday. His eyes seemed a little brighter, and his smile a little quicker. We still didn't talk about our date. I didn't know how to bring it up.

Class was over and I still hadn't said anything meaningful to him and he hadn't said anything to me. I felt he wasn't mad at me, but I didn't know for sure. Then, just before he left, he came up to me and grabbed my arm. He turned me a little to the side and in a low voice so no one else could overhear, he said, "I'm going to call you, Amy. Is that ok?"

It took me a few seconds to react, but I kept my voice normal. "Sure, Steve. You can call anytime."

He took a quick look around, then leaned in and kissed me on the lips, before he left. We were both smiling as he went out the door.

On the way back to the dorm, Brenda asked, "Do you think he's going to call you again, now?"

I thought he'd been quick enough that no one had noticed, but I should have known she'd be spying on us.

He didn't call that night. I stayed in my room with my phone plugged into the charger, just in case. When he called, I didn't want anyone eavesdropping on my conversation.

He didn't call Saturday morning either. Chuck or Di was supposed to pick us up around noon, as usual, and I was really hoping he would call before then. Just as I was getting ready to go downstairs to wait, my phone rang.

"Amy? Is this a good time to talk?"

"Sure it is, Steve." I'd noticed how he always used my name when he talked to me on the phone, and had decided to give him the same courtesy, whenever I remembered to.

"What are you doing today, Amy?"

"Well, me and Brenda were going over to her aunt and uncle's house for dinner."

"What time do you think you'll get back?"

"We usually spend the night and come back on Sunday evening."

"Amy, do you do this every weekend?"

"Pretty much."

"Don't you ever get tired of the same routine, Amy?"

Well, now that he mentioned it, it did seem to have become more of a habit than a welcome break from school. Aunt Di was an excellent cook, but with her doctor's rounds she didn't have time to cook every weekend. We often just went to restaurants or ordered take-out.

But I just said, "It's all right. Chuck and Di sort of expect us."

"I have a better idea, Amy. Why don't we go out, just the two of us. I have a car. I can drive us out to dinner."

"They sort of expect me to go with them."

Whenever I say something stupid and lame like that, I realize it right away, but after I say it, it's too late to pull the words back.

"Every weekend? Well, Amy, if you aren't interested..."

This was maybe my last chance with Steve. Skipping one weekend with Chuck and Di wouldn't hurt. I'm entitled to a life of my own, I thought.

"Ok, Steve. You're right. I'd be happy to. I'll let Brenda go by herself this weekend."

"Great! I'll pick you up at six. Wear something nice."

I almost *ran* across the hall to tell Brenda.

"I can't go with you to the house this weekend," I told her.

She looked up with a frown. "Are you Ok? Aren't you feeling well?"

"I'm fine," I said. In fact, I was more than fine. I was ecstatic. I had a second date with the handsomest boy in the dance class.

Brenda asked, "Do you want us to stick around the school this weekend?"

I could sense a small bud of suspicion start to sprout in her.

"No," I said. "You go. I just want to be by myself for once."

The bud of suspicion blossomed completely.

"This is about Steve, isn't it? You're going to see him again. Another date."

"Brenda, you're my friend, but you're not my mother. When you bad-mouth him, it tells me that you don't trust my judgment, you don't trust my ability to take care of myself, you don't trust *me*, and you don't think I should have a life of my own. You are wrong on all four counts."

"What I don't trust," she replied, "is that word, 'trust'. You know that about me. And, I *am* your friend. I want you to be happy. And safe."

"I've made up my mind about this," I told her, "give my apologies to your aunt and uncle."

Brenda's frown deepened. She pursed her lips, but kept them shut tight. I knew she wanted to tell me not to go with Steve. Brenda had never been jealous of me before, but her relationship with Ricky wasn't progressing like the one between me and Steve. She was just going to have to accept that she and I were different people. We wanted different things and had our own individual priorities.

"At least tell me where you're going."

"Someplace nice."

Brenda rolled her eyes at me.

"Do you even know where he's planning to take you?"

I rolled my own eyes right back at her.

"It doesn't matter," I said. "I'm sure it'll be someplace nice."

Steve picked me up a little after six-thirty. He explained that traffic had been bad in his neighborhood, so I didn't mind. The car was a silver BMW sedan.

"This is a nice car, Steve."

"It's ok. It's my mom's car. It's two years old."

"It's still very nice."

"Yeah," he said, "except it doesn't have any cup-holders."

I laughed and it felt good to laugh. The car was warm, I was on a real date with a guy who liked me and I felt free.

We pulled up in front of a well-known steakhouse behind the convention center not far from the inner harbor. A guy in a vest came up to the driver's side and Steve handed him the keys. Another red-vested guy opened my door and helped me out. I'd never experienced valet service before.

Steve came around quickly and took my arm and led me inside. He'd made reservations and the maître d' led us to a table in the back. Steve was a perfect gentleman, even pulling out my chair for me. Nobody had ever done that for me before either.

When the waiter came by, Steve ordered two glasses of red wine.

"I'm sorry, sir," the waiter said, "but I'm required to check ID's. Of course, if you would care for something else, we have excellent sparkling water or any other beverage."

Steve looked upset, but he said, "Just two ginger ales. Is that ok with you, Amy."

"Ginger ale is fine," I said.

The truth is that I didn't care for ginger ale. Ice tea would have been better, but I didn't want to break the mood.

Everything on the menu was expensive, but Steve encouraged me to order whatever I wanted.

"I don't know," I said. "What are you going to get, Steve?"

"I usually get the double-cut filet."

"Double-cut?"

"Twice as thick."

I thought about that. I knew a lady should at least pretend to have a modest appetite.

"Do they have single-cut?"

"Of course."

"I'll have that then. With a small salad, please."

The salad came almost immediately, and I didn't want to talk while with my mouth full, so I let Steve do most of the talking. He liked to talk, and I liked to listen. He talked more about his plans for after college.

"The whole reason I'm going to Yale is for the networking," he told me. "If you look at the list of the alumni, you can see how true that is. Tops of the field in every field. It really doesn't matter what you study, it's the contacts you make in college that make or break you later."

He'd already told me this on our first date, but I didn't mind hearing him repeat it.

"Of course, I'll get a law degree. I can do so much more with that, and being a member of the bar opens up a whole other level of contacts and networking that's closed off to non-lawyers. If I decide to go into politics later, I'll have to be a lawyer. If you're a lawyer, you can do anything. Most bankers are also lawyers. The reality is that bankers and lawyers own this country."

I thought he was smart to be planning so far ahead. Brenda and I had The Plan, but that didn't cover specifics for so far ahead. We kept our specific plans no farther ahead than a month or two at a time. I wondered if it was time to change that.

"Amy, have you given more thought to your college plans? You were still undecided last month."

"No," I answered, "we haven't thought that far ahead, yet. We probably won't get serious about it until summer vacation starts."

He frowned.

"Amy, you're back to that 'we' stuff again."

I blushed.

"You need to think of yourself and your own life, Amy."

Steve was right.

"Someday, Amy, you're going to have a family. Your first loyalty then is going to be to them, not to your childhood friends, right?"

"Yeah," I said, "it's just that we've been... working together... for so long, it's hard to shift gears now."

"I understand," he said. "The two of you were the only two smart girls surrounded by a sea of ignorant brats and hood rats, so I guess you had to stick together to survive."

It hadn't been that bad, I thought. And we were real friends, too.

"But it's different now," Steve continued. "Now, you're surrounded by a better class of students, you have a lot more resources, you don't really need each other like you did before."

He reached over and touched my hand.

"You're not alone anymore, Amy."

I was glad I didn't get the double-cut filet. The thing was enormous. We finished our main course with very little conversation, but Steve did get me to be a little more talkative.

"I heard a little about you having problems at school, too."

"It's nothing I can't handle," I told him. "The schoolwork isn't too tough. I'm used to hard work."

"That's not what I mean, Amy. I heard there were rumors of witchcraft and magic spells and stuff."

"Just some silly talk," I lied, "just girls being catty and letting their imaginations get the better of them."

"I know," he said, "girls are like that, sometimes. Don't let them get to you."

I felt too stuffed for desert, but Steve ordered the carrot cake for both of us, and I have to admit it was very good. The whole meal was good, maybe the best meal ever. But I think even Steve was a little bit stuffed, because we slowed down and lingered over desert.

"This is good," he said, "but it would go even better with a nice red wine."

"We don't drink," I said, and regretted it immediately. Especially the "we" part.

"You know, Amy, I don't want to bad-mouth Brenda, and I don't want to do anything to hurt your friendship, but don't you ever think she is holding you back sometimes?"

That thought *had* crossed my mind one or twice. I nodded my head.

"Brenda doesn't have a boyfriend, does she?"

"Well," I said, "you know she likes Ricky."

"But has she actually gone out with him?"

"Not really, not yet, I think."

"But, does she disapprove of you going out with me?"

"Well, she is just being a little overprotective, maybe."

"She's not your mother, Amy. Is it possible she could be a little jealous of you?"

I didn't reply right away.

I didn't want to say what I thought out loud.

"See, Amy, she is holding you back. I'm sure she means well, but you deserve a life of your own. You came here from the Midwest and shouldn't waste your time while you're out here. There are lots of things to see and do, and you're not going to see or do any of them penned up behind the walls of your school or cooped up in Brenda's aunt's house."

"Broaden your horizons. Take advantage of the opportunities that come your way."

"I know," I finally replied. "It's hard to change old habits. Brenda and I have gotten where we are because we worked together and supported each other when no one else did."

"And that made sense at the time, Amy. But it's different now, like I said."

"I know." I was repeating myself again. I did that a lot with Steve.

"I'm not suggesting you give up that friendship. Only that you start thinking more of yourself as an independent adult, and not a part of something like a two-cell organism."

That last comment made me smile.

"Two-cell organism" was not the kind of phrase I expected from Steve, but it was actually pretty accurate, when I thought about it.

He paid for the check with a credit card, and I remember thinking that it was time Brenda and me got a credit card. Cleo had a credit card, so being sixteen shouldn't be a barrier to having one.

When they brought the car around, Steve tipped the valet with cash. I didn't see how much, but the valet looked surprised by the tip. Of course, I had no idea what the proper amount should be, and I didn't ask.

On the drive back, Steve made another good point.

"When you are thinking of what is best for you and Brenda, as a couple, you are not thinking of what is best for either of you as individuals. It's not good for you, and it's not good for Brenda either."

We talked about cars some more.

"I've pretty much settled on a Porsche," Steve said. "But haven't decided on either a Boxter or a Cayman."

"I don't know the difference," I admitted.

"The Boxter is a convertible, the Cayman is a coupe." He looked over at me. "A Porsche doesn't have cup-holders either."

I laughed; then asked, "Won't the insurance be higher on the convertible?"

"That doesn't matter. It'll be high until I'm twenty-five no matter what. It's discrimination against younger drivers, even though we have better vision, better health, and quicker reflexes. It's fucked up."

"Anyway," he added, "I won't get the car until I get my full license."

My brain froze for a moment, then I did the math.

"Steve, you have a provisional license now, right?"

"Yeah, but I've had it for a little while. I've logged the hours. I'm a good driver, Amy. No accidents yet."

"But are you allowed to carry passengers on a provisional? At night?"

"That's just a technicality. Besides, the cops aren't going to hassle a white guy in a BMW in this neighborhood."

We parked on the street outside the school. Through the trees and over the wall, I could see the lights of my own room high up in the dorm. I'm slow sometimes, so it took me a minute to figure out why we were parked out here, but when he reached over for me, I was ready.

Steve was a good kisser. Not that I had a lot of expertise, but I was learning, I thought. I even let him put his hand inside my blouse, but it was very awkward in the front seat. If he had asked me to get in the back with him, I probably would have said yes, but we just kissed some more and then he just said, "Next time, Amy."

He started up the car again and we drove around to the gate and into the parking lot. He gave me one last kiss and I opened my door and got out. I stood by the garden gate and waved as he drove off, but it was dark and I don't think he saw me wave, because he didn't wave back.

While I climbed the stairs, I kept thinking, second date, second base, no need to tell Brenda that.

40. SCARFACE
AMY

Not everybody knows that Al Capone used to live in Baltimore.

Before he became a big-time crime boss he had a reputable job as a bookkeeper for Aiello Construction Company. Aunt Di had her main office at Johns Hopkins, but she shared a smaller office at Union Memorial Hospital a block away. She even pointed out a Japanese cherry tree on the grounds that had been donated by a grateful Al Capone after Union Memorial had treated him for syphilis.

For some perverse reason, Valentine's Day always reminded me of Al Capone and the V-D massacre more than it reminded me of cupids and candy hearts.

The day fell on a Tuesday, and we had a dance class that evening. To everyone's surprise, Ms. Dunham had decorated the gym with red paper hearts on the walls and had a heart-shaped cake and sodas set up on a table. There was even a bowl of candy hearts.

"All right, Ladies and Gentlemen," she began, "I thought a small celebration might be in order. You've learned your lessons very well. You can all dance reasonably well now, but you still need practice and refinement. Dancing is not about romance, it is about movement and knowing the balance between freedom and control. The cake is for after class, so let's begin."

I didn't quite understand what her point was at the time, though I was pretty sure she thought she had one.

We switched around partners as usual the first half-hour, but after a brief rest and the usual lecture about leading and following, she allowed us to choose our own. Rarely the shy one, Brenda invited Ricky to dance. I noticed Bobby was looking at me, but thankfully, it was Steve who got to me first.

"Amy. Will you be my valentine tonight?"

That was the line he used to ask me to be his dance partner and at the time I thought it was cute, original and charming, and I smiled and nodded.

The next few dances were Waltzes, which allowed us to hold each other close and talk a little. I was worried he might bring up the sex thing again, but he didn't. I decided I was wrong to think he'd been trying to pressure me. After a short break to catch our breaths, the next series of dances were foxtrots, and after that, the merengue.

I'd been having frequent headaches lately. Brenda said it was all in my head.

No shit. Where else would I have a headache?

She actually told me it was because I was obsessing over "that boy", but that was bullshit. I wondered if it had to do with me worrying about all this magic bullshit. I was probably just studying too hard. I needed to take a break and relax. I was getting tired too easily. My lacrosse game sucked, but they wouldn't let me drop it. More stupid school rules.

But I felt good that night. No headache and being in the same room with Steve cheered me up a lot.

The dancing itself went well, and I don't think anyone screwed up. We were all doing our appropriate parts and at one point I mentioned it to Brenda.

"We're actually dancing," I whispered to her.

I'm sure my voice betrayed my amazement, because she just grinned.

"I mean," I added, "with every partner, we're doing our steps in unison, the right way. Before we were two separate people moving beside each other, but now we're almost a single unit."

"Four legs good, two legs bad," she said.

It took me a second to recognize she was quoting a line from Orwell's Animal Farm. It was eerily appropriate.

Ms. Dunham called a halt to the lesson with a half-hour to spare, and addressed us all.

"That's enough for this evening, ladies and gentlemen. We can cut the cake and you can catch your breath."

"Ms. Dunham!" It was Bobby. "Before you do that, I have something to say, if I may."

She blinked in surprise, but replied, "Certainly, Mr. Ayala. Go ahead."

Bobby went over to where he'd draped his coat and retrieved a tote bag.

"First of all," he said, "I'm sure I speak for all of us when I say that we are very grateful to Ms. Dunham for her efforts in trying to teach us how to put our right foot forward. Or our left foot, depending on the dancer."

From the bag, he pulled a red heart-shaped box of candy and presented it to her. "With respect and gratitude, Señora," he said, "Please accept this small token of appreciation with regards to the day."

Again, she blinked in surprise, and for the first time, she seemed a bit shy, but accepted her gift with a smile.

Bobby wasn't done.

"Every lady," he said, "needs to be remembered on Valentine's Day."

He pulled another small heart-shaped box from his bag and handed it to Sue Spence who was closest to him at the time. She let out a very faint little squeal of either surprise or delight, probably both.

He continued to pass out boxes of sweets to every girl there. When he gave Brenda hers, she leaned over, gave him a kiss on the cheek and whispered something in his ear. The kiss, though very brief, annoyed me for some reason. Or, maybe it was the whispered secret that got to me.

He saved me for last. It seemed like it took forever for him to walk the few steps to me. He reached down, took my hand and guided it up to level with my chest, then placed the box in my hand. I noticed it had my name on the little tag. I looked around and saw some of the other girls looking at their tags, so he'd personalized each one.

"I haven't forgotten you, Amy," he said. "Happy Valentine's Day."

I blushed.

When I glanced over at Steve, I could tell he was pissed. I couldn't blame him. Bobby knew Steve and I were dating, or trying to, and Bobby was trying to interfere with us. He was just like Brenda, trying to split us up. He just had a different reason.

Still, I didn't throw it back at him. It was a sweet gesture, regardless of his motives. I held the heart close and didn't let it go.

Bobby went back to one of the other girls, while Ricky took the initiative to cut the cake. Brenda went over to help him. She and Ricky were obviously getting more friendly. I was ok with that. And if I was ok with her trying to hook up with some guy, she ought not to be interfering with me trying to do the same thing.

Steve came over to me and put his hand on my arm. "Are you going to keep that?" He nodded at my candy heart box. I didn't understand his question at first, but he took it away from me and looked at it, turning it over to check the label on the bottom.

"It was a nice gesture," Steve said, "but he sure didn't spend much money."

Steve was right. I could tell from the label that it was just cheap candy from the grocery-store's seasonal aisle.

"Godiva would have meant something," he said. But then he added, "Still, I have to admit I should have thought of doing that. It's not really a good excuse, but I've been really tied up with mid-terms. I haven't been doing anything but studying. I hope for his sake Roberto hasn't been neglecting his schoolwork to go shopping."

He handed the little box back to me and I clutched it tight to my chest for some reason even though it was just a stupid box of cheap candy.

I managed to take my last dance with Steve. When it was over, he leaned in and gave me a kiss on the cheek.

"Amy," he said, "I know our last date wasn't very exciting."

"That's ok, Steve. It was fine. It was very nice."

I knew it was a pretty lame response.

"Well," he said, "Maybe next time we can get together for something more meaningful. Would you like that?"

I could feel my heart skip a few beats, just like those cheap romance novels say it does sometimes. I'd always thought that was just a dumb cliché.

I managed to croak out an answer, though.

"Yes. I'd like that, Steve."

He just smiled.

The cake wasn't very good, but I suppose it was still a nice idea. I tried the candy from Bobby's heart later, and it tasted stale. On the other hand, it might have been me. Even the food they served up at school was starting to taste like cardboard to me lately.

41. SNOMAGEDDON
AMY

The very next day, after Valentine's Day, there was another incident.

I was walking down the hallway, and I admit I probably wasn't paying attention, when me and Putnam bumped into each other. It felt like she had deliberately bumped into me, but I was so out of it, I suppose it might have been me who blundered into her.

"Gee, Amy. Watch where you're going, ok?"

I was about to apologize, but something about the expression on her face stopped me.

"You watch it," I muttered.

"Is that a threat?"

"Just leave me alone."

"Or what?"

I was too tired to reply, I just waved her away with my hand.

The day after that she was sitting on the bench at soccer practice when, seemingly from nowhere, a stray cat attacked her.

She got a lot of scratches on her hand and wrist, but she was fine. They took her in for some tests but I heard they just dosed her up with antibiotics as a precaution. The cat disappeared. We'd all seen one or two feral cats on campus. It wasn't a big deal. The groundskeepers kept the place pretty clean, so it was a rare thing to see one.

The rumor mill started up again. I'd been on the soccer field at the time, but at the other end, far from Mary's bench. That distance didn't seem to matter. Cats and witches go together. Some girls were saying it had to be me again.

As soon as one thing passed and people thought I was normal again, then something new would happen and it would be the same crap all over again. Maybe it was even true. After the incident in the hallway, I dreamed about Mary being attacked and torn apart by a pride of lions on the African savannah. But that was only a stupid dream.

Baltimore only got one big snowfall that year. It was near the end of February and even then it was only a little more than twelve inches. The newscasters on TV made it sound like the Apocalypse, using the term "Snomageddon" over and over. I guess none of them had ever been to the Midwest.

For me, it might just as well have been the end of the world, at least the end of the world as I'd always known it.

I wasn't normal. I knew that now. Something was very wrong, and it was me.

The headaches were less severe, but they were nearly constant now and had been for the last two weeks since the cat-Mary thing or maybe even before. It was hard to remember.

When I got up in the morning, first thing I would do was kneel over the toilet bowl and try to puke while Brenda held my hair. It was always the dry heaves, or maybe a little bit of water would come up. Brenda tried to cheer me up with her dumb jokes, "Maybe you're just pregnant, Amy, morning sickness is a natural part of the process." But that only made me feel worse. No guy wants a future with a freak. He won't want to kiss some girl whose lips stink of vomit, much less do anything else with her. And word would get around; girls talk. He would find out.

Brenda had traded beds with Xuěyàn so she could watch me better. We weren't supposed to do that--rooms were assigned for a reason. If she got in trouble, it would be my fault, I told her to go back, but she just told me to shut up. She could look out for herself, she said. She tried to play it cool, and be her usual happy self around me, but I could feel Brenda's tension and concern. It was like she radiated tight tendrils that filled the room like a spider web, with her at the center. I couldn't tell if she was the spider or the fly, though.

I was always complaining about how bad the food had gotten. It was bland and tasteless and chewing it had become a tiresome chore. Brenda and Cleo and the Jins kept encouraging me to eat, but I could never eat enough to satisfy them.

Di thought I might be sick and she kept taking me in to the hospital for more pointless tests. She never found anything. I just let her lead me from place to place and do whatever she said, but later, when I tried to recall what tests I'd done, I couldn't remember them. Maybe I was turning into a zombie. Maybe zombies weren't made by being bitten; maybe it was just a virus you caught, and then a slow and steady process where the patient degenerates into a walking, rotting corpse.

It was better when I slept. My dreams were very vivid. Sometimes they were full of bright colors, and I would be flying, like Superman, over strange landscapes. Other times they would be dark and I would be on foot. Always, I was wandering, searching for something, but not knowing what I was searching for. And in my dreams, I was never sick or weak, but always strong.

I still went to classes. I got mediocre marks on my tests, and worse marks on my papers. Doing papers was a nearly impossible chore. I would just stare at the blank screen, unable to start. Brenda or Xuěyàn usually wrote the first few lines for me, and then I could get something done, but there was no joy in it. Even math seemed like a waste of time to me. Everything did, truthfully. Every day seemed to drag on hour by hour, minute by minute. I would sometimes stare at the clock and watch as the second hand took an eternity to tick away one second at a time.

I remember sitting in Dr. Kramer's office one evening, watching the clock tick away. Aunt Diane was there and they were talking about me. I paid attention only long enough to hear Di tell her, "It's still too early to consider something like Prozac or Zoloft, she's functioning and..." I lost interest in their conversation after that.

When Brenda led me arm in arm back to my room, we passed over the glass corridor connecting the buildings. The grounds were covered in a soft white blanket of snow, clean and bright and fresh. I used to love the way snow covered up the dirty streets, but now it just looked empty and cold.

42. SOROROCIDE
AMY

Algebra class had just started when I began to feel light-headed. The teacher was droning on about determinants, old stuff to me, and my mind wandered.

Brenda didn't understand how I was feeling. We'd been together for so long, and yet, she just didn't understand. The bitch kept telling me to "snap out of it" or to be more like how I used to be, whatever the hell that was. Worse, she was treating me like a child, after all I'd done for her. She didn't know how I felt.

Nothing bad ever happened to Brenda, the golden child, for whom everything came easy, who danced through life without a care in the world, never knowing what it was like to feel bad. Nothing ever disturbed Brenda's happy little life. Maybe if she got knocked down hard, she might be able to sympathize.

It would be good for her to get hurt once.

It would teach the bitch some compassion.

I gasped. There was a sudden sting in my right hand that made me jerk my whole arm as if I'd been stung by a bee. My head felt like it had been slammed against a wall and my stomach and chest felt like I'd been kicked. I stifled a scream.

Now what, I wondered?

The pain seemed to reach a quick peak and then slowly eased. I was wondering if I should ask to be excused, but that would require me to stir myself to speak, and I hadn't been talking much lately. My mind was racing but I couldn't focus on anything, not on the lesson on the board, not on my body, not even on my own thoughts. I started to feel disembodied, as if I was floating. I wondered if I was going to faint.

The pain had become a set of minor irritations, but something was gnawing away in the back of my mind. I was missing something important. The seconds and minutes ticked by, but the feeling of dread grew.

The hour was nearly up when the image of Brenda's face, contorted in pain, flashed into my mind and I jerked to my feet.

The teacher and the whole class looked at me. I spoke before any of them did.

"I have to go," I said.

I ran all the way to the nurse's office. Drs. Davis and Kramer and Ms. Dunham were standing outside the door talking with the nurse. I was nearly out of breath but managed to gasp out the only question that mattered, "Is Brenda ok?"

Dr. Kramer spoke first. "Everything is under control, Miss McDonald; she is going to be fine. We've called her aunt, and the ambulance is on its way. There is nothing for you to do here."

"I have to see her."

Dr. Davis put her hand on my shoulder. "I don't think that is a good idea, just yet, dear. The EMT's have given her first aid; she needs to rest while we wait for the ambulance. I'm sure Miss Dickens' Aunt will let you see her once they get her evaluated at the hospital."

"I have to see her," I repeated.

"It's really not a good idea to bother her right now," the nurse said. "As Dr. Kramer says, there really is nothing you can do for her right now, except disturb her rest. You don't want to do that, do you? I'm sure you'll be able to see her later."

Run along, little girl.

That was the message.

Let the grown-ups handle this.

It did make sense.

There probably was nothing I could do.

I needed to see her, but my selfish needs weren't really important. Brenda's health and safety was all that really mattered. I was just in the way here.

I was about to leave quietly, when Dr. Davis made a mistake.

"Amy," she said, "If you were in there, and Brenda was out here, she would know you needed your rest, she would let us take care of you, and she would go back to her classes."

No.

That was wrong.

If I was hurt, there would be no force in the world that would keep Brenda from my side. Certainly not this group. I felt stronger than I had in a long time, and I suddenly seemed to see everything sharper, and clearer, with brighter colors, like in my dreams.

"Dr. Davis: Brenda is my friend." I told her. "You can expel me, you can call the cops and have me arrested, and you can try to restrain me physically. But you can't keep me out. There are only four of you and that's not enough to stop me, if you try. I am going to see her. Now. Please don't get in my way."

Before they could recover from their shock, I squeezed between them and went inside.

Brenda's forehead was wrinkled and dotted with beads of sweat. I knew they wouldn't give her anything for the pain until the ambulance arrived and maybe not even until they got her evaluated at the hospital. I snatched a paper towel from the dispenser, ran it under the faucet quickly and placed it on her forehead. She said, "Oh," and she managed a tiny smile.

"You're going to be ok," I told her, brushing her hair back. "Don't worry."

She nodded her head slightly.

"How did this happen?" I asked her.

"Amy, don't make her talk…" It was Ms. Dunham. They had all followed me into the little room.

I turned my head to glare at them, and they all took a step back, in unison, like puppets on strings. They had correctly interpreted my glance for the threat that it was. I probably was going to be arrested for this, and definitely expelled. Well, at least I wouldn't have to wear the stupid uniform anymore.

My focus returned to Brenda. Her hand was heavily bandaged and I could see a big bruise developing on the side of her face. But I knew it was her stomach that hurt the most. I put my palm over her tummy, it felt hot. I tried to imagine drawing the heat into my hand, but I couldn't tell if I was helping or not.

"It was an accident," Ms. Dunham said. "She and her partner lost their balance at the same time and collided. They banged into each other pretty hard. Her partner's foil snapped and punctured Brenda's ungloved hand. Injuries in fencing are extremely rare. This was just a freak accident."

"I got punched in the solar plexus, too," Brenda said. "When we collided. Her elbow, I think. Something feels broken. They cut off my jacket. The new one I got from Karen."

I very lightly caressed the area at the bottom of her ribcage.

She was still wearing her knee britches and there were big brown splotches on the white fabric of her thigh. I involuntarily sucked air in through my teeth at the sight and asked, "What's that?"

As soon as I said it I knew I shouldn't have, but Brenda answered anyway.

"Human circulatory fluid. It will come out in the wash--just rub in a little salt."

Human circulatory fluid.

Blood.

This was all my fault.

The one person in the world who had always been there for me, and I had hurt her. The one person I should never hurt.

This is how I use my so-called powers.

Me: a worthless piece of shit.

"The ambulance is coming through the gate," someone said.

"I'm riding in with her," I said.

Anticipating resistance, I fumbled for my phone. The one good thing about these stupid uniform blazers was that they had pockets and I could always carry my phone. I turned it on and called Aunt Diane. It rang once and then clicked off.

"I can't get a good signal here," I told Brenda, "I'm calling Aunt Di."

I stepped outside the office, and then outside the building. There were only a few patches of snow left, but it was bitterly cold. I got a good connection, but it just rang to Di's voice mail. I was about to leave a message when the ambulance pulled up and parked right in front of me. Seeing them unload the gurney, the words caught in my throat, and my mind went blank. I started to cry then, great heaving sobs that astonished me. I hadn't really cried in years. Dumb, I clawed at the door to open it for the EMT's, but I kept missing the handle. One of them opened the door instead while another took pity on me and pushed me inside where it was warmer. I pointed to the nurse's office, and leaned against the wall, still crying. I tried to keep quiet, I didn't want Brenda to see me like this, it would only upset her to see me such a mess, but I couldn't stop. I took a deep breath and ran away back up to my room, trying to dry my tears with my sleeve.

My phone rang after dinner. I'd skipped the rest of my classes, hadn't gone to dinner and had chased poor Xuěyàn out of the room when she'd tried to look in on me. It was Aunt Di on the phone.

"Brenda's ok, Amy," she told me. "You can talk to her on the phone in the morning, she's a little doped up right now. Tomorrow night, I'll probably come get you so you can visit her, but she'll most likely be discharged the day after tomorrow."

"Are you sure she's ok? Her stomach was hurting."

"Her stomach is fine. She has a cracked rib, but that will heal on its own. We did some minor surgery on her hand..."

"Surgery! Will she be able to use..."

"Don't worry, Amy. It was *minor* surgery. I'm confident she'll have full use of her hand. We may send her to physical therapy later, but she'll be fine. Just a tiny scar. Maybe not even that."

I could feel the tightness in my chest. I was going to start crying again.

"I'm sorry," I said.

"Amy, don't say that. This wasn't your fault. Now, you get some rest tonight. I'll call you in the morning when I check on her, and I'll give you an update and probably let you talk to her yourself. Brenda is going to be fine, she'll probably be back at school by the end of the week. "

I didn't think I'd be able to sleep, and for a long while, I just lay awake in bed, but sometime before midnight I did fall asleep. It was a deep, dreamless sleep. I woke up just a minute or two before the alarm went off. I was brushing my teeth when I heard the ringtone.

"Good morning, Amy," Aunt Diane said.

"Good morning, Aunt Di," I replied.

I waited for her to say something else.

"I have someone here who wants to talk to you," she said.

"Good morning, Amy." Brenda's voice was slow and she sounded tired, but I felt excited just to hear it again.

"How are you feeling, Brenda?"

"Di says I have a cracked rib. It only hurts when I breathe."

"Brenda, I'm sorry. This was all my fault."

"Don't say that. I'm fine. You'll have to cut my food for me though, now that I'm a damned cripple."

"Whatever you need," I told her.

I could hear Diane taking the phone away from her.

"Amy, this is Di, we're probably going to discharge her this evening instead of tomorrow, so I'll take her home tonight and bring her back to school tomorrow. I wanted to keep her home for the rest of the week, but she insists on getting back to school right away. So, I won't bring you over to see her tonight, like I said, I hope you don't mind."

"No ma'am," I said. "Just make sure she's ok. I'll take care of her once you bring her back. Just tell me what you need me to do, and I'll do it."

"Ok, Amy. We'll call you again tonight and you can talk to each other some more then."

I looked at the clock when we hung up. If I hurried, I could still get some breakfast before class. I was hungry.

43. WEDGE OF DOUBT
BRENDA

The worst part of having a bandaged hand was getting myself ready in the morning.

Using toilet paper with the "other" hand was much harder than I had imagined it could be. I guess I wasn't as ambidextrous as I thought.

I was surprised to learn that I'd always been putting my left arm into the sleeve of my blouse first when I got dressed and that was a problem now. I needed to put the bandaged right hand through its sleeve first. That felt awkward and simply "strange".

I was supposed to change the bandage twice a day. Amy tried diligently to help with that, but Karen did a much better job. Karen had been a candy-striper at UCSF hospital in San Francisco, and had assisted with bandages before. Karen was much less squeamish than Amy too. Chuck and Di took turns and one of them came to the school every evening to check on me, and even they were impressed with how well Karen did.

I'd joked with Amy that she'd have to be cutting my food for me, but I didn't need any help with any of that. I just switched the hands holding the knife and fork and was fine.

I only had the bandage for about a week and a half.

What was most interesting was how everyone treated me.

As a "cripple" nearly everyone's attitude towards me changed. Some people went out of their way to show exaggerated sympathy, holding doors open for me, offering to carry my bag, or buss my table for me after meals. But there were others who viewed a cripple with contempt. They saw me as a weaker member of the pack who should be expelled from the herd lest she contaminate the healthy members. The amazing part was that even though their attitude was blatantly obvious, they themselves didn't see it. They weren't even part of Putnam's posse.

Aunt Diane had promised me only a tiny scar, and her word proved good. She'd had a friend of hers do the actual surgery and he'd done a superb job. The blade had broken off clean, as I thought maraging steel is supposed to do, and it had punched through between the long bones of my hand. Even right when it happened, I'd been lucky no major vein had been clipped, so there wasn't a whole lot of blood. They sent me to the physical therapist, and he gave me a few exercises to do, like crumpling a sheet of newspaper one-handed, but said I didn't need anything else. It was the cracked rib that bothered me the most, but even that got better in only a couple of weeks.

I was proud of my little scar.

Amy felt guilty, but I didn't blame her.

Amy seemed to be over her depression. It had disappeared like magic, but she was still fixated on that boy.

Anytime we talked about it, she would get all defensive, so we stopped talking about that completely. Instead, we talked about our schoolwork. She helped me with my Algebra, and I'll give her credit, she was able to explain the "Limits" they talked about in the pre-calculus chapter better than my teacher.

The one thing we did *not* discuss was this whole "witchcraft" business. I didn't know if she was still in denial about it, or had moved on to the acceptance phase. I did know it was a topic I did not care to touch even with a ten-foot pole.

44. GIRLFRIENDS
BRENDA

Amy and I needed to talk in private.

If we'd both still been in the laundry room, that would have been ideal, but I'd given up my key and going there with Amy now would not be a good idea.

We headed outside to the garden. It was a little chilly, but that just made it less likely we'd be disturbed.

"So," I asked, "where do we stand?"

"Those bitches are trying to get rid of us. They're going to be trying to frame us for something."

"Which 'bitches' do you mean?"

Amy rolled her eyes at me.

"Don't play *me*...," she said. "You *know* who."

"Well," I said, "Putnam, pretty clearly. And Abby too. But what about Ann and Betty?"

Amy glared at me.

"Of course them too!"

"You don't think it's possible a couple of those could be innocent pawns? Maybe Ann and Betty?"

"No, they're all in it together, they have their own little gang. Putnam's the ringleader."

"I agree about Putnam, for sure. But I think we should be cautious about assuming evil intent from the other members of their little gang. They might only be guilty of being gullible."

"You honestly think any of their little clique doesn't know what Putnam is trying to do?"

"No, but we don't have proof."

"We should just grab Mary Putnam and beat a confession out of her."

"You don't mean that," I told her.

"Sure I do," Amy answered.

"No you don't. Not really. That would backfire on us. We should just let this crap roll off our backs, sit tight, and gather evidence."

"Or," Amy said, "We could tell Putnam, politely, and to her face, that we know what she is up to. That should put the fear of God in her."

"I don't think we should confront them at all. Confrontation is what she wants. I don't want to give our enemies *anything* that they want. Do you?"

Enemies.

I'd given them the name.

They, or at least Mary Putnam, had declared themselves to be our enemies. If that is what they wanted to be, then I would give them that much, at least.

"If we don't confront them," Amy pointed out, "they'll think we're a couple of punks who can be pushed around. It'll only encourage them."

"And if we do, they'll just become more careful and more subtle. I'd rather have them careless and open. I want plenty of witnesses next time they pull something."

"I'm cold," Amy said, "let's go back inside."

There were more girls in the hallway inside, so our discussion became more general.

"Ok, Brenda, I'll go along with you for now. But I think you're wrong."

"Don't say that unless you mean it," I said. "I don't want you to agree with me just to shut me up. We need more."

"I said I'd go along with you, for now. That doesn't mean this discussion is over. Far from it."

"Look, Amy..."

"You are wrong, Brenda."

"Amy, look. I just...," I was repeating myself.

"You're the one who's going to see. Your way won't work. You think we can just 'be nice?' and everything will work out?"

Other girls were staring at us.

"Amy!" I wanted to her to hush up. The public hallway was not the place.

She frowned at me.

"You're not being smart," she said, before stalking off.

Karen came up to me right then.

"You two fight like an old married couple," She told me. She smiled as she said it.

"Yeah, but we don't fight about sex or money, so, obviously, we're not."

My response earned a laugh, but I didn't really think Amy and I fought all that often.

We had our disagreements, sure. We always did. But I didn't think we'd ever be arguing in public. I knew that couldn't lead to anything good, but I didn't anticipate what else it would lead to.

It happened sooner than I expected, when one of the girls cornered me in the alcove outside the biology lab. This was a little dead space in the floor plan, right off the hallway, where girls would sometimes get together to trade gossip and whispers. Joan Marshall was a short, brown-haired girl who'd made little impression on me till now. She was quiet, and I thought, a loner. She came up to stand directly in front of me and said, "Brenda, can I talk to you for a minute?"

I think those may have been the first words she'd ever said to me.

"Sure," I said, and she immediately pulled me into the alcove.

"I heard what Amy said to you," she said, "and I'm sorry." Joan rested her hand on my upper arm for a moment.

"It's not a big deal," I replied. I wondered where Joan was going with this but I gave her the opportunity to continue.

Joan eased a little bit closer and lowered her voice just a little bit more.

"You and Amy have been friends for a long time, right?"

"Yeah, a very long time. Since pre-school."

"It's rare that any friendship lasts that long. It's natural for all relationships to change over time, I think. It's probably inevitable."

I could tell that Joan had rehearsed this little speech, but still couldn't see what point she was trying to make.

"I broke up with my own girlfriend a couple of months ago," Joan added. "She's going to a different school now, and once we were not seeing each other every day, I guess we started to see how different we were. It's probably a good thing, even though I missed her a lot at first. We'd been 'friends' since before junior high, and now I think we just stayed together out of habit more than anything."

Something about the way Joan said the word 'friends' tickled the back of my mind. I took a deep breath.

Joan took a deep breath too. "If," she said, "you and Amy, if you're not as close anymore, then maybe that's not all bad. I think you should take the opportunity to make new friends. I don't think you've been doing much of that since you've been here." She reached out again, this time placing her right hand over my left, snaking her fingers inside mine to hold my hand.

"Uh...," was all I could get out.

"I just want you to know that I think *we* could be friends, Brenda. Once we got to know each other better." She gave my hand a little squeeze, but I still wasn't exactly sure what I was hearing, not totally.

"You're very pretty, Brenda. I've always thought that. I hope you think I'm maybe a little bit attractive, too."

Ok.

Now I was sure.

Joan was still holding my hand with her left, and with her other hand, she reached up to caress my shoulder. "I just want to let you know I'm here for you, Brenda, if you want. Why don't we sit together in the cafeteria, so we can talk?"

Shit.

I took another deep breath.

But I made no effort to pull away.

"Joan," I said, "What kind of relationship do you think I've had with Amy? Something more than just simple friendship?"

Her eyes widened a bit.

"You're, you were, you've been girlfriends, right?"

"Joan. I know that sometimes, in the past, some people have assumed that Amy and I are or have been lovers."

Joan frowned.

"But we are not. Never have been. Not with each other, and not with any other girls, either."

Joan's face flushed. She moistened her lips and she removed her left hand from my shoulder.

"I didn't think...," She said, "I just meant we could be friends, normal friends..."

"It's ok, Joan. We *can* be normal friends. I'm not mad at you. I just want to be clear. I know some people have the wrong ideas about me and Amy. I've heard the rumors, too."

She tried to pull away. She was going to run off, but I kept a firm grip on her hand.

"I'll keep our little conversation secret, if you want, Joan. I promise. But I want to know where you heard that I was gay."

She shook her head and blushed, hard, making a little choking noise deep in her throat.

"Joan. If you are as smart as I think you are, you'll tell me. I won't tell anyone else."

Again, she tried to pull away, but I grabbed her wrist with my other hand and held tight. Her eyes widened as my eyes narrowed. She lost the staring contest and relaxed.

"I'm sorry," she said.

"It will be ok," I told her, "just tell me who and we'll be able to forget this whole thing."

The name she gave me was not a surprise.

45. THE PUTNAM PLAN

"You shouldn't be afraid of me," Mary said.

Ann froze in place, but out of the corner of her eye she noticed Betty flinch and Abby smile.

"You know," Ann said, "Everything you've tried has failed to work. Maybe we should just lay off, at least for a while."

Mary scowled, "We just need to stay focused. Those two have been lucky so far, but now is the time to take this to the next level."

"Yes," she added, "They've been very lucky. But we *have* made a difference. They're off-balance, under stress, and not as close as before. They've even been arguing in public, something we didn't see before."

"Maybe they're not as tight as they were, but they're still friends and I'm not so sure it's all been just luck with them. There is something else."

"We all agree they have to go. This is the time to strike. I've learned from our earlier attempts. You shouldn't think of them as failures, they were more like trial balloons. I know what to do now. Trust me."

"Look," Ann said, "I think the school could do without them, but aren't we overreacting? They're not that bad. Why do we have to do anything?"

"You're still stuck on that 'do-nothing' strategy? You really want this school to be taken over by a pack of lesbo hood rats?"

"I really don't think they're gay. And they're not causing any real trouble. It was us who brought pot into the school, not them."

"You going soft on us now, Ann?"

"I just think this is getting out of hand. We keep escalating things, and I'm worried about what would happen if something backfires. *We* could be getting in trouble instead of them."

Mary leaned forward and lowered her voice.

"You're afraid."

Ann stiffened.

"I guess I am," she said, but added, "So, what's your new plan?"

"I'm not sure I should tell you. It's not that I don't trust you, Ann. I just think the fewer people who know the details, the better."

"But you do have a plan, right?"

"A very good plan. If you don't want to help, maybe Abby will be willing to take your place."

Abby straightened up in her chair and tried to suppress a grin.

Ann glanced over at Betty.

Betty reminded Ann of a frightened deer trying to decide if she should cross the road or not. Ann had seen enough dead deer on the side of the road to know that deer often made the wrong decision.

"If you walk out on us now, you're the one who risks getting hurt, Ann. It means you're declaring that you don't want to be one of us anymore, it means you're telling us we shouldn't trust you anymore. You're saying you want to be alone."

"We have two more full years of school here after the end of this year, Ann. It's a difficult enough job to get through this with friends, it may be impossible to do it alone, without any help. Don't be stupid, Ann. Besides, you don't owe those girls anything. I think you do owe us, though. Why would you risk yourself for them?"

"I don't care about them, not really," Ann replied. "I care about us, about myself. When Amy and Brenda first showed up here, I could tell they were out of place and maybe didn't belong here. And I wanted them gone, too."

"And now you don't, is what you're saying."

"No, I'm not saying that."

"Do you even know what you want, Ann?"

"I just don't want trouble."

Ann took a deep breath.

"If they deserve to be kicked out, let them prove it. If you're right about them being so 'wrong', they will prove it eventually. They'll take care of it themselves."

"You used to be on our side," Mary said, "but something has turned you against us. Against all of us, against the school itself."

Mary paused to let her 'with us or against us' message sink in before continuing.

"They did this. Don't you see, Ann? You were always one of us before. We did everything together, and now you're not with us anymore. They'll keep doing this to others until the whole school is split up. I'm not sure how, but they've turned you against us. Come back to the fold, Ann. Help us get rid of them. Don't try to go it alone, you won't make it. Commit to the plan and you can still be one of us."

"Besides, what are you going to do? Go to Kramer and tell about your involvement in this. You were the one who put the joint in Amy's coat. Are you going to confess to that? That would be the end of you."

Ann swallowed hard but tossed her head back.

"Amy and Brenda didn't break us up," she said, "You did that."

Mary didn't reply right away. She just stared at Ann for a long time before answering her.

"I know you'll at least keep your mouth shut. I still have the receipt for the itching powder you bought. And that's not all I've got on you. Don't make me use any of it."

46. THIRD TIME THE CHARM
AMY

I had been reading books and the relationship advice in the teen magazines and on the internet and most agreed that a girl shouldn't have sex on the first date. They did not agree on how many dates you should have before it was time.

I didn't take their advice and info at face value. I knew a lot of it was bullshit, probably written by 40 or 50-year old professional writers working on a publication deadline, but I had to start somewhere.

The consensus seemed to be that you shouldn't put out until the third date. I wasn't stupid. Well, maybe I was, but at least I knew it depended on the guy, the level of commitment, the circumstances, and the girl.

This was going to be our third date, and I felt ready. Third time is the charm, I thought.

Third time would be the first time. For me.

If I decided to do it.

I didn't even have to tell Brenda. I'd gotten past the second date with Steve and that made me free of our bargain. I could act with a clear conscience as far as that was concerned.

I remembered Aunt Di's offer to help with "anything I needed" but I didn't want to involve her. I didn't even want her to know.

Fortunately, there was the internet. And a drugstore only two blocks away.

Whatever I decided to do, or however far I decided to go, I knew I should be prepared.

I knew there was no reason, but I was still nervous. I could have ordered supplies on-line, but I didn't have time with our date only a couple of days away. Besides, I could just imagine getting a call from the mailroom; *"Miss McDonald, your package from Condoms-R-Us has arrived."*

I was sure my nerves were showing when I entered the drugstore. I kept imagining some clerk would mistake my nervousness and think me a shoplifter instead of a stupid girl getting ready to maybe get laid for the first time. I'd planned a quick in and out. I picked up a basket at the door and went straight to the feminine hygiene section. I found what I needed, threw the condoms in the basket, added a bottle of aspirin to make it seem like the condoms weren't my only purchase, and then, to try to make me seem older, went to the periodicals section and added a copy of the Wall Street Journal.

I nearly lost it when the check-out girl asked me if I had a drugstore loyalty card, but she rang me up and checked me out without any other problems. Once outside, I was actually shaking. I shouldn't be shaking, I thought. I'm old enough to buy condoms, for Pete's sake. If I'm old enough to plan on using them, I should be old enough to buy them without being embarrassed.

I calmed down on the walk back. The plastic bag was transparent enough to show the condom box, so I wrapped it in the newspaper and stuffed the aspirin bottle in my pocket until I got back to my room.

Steve picked me up at seven-thirty Saturday night.

He had his mom's Beemer again and when I put my butt in the seat, it seemed to fit just right, like I belonged there.

As we pulled away, I asked, "Where are we going tonight, Steve?"

"My house."

I nearly gasped. I thought I was ready, but that seemed bold, somehow.

"Am I going to meet your parents?"

"No, they're up in Philly for some benefit. They won't be home 'till tomorrow. We'll have the house to ourselves."

I wondered if I was starting to get cold feet.

"I'll fix us dinner tonight," he said. "I'm an excellent cook."

"Oh." A second later, I added, "can I help?"

"Sure. I'll think of something for you to do. Can you handle carrots or cucumbers?"

"You mean to fix a salad?"

"Sure. What else would I mean?"

It took me another second to catch the double meaning. I was always slow on the uptake.

"Don't worry, Amy. It'll be fine. Trust me."

I *did* trust him.

"We'll have Chicken L'Orange," he added.

Once we were inside, he led me to the kitchen.

He pulled out the carrots and a big cucumber and handed them to me.

"Careful with the knife, Amy. Don't cut anything that shouldn't be cut."

I knew how to fix a salad.

I remember setting the table and dishing the salad.

I remember Steve putting out two wine glasses.

I remember the sweet taste of the orange chicken.

I remember Steve telling me not to clean up, the maid would take care of that in the morning.

I remember looking at a bottle of wine and almost saying "we" don't drink, but catching myself and saying "I" don't drink instead.

I remember being a little surprised that the wine didn't burn my throat the way the Cognac and the Amontillado had.

I remember my hands being numb and unfeeling.

It was cold outside. I had my coat, but kept thinking I had forgotten something.

I was stumbling.

I was next to a wall. It was either stone or brick. I remember thinking it was odd I couldn't tell the difference. I didn't know where the wall was, and that was odd too. I ran my hand across it and felt the grit crumble under my palm. It was dirty. I tried to brush the dirt off on my jacket, but it wouldn't come off. I brushed harder and harder, but I couldn't get rid of it. I started to gag, thinking of the filth.

I felt faint and put both palms flat against the filthy wall. Without any apparent warning, I puked. The vomit sprayed over my shoes. I braced myself and threw up again, then lost my balance and slid to my knees, landing them in the pool of puke. The smell of it was in my nose and I tried to retch again, but nothing came up but spit. I retched and retched but nothing more came up.

The next thing I remember was sitting at a bus stop, twitching and trembling. At least two buses stopped, then passed me by. I don't remember even trying to get on either one. It was like I just wanted a place to sit and the buses were just passing scenery.

At one point I had my phone in my hand. It kept playing a ringtone that I recognized as Brenda's but I didn't answer it. I don't know if I had forgotten how, or if it just didn't seem important.

"Come with me, Miss."

The voice was deep, sad, and strangely familiar.

I felt a blanket around me, and then I lay down on something soft and warm. At the shock of the sudden warmth all around me, I retched again.

"Don't worry about that, Miss," the voice reassured me.

Why would I be worried about that? Why would I be worried about anything?

At some later point, I realized I was sitting in a waiting room of some kind. I felt cold again, but I knew I was asleep.

That part was very odd. I couldn't remember ever before being asleep and also knowing I was asleep.

But that feeling faded and I sank into a deeper sleep where I dreamed. I dreamed I heard voices talking about me while I drifted like a boat lost at sea floating through a fog bank or a cloud.

"So, she was just outside the campus?"

"That's right, Brenda. Azim found her at the bus stop. There were tracks that led from the campus parking lot to the bus shelter, so it looks like she walked there from the lot."

"Where was she going?"

"I doubt she knew. I doubt she even knew she was on campus. Some part of her may have thought she could take the bus back to the campus, not realizing she was already there."

"So, Steve probably just brought her back and dumped her in the parking lot."

"Maybe. We'll let the cops figure out that part."

"No, Cleo. We won't involve them."

"I don't like involving them either, but we have to call the cops."

"Not without Amy's ok."

"She's not in any position to give her consent."

"We'll wait until she is."

"You can't let him get away with this, Brenda. Amy's been drugged. She might have been killed. She still might have suffered brain damage. Some of these date-rape drugs are far from harmless. Some of them are actively toxic. You have to call the cops."

"He won't get away with it. But we don't *have* to call the cops. We'll take care of him later. In the end, Steve's not important. He is *nothing*. Amy and I are playing a bigger game. We're very grateful for all your help, Cleo. Don't ever doubt that, or doubt that we'll someday find a way to repay you. But this is our thing. How we handle it is not really your concern."

"So, what are you going to do?"

"Don't know yet. We'll think of something. There's no hurry. The only thing that matters is getting Amy back on her feet."

"You don't think you have a duty to other women to report this guy? You don't think this is the first time he's done this sort of thing, do you?"

"No. I don't think this is his first time. But I only have one sister that I have to worry about, and that's a full time job in itself."

There was a moment of silence.

"Amy is a lot of work for you."

"That's just this year. She's always been trouble-free before we came to the Academy."

"Would she put out this same level of effort for you?"

Another moment of silence.

"The doctor is ready for her. I'll help you get her undressed."

"Thanks for finding this doctor, Cleo. We want to keep this as quiet as possible. At least for now. And Cleo; it doesn't matter what she would do for me. It's not like there's a scorecard where we're keeping count."

At some point I knew I was lying on something hard and I was covered by a paper sheet. I was still cold. The voices in my dream were still talking about me, two that sounded familiar, and another I'd never heard before.

"There is no evidence of rape, or sexual intercourse, but there is some bruising on her arms and her neck, as if she was restrained or in a fight. Not a big fight, maybe a brief struggle."

"She was drugged?"

"Yes. She tested positive for PCP..."

"PCP?"

"But the symptoms don't match PCP. It's probably Ketamine. There is no specific test for Ketamine, but users often test positive for PCP. Both Ketamine and PCP are technically classed as NMDA receptor antagonists."

"Special K."

"I found only a trace of alcohol in her blood. Do you know what other drugs she takes?"

"She doesn't take drugs. Someone had to have given it to her, without her knowledge. Will she be ok?"

"Probably. We don't know the dosage. Ketamine acts fast, but it also wears off fast, most of the time. A matter of a few hours, not days. We just wait for it to clear her system, there is no antidote for it."

I dreamed I was a little girl, running over a grassy field, my hair streaming behind me, a cool breeze on my face. From time to time I would

run into a fog bank and then I'd punch through it into the clear again. I was
running away from something, but I couldn't remember what it was.

I woke up in the wee hours of the morning, in my own bed in my own
room. I lay on my side. My stomach was growling and felt empty. I could tell
my breath stank. I looked over at Xuĕyàn, but saw Brenda asleep in her bed
instead. I just watched the small, slow rise and fall of her blanket as she
breathed, I don't know for how long.

I felt fuzzy headed and dry-mouthed and knew only that something had
happened and I couldn't remember. Just then, the alarm went off.

Brenda bolted up onto her elbows, looking over at me.

"Amy. Are you ok? How do you feel?"

It took me a while to get my mouth connected to my brain.

"I don't know," I said.

"What do you remember about last night?"

"I don't know."

"Do you remember going out with Steve?'

"Was that last night?"

"Yes. Where did you go? Do you remember?"

My face flushed hot.

"We went to his house," I admitted.

"What happened then?"

"We had dinner?" I wasn't sure at first.

"What else?"

"I don't remember."

A part of me knew that my answer should alarm me, but it was like I
didn't think there was anything odd about it.

"Did you drink anything there?"

"I think I drank some red wine?"

Brenda frowned at me.

"One glass or two? More than two maybe?"

"I don't remember. Was I drunk?"

She didn't answer me, but said, "Take a shower and get dressed first.
Then we'll talk. Don't worry about anything."

I wasn't worried, then. The worry came later.

Brenda took her shower after me and got herself dressed quick, not even
bothering about her hair.

She sat beside me on my bed and put an arm around my shoulder.

"Amy. I have some bad news, but it's not all bad. You don't remember much of last night because you were drugged."

The word "drugged" got my attention and I could actually feel my eyes pop open wide.

"It was 'Special K', Ketamine, in the wine. Cleo and I took you to a private doctor she knew. You're fine now."

For some strange reason, this didn't surprise me as it probably should have at the time.

"I got a couple of phone calls from you around ten o'clock last night, but you didn't talk, you just rang my cell. I got scared and went to Cleo. She called Azim and we went looking for you. We found you just outside the campus. We found your purse in the school parking lot, so you made it here, but then wandered off. Ketamine causes memory lapses which is why you have problems remembering last night."

"Steve."

"Yes," Brenda said, "Steve."

"Did you talk to him?"

"No."

"Steve," I repeated.

Yesterday, if Brenda had even implied Steve was less than perfect, I would have been at her throat. Now, I just didn't know what to think. I wasn't even thinking at all, my wits seemed so dull.

"Amy. Do you believe Steve could have drugged you?"

"Yes."

The answer just popped out of my mouth.

I was only a little bit surprised at my answer, but I turned the idea over and over in my mind and I guessed it made sense. I wasn't mad at him for some reason, but I could feel something climbing up from my stomach that I was able to recognize as frustration with myself. *Why hadn't I seen this coming?*

"The doctor said you would probably feel dull and detached today. Mentally slow and thick, maybe. Don't worry, it'll pass."

She gave me a little one-armed sideways hug and said, "I think you should skip classes today. Just stay here and rest. But let's get breakfast first."

We both stood up. I swayed on my feet for a second, but I steadied myself and I was ok.

"What do we tell the Jins?"

"We'll just tell them you didn't feel well and came back early. It's the truth; there's no need to elaborate."

After breakfast, I checked in with the nurse. All she did was take my temperature and blood pressure. Blood pressure was only a little high, but she excused me from classes for the day, so I went back to my room and took a nap until mid-afternoon.

When I got up, I tried to remember what had happened, but could only recall a few fragments. According to Brenda, the doctor had said that if I remembered only fragments, those fragments were likely to be all I would ever remember.

I thought if those specific memories were gone, maybe I could at least remember my feelings and what they were from before. I think I had thought I was in love with Steve. Now, that idea seemed totally alien.

Brenda came back to the room around four, after her last class.

"You're awake," she said.

I just nodded my head.

"You had a good long nap, I checked on you a couple of times between classes and you were always asleep. That's good. Do you remember anything more?"

"I don't know. I remember dishing the salad and sitting down, pretty clear. But only a few brief fragments after that. I remember this morning, here."

Brenda just waited for me to say something else. Finally I did.

"Did Steve really slip me 'Special K'? Did he really drug me?"

"We don't know for sure, but you were definitely drugged with it about the time your memories turn to shit. That puts it while you were with him in his house. Somebody, apparently him, dropped you off in the school parking lot last night and left you there. The doctor says you still have your cherry, but at some point, you were in a physical struggle."

Brenda picked up my phone. She'd plugged it into the charger earlier. Now she turned it on and checked it for calls.

"No messages," she said.

She picked up her own phone and made a call. It rang for a long time.

Then I heard Steve's voice.

"Hello?"

Brenda put her phone on 'speaker' and signed me to keep quiet.

"Steve? This is Brenda. What happened with Amy last night?"

Brenda's voice was casual and carefree as if she was only mildly curious. She sounded almost sweet.

"Uh, mmm..."

Brenda waited him out.

"Well, we had dinner and I brought her back to the school..."

"How did she seem to you last night, Steve?"

"Well, I guess she did seem a little out of it."

His voice grew bolder.

"I think she'd been drinking," he added. "In fact, I'm sure of it. I mean, I've had a beer a time or two, but your 'friend' was blind stinking drunk. That's why I took her back early. I can't deal with chicks who get all sloppy drunk and aggressive and start imagining things. Amy's got a hot temper too. I didn't expect that from her. She's a mean drunk. I'm no expert, but I think she was taking some kind of drugs too. She probably got it off the street. I don't know if she's smoking crack or what it is, but you need to keep that bitch on a shorter leash."

I could hear the phone disconnect as he hung up.

Brenda and I just stared at each other.

She let me speak first.

"I am so fucking stupid."

"You just made a mistake, Amy. It could have been worse. I'm guessing you had enough sense to know something was wrong and to fight him off when he made his move. A lot of girls would've just blacked out and woken up later with their..."

"What kind of guy even wants to have sex with an unconscious girl?" I wondered aloud.

"What should really piss you off is that he drugged you even though you were probably ready to sleep with him on your own. He just wanted a sure thing. He was too fucking stupid and too insensitive to know you were ready."

"I trusted him," I said.

"It's ok, Amy. Even smart people do stupid things."

She gave me a light punch on my upper arm as she said that.

I looked at her.

"You hit like a girl," I told her.

She grinned. "Thank you," She said, "that's such a sweet thing to say."

47. THIEF
BRENDA

Amy bounced back pretty quick. I so was surprised at *how* quick, I thought she might be faking her recovery. Her date had been on Saturday, and by Tuesday, she was back to normal, but subdued. Our last dance class was on Tuesday, but she stayed in her room. I went, of course. I wanted to see who else showed up.

Ricky and Bobby were there, but Steve was absent. We had a chance to talk while we waited for Ms. Dunham to arrive.

"So, Ricky," I asked, "where's Steve?"

"Where's Amy?" Bobby countered.

I smiled at him.

"I asked first. Where's Steve?"

"Don't know," Ricky replied. "He said something... I don't even know if he'll be at the dance."

"He 'said something'? What did he say, exactly?"

"I don't want to repeat it. It's not important."

"Where's Amy?" Bobby asked again.

"She's just not feeling well today. She'll be fine."

We all stared stupidly at each other for a few seconds before I threw Bobby a bone.

"Amy broke up with Steve," I said.

Both guys raised a single eyebrow simultaneously.

Bobby asked, "do you think this is a temporary thing, or ..."

"No. It's permanent."

"Amy can do better," Bobby said. The note of hope in his voice was undeniable.

"Steve's an asshole," Ricky added firmly.

The class was just a review of everything we'd been taught.

Ms. Dunham's last words to us were:

"You have all done very well. I expect you will be some of best dancers at the ball. Just remember what you've learned and you will surprise a lot of people. I'm sure you will make me and my teaching look very good. Don't forget to have fun, either."

Just before they left, I pulled the guys aside.

"I'll see you both at the dance. Amy will be there if I have to drag her by her yellow ponytail. I want you to save a lot of dances for us."

Both guys grinned. I put my palm flat on Ricky's chest.

"I want *most* of your dances, mister."

His grin disappeared and he placed his hand over mine and looked directly into my eyes.

"As you wish," was all he said.

48. SAFE OR SORRY
BRENDA

"Mary Putnam lost her new laptop."

When I overheard someone say this at lunch the next day, I immediately glanced over at Mary. She was looking right back at me and whispering to Abby Parris. I felt the hair on the back of my neck stand up and next to me, Amy straightened her back as if she'd been stabbed with a fork.

She caught on right away.

"We need to make sure we're clean," she said. "What if we find it?"

"We *can't* find it," I insisted. "We *absolutely* can't."

She nodded.

We finished lunch quickly, but I stayed at the table to keep an eye on Putnam while Amy headed upstairs to make sure.

She came back just before the bell. She didn't approach me, but gave me the hand signal that we were ok.

We had History class together later and I asked her directly, just to make sure.

"You searched both our rooms?"

"Don't worry, Brenda. We're clean."

"This could be an excuse to do a shake-down. If they found something smaller, like another joint..."

"I thought of that. I did a very thorough sweep. I didn't find anything compromising at all."

"Maybe we're just paranoid."

"Yeah, it could be she really did just lose it. She might have misplaced it and will remember where tomorrow. Or somebody else actually stole it."

"You're probably right. It's not always about us, Amy."

"Still," she said, "better safe than sorry."

49. EASTER BALL
BRENDA

It turned out that the junior class had responsibility for decorating the gym for the dance, so the only thing the rest of us had to do was just show up. They did an ok job on the spring theme, only a few Easter eggs and bunnies, but flowers everywhere. Amy looked great in her cream sleeveless dress, but my white gown drew the most compliments that night.

I know, because I was petty enough to keep count.

Ricky had told me that Steve would not be showing up at the dance, but I was still a little concerned, and I know Amy was too.

When Ricky and Bobby showed up together, I grabbed Amy.

But Amy pulled away from me. "No," she said. "I don't know if they want to talk to me."

I wagged my finger in her face.

"We've already discussed this," I reminded her, "you agreed to make an effort tonight. To give other guys a chance."

"I know," she said. "Just give me a little time. Please."

Shaking my head, I indulged her with a tiny smile and headed toward the guys. They met me half-way.

"Wow. You guys look great in suits. You both do."

"Hey! You're not supposed to tell us that," Ricky scolded, "We are supposed to be the first to tell *you* how great *you* look."

"You do look great, Brenda," Bobby said. He looked around until his eyes found Amy. "Amy looks good, too."

"Why not go tell her, Roberto?"

He gave me a shy smile and left to do just that. I turned back to Ricky just in time for him to hug me and give me a kiss on the cheek. That brought a smile to my own face.

But I noticed something odd about his glasses.

"Ricky, did you break your glasses?"

The poor guy actually blushed.

"Yeah," he said, "I haven't had a chance to fix them yet. I'm sorry. I need to get new frames, I think. I'm using a little piece of wire to hold the end-piece on. The hinge is broke."

"How'd that happen?"

"It was just a dumb accident. I dropped them on the floor and stepped on them."

I had been biting my tongue for months, but I recognized an opportunity when I saw one.

"Those glasses aren't right for you anyway," I told him. "This is your chance to get frames that suit you better."

"Yeah," he said. "I know. My sister says they make me look stupid. Even more stupid than I am, she says. I just got them because they felt like they had a good fit. I didn't care what they looked like at the time."

Good answer, I thought. He's smart enough to know they don't improve his appearance, but not vain enough to make a big deal of it. I actually felt bad then. I was the one who was caring more about his appearance than his substance. But as long as I kept my mouth shut, he wouldn't know how shallow I was.

"That's a very nice dress, Brenda. You look like an angel."

My laugh surprised me. It's remarkable how a few simple words can warm the heart.

I was about to drag us over to Amy and Bobby, but the music started up for the first dance, and Ricky took my hand. We fell right into the dance frame and stepped out onto the floor together, sliding into our steps without a second thought. Another couple followed our example, then a few more. He gave all the right signals so it was easy to follow his lead. I thought how nice it was to dance with someone I'd practiced with. One step followed another naturally and I understood what Ms. Dunham had meant when she said that "the dance is a poem of which each movement is a word." A part of me wanted to look around for her to see if our teacher was watching, but I remembered that my proper focus was on my partner and I kept it there.

There was only the slightest pause before the next song started. The first tune had been a waltz, the second was a foxtrot with a slightly faster tempo. Ricky led us into longer strides as we wheeled around the floor. We'd learned our lessons well, but not everyone on the floor had. I kept waiting for someone to bump into us, and after a while someone did. It was Amy and Bobby. We recovered immediately and the guys kept us in sync dancing next to each other. Amy was actually smiling.

"Just like a dumb blonde," I said, "they never pay attention to where they're going."

"If your black butt wasn't so big," she replied, "there wouldn't have been a problem."

Of course, the only comments I ever got about my booty was that I had "no ass at all," or that I was too skinny. But a joke never needs to be backed up by facts. And I can always give back as good as I get.

"The real problem is that white chicks got no rhythm. They can take all the lessons they want, but white girls still can't dance."

"Ah," Bobby interjected, "but her partner is Latino. We *invented* all the good dances. She'll be fine with me."

We all laughed and kept dancing.

After a couple more songs, there was a break, so we all went over to the table to get some punch. I could tell Amy was hesitant, so I tasted it first and nodded to her that it was still fine. The seniors hadn't spiked it yet.

"Bobby was telling me his family has horses on their farm," Amy said.

"They are working horses," Bobby added, "not fancy horses for show or racing."

"I've never ridden a horse," Amy said.

"That's not true," I reminded her. "We went on the pony ride a bunch of times at the state fair in Sedalia."

"That doesn't count. We were too little, and they just led us around in a circle. Bobby told me he rode his horse to school every day back home."

I looked at him. I could picture a tiny tyke-sized version of Roberto perched on his steed, reins in one hand, books in the other, trotting down the streets of some country village.

"Our farm is up in the hills," he said, "and there was no school bus, so I always rode my horse. I wasn't the only one. Several other students rode their horses to school. If you ever visit Antigua, you can learn to ride at our farm. My parents would be happy to have you as our guests. It is an old house with plenty of extra rooms."

I'd just noticed that Bobby had what was almost certainly a black eye. A quick, more critical look back at Ricky revealed what was probably a bruise on his jaw. His story about stepping on his glasses suddenly lost some credibility.

I may not be the math whiz that Amy is, but I can still put two and two together. I doubted Bobby and Ricky had been fighting each other. The only way they'd be covering up a fight is if it had been with someone I knew.

Someone who was not here at the dance tonight.

The next question is how they would have found out about what happened with Steve and Amy. The Jins certainly suspected something, but only four people actually knew: Amy, myself, Cleo, and Steve. Amy, Cleo, and I weren't talking about it, so that left only Steve. I wondered what story he'd told. Whatever it was, I doubt it had been believed.

Ricky had said Steve wasn't feeling well. I hoped that was true. I felt confident I'd been dancing with one of the causes of his unfortunate illness, and that Amy had been dancing with another.

Guys like to argue with their fists sometimes. I knew I shouldn't approve of that macho bullshit, but it was hard to be angry with Ricky or Bobby.

Later, maybe, Amy or I would take care of Steve ourselves. There was no hurry.

We sat out only a couple of dances, but then got back onto the floor and spent most of our time there. We switched partners a few times, but mostly stuck with our own guys.

Karen and Xuěyàn didn't have regular boyfriends at the dance. Karen had hinted that she had a boyfriend back home, and I know she talked to some guy on the phone sometimes, but Xuěyàn refused to say one way or the other. At the dance, they just made themselves available and danced with everybody. They had told me they could dance, but I was surprised that they could dance so well. They each danced a couple of times with Ricky and Bobby, and they not only impressed both guys, but looked good doing it.

There was a piercing scream. I felt cold run deep in my bones. My immediate thought was that it was going to be another Amy thing, especially when I saw Bobby break away from her and run to the scene of the commotion. Sue Spence was lying on the floor, crying. I eased over to see one of her shoes lying beside her, the heel broken off. Bobby was holding her ankle. He was telling Sue's date to call security.

So, it was just a broken heel. They weren't even very high heels; Sue had been showing off her brand new shoes earlier, which meant she had never danced in them before.

Just as a soldier should never take an unfamiliar weapon into combat, a woman should never take new shoes to a dance. This was my first real dance, but even I knew that much.

Amy was standing alone, looking lost, so I let go of Ricky and went over to her.

"I heard the scream and he ran," she said.

I looked over at Bobby again. He was gently flexing Sue's foot.

"I'm no doctor," he said smiling at her, "but it doesn't feel broken. I think it's just a simple sprain. Wait for security and they'll take care of you, but I think you'll be fine."

Bobby was examining her ankle as if she were a horse who'd thrown a shoe. Probably not a thought I should share with poor Sue.

Sue calmed down quick and her breathing slowed to almost normal, her wailing turned into soft whimpers.

Bobby had moved fast. The Chaperones had been more bewildered than helpful at first, but Amy's guy had not hesitated.

As soon as security showed up with their EMT bag, Bobby let go of Sue and came back to Amy.

"I'm sorry if it seemed like I just dumped you, Amy, but I heard her scream and I had to see if I could help."

Amy was still looking confused, so I spoke up, "Don't apologize, Bobby. That was quick thinking. You did the right thing, we all appreciate that."

Amy nodded her head, once slowly, then twice more with real conviction.

Sue got hauled off in a stretcher, to her immense embarrassment, but the rest of us gave her a round of applause like she was a football player being carried off the field due to an injury, and that seemed to cheer her up, especially as her date stayed by her side. Bobby remembered to collect the broken shoe and its heel, which he entrusted to her date.

After a brief intermission, the music started up again and we danced away the evening until they flicked the lights, signaling the end of the night.

What I remember most about the dance was the pure exhilaration of dancing. Whirling, twirling, gliding; the simple joy of movement, the arms of a strong, decent guy, the bright smile on Amy's face, and my foolish dream that the carefree night could last forever.

We didn't anticipate the challenge ahead, and so we were able to enjoy the evening.

Dreams are merely dreams and morning always follows, bringing the hard light of reality.

Putnam and her posse hadn't made an appearance at the party. We were both glad of that, but our relief should have been a reason to be wary rather than a reason to be cheerful.

The four of us made a date for the next Saturday. Neither of our guys had a driver's license yet, but Ricky said he'd get his sister to drive us to Arundel Mills mall, drop us off and then come back for us later. Teresa was a grad student at nearby UMBC and would be working on her thesis all weekend, so it wasn't too big of an imposition on her. I got the clear impression that she liked doing an occasional favor for her baby brother.

We could drag the guys around while we window-shopped, the mall had a 24-screen movie theatre, there were plenty of places to eat, and what Ricky claimed was a very big arcade. It would all be innocent fun, which I figured Amy needed, and plenty of time for me and Ricky to just spend more time together in a relaxed, low-pressure environment.

We all walked out to the parking lot to say our goodbyes. Ricky and Bobby had car-pooled with somebody from their school. Their ride came looking for them, some guy I'd never met. Ricky hugged me tight and gave me one last lingering kiss before breaking away. Both our guys gave us a last look as they climbed into the car. After the car drove off, both craned their necks to watch us get smaller and smaller.

Amy and I were standing under the parking lot lamps and these were starting to draw a lot of bugs that fluttered around our heads. I batted a few away and said, "Let's go home, Amy."

She followed me silently at first, but then said, "Shouldn't they have escorted us to our door?"

"Amy! You know boys aren't allowed past the garden gate. Certainly not at night."

As we were climbing the stairs to our rooms, Amy had another question for me.

"Brenda," she asked, "back on Valentine's day, when Bobby gave you that candy heart, you kissed him..."

"I hope you're not jealous of that, it was just on the cheek."

"No, that's not it," she said. "You whispered something to him. He won't tell me what it was. Was it about me?"

"Not everything is about you, Amy."

She nodded slowly. "I know."

I wasn't going to tell her, but she looked sad, so...

"It wasn't about you, Amy. It was about him. I told him his mother would be proud to know that her son was so thoughtful and knew how act like a gentleman towards the ladies."

There was a smile struggling to surface on Amy's face.

I asked, "Were you pissed off when he abandoned you to go check on Sue? You know it was the right thing. Everyone else was just standing around with their thumb up their..."

"He's a good guy," Amy said.

"A decent and honorable guy," I replied.

Amy's smile came out.

VESPERS

Softly falls the light of day,
While our campfires fade away.
Silently each Scout should ask:
Have I done my daily task?
Have I kept my honor bright?
Can I guiltless sleep tonight?
Have I done and have I dared,
Everything to be prepared?

- Scout Vespers (Girl Scout Songbook)

51. SACRIFICE
AMY

I'd been thinking about our upcoming double date with the guys on Saturday, and having a hard time focusing on my history paper. I went to the library before my first class to ask Cleo to help me with some research, but she wasn't there, so I found a study carrel in the corner and settled in.

Did I really want to go on a date with some boy after that disaster with Steve? Swearing off boys forever was tempting, but not realistic or practical. They weren't all like Steve, and Brenda was right, Roberto was a real guy. A true gentleman. On the other hand, that's what I thought about Steve at first too. This double-date thing wasn't going to be a romantic date, though. We were just going to the mall, really not anything more than that. Brenda would be there and we could watch each other's backs. I was mostly going just because Brenda wanted me to.

No matter what trick I tried, I just couldn't concentrate. After about ten minutes, I put the paper aside, and pulled out my notebook. Working math problems always relaxed me.

I know that sounds crazy to most people, but everybody is different. Some people use exercise to relax. Some just vegetate in front of the tube or listen to music, or read a book to relax, or do crosswords, or whatever. Ms. Dunham had said that dancing was the thing that relaxed her, and I know my mom used to do yoga. Of course, some high-energy people, like Xuěyàn, never relaxed or seemed to need to. But for me, solving math problems always helped. My mind would clear of everything but the simple logic of the equations, numbers and patterns, and their elegant beauty always calmed me. I would often take a math break when studying, and when I returned to my other studies, everything would be much clearer.

I was doing that, and at first, it seemed to work, but then I couldn't concentrate on that either. Even holding the pen was difficult. I looked at my hand and wondered why I had a pen in it. It didn't even look like my own hand. Shouldn't I be holding it in my left? Or, maybe it was my hand, but it didn't seem connected to me. It was like my arm had fallen asleep, but without the tingling you usually get.

The full transition began with a creeping sense of unease, but it was the voice that took me by surprise.

"I need you to come with me right now."

I looked around, but didn't see anybody. The voice was clear as crystal and sounded very close.

I had an ear infection a couple of years before, and it lasted about a week and I was temporarily deaf in one ear. When that happened, whenever anybody said anything, I always had to look around to see who it was, I wasn't able to tell where the voice was coming from. It was like being in a thick fog. We forget how much we depend on both ears.

This was something like that. The voice was clear, but lacked direction. It sounded familiar, but I couldn't identify it. The next voice was just as clear, just as close, and just as non-directional. But this voice I recognized as Brenda's.

"Can I drop my stuff off in my room first?"

"No, you can't go to your room. Come along right now."

My whole body seemed disassociated from me. The notebook in front of me, and even the desk seemed fuzzy and transparent, and I saw the long hallway of the main building stretched out in front of me. I was walking down that hallway, but I was also sitting in the library, as if I were two people in two different places at the same time.

The feeling of dread became almost a physical thing that I could feel surrounding me, like walking down a passage choked with molasses. It had a sharp, metallic-pepper-like smell to it.

Brenda asked, "Is this about Amy? Is she ok?"

"We're going to talk about you, first. You're going to answer a few questions."

I bent my neck around the study carrel and even lifted myself up a bit to look around, but I couldn't see Brenda or anyone else. The library seemed distorted, as if it had been stretched out into a hallway. The long row of bookshelves on one side had magically disappeared.

I must be trippin' for real, I thought.

The other voice was Dr. Kramer's.

She led Brenda down the hall, past her own office and directly into Dr. Davis' office. There were a couple of girls in the anteroom, but they quickly looked away. Our English teacher was there too, but she also refused to meet Brenda's eyes.

Inside the office, Brenda was directed to sit down in a chair in the center of the room, in front of the desk. Dr. Kramer went to sit at Dr. Davis' side. Mrs. Thompson, the head of security was also there. No one was smiling.

Kramer said, "Start the recording."

Dr. Davis asked, "Do you object to us recording this session, Miss Dickens?"

Her tone was polite, but she still wasn't smiling.

Brenda flushed. It felt like she'd swallowed something hot that burned all the way from her lips to the bottom of her stomach. She didn't answer, but she shook her head.

"Speak up for the recording, please," Thompson told her.

The fire in Brenda's belly sank deeper in her gut.

"No. No objection," she managed to say.

Kramer pointed to a laptop on the desk.

"Do you know what this is?" She asked.

Brenda hesitated before replying. "It looks like a laptop."

"Who does it belong to?"

"I don't know," Brenda replied.

Even through the molasses, or the fog, or whatever it was, I knew.

It could only belong to one person.

"Are you sure you don't know?" Mrs. Thompson asked, "Doesn't it look familiar?"

"No. It's not mine."

Dr. Kramer gave a little snort. "Now we're getting somewhere."

Dr. Davis made a gesture to silence her.

"Miss Dickens," she said, "We found this in your room. Can you explain how it might have gotten there?"

Brenda's heart thumped once, hard. Her mouth was dry and she shook her head.

"I can't help you unless I know the truth, Brenda."

Brenda took a couple of fast, shallow breaths, then a deep one. She held it, then slowly let it out.

She asked, "Where did you find it?"

Dr. Kramer asked, "Where do you think?"

Mrs. Thompson said, "It was found in the bottom of a suitcase in the back of your closet."

Dr. Davis just stared at Brenda.

"I didn't put it there. I haven't seen that laptop since the first day when Mary was showing it off."

Dr. Kramer pounced. "So, you *do* recognize it. You just said you didn't know whose it was, but now you admit knowing it belongs to Miss Putnam. Did she give it to you?"

You're trying to trick me, Brenda thought. But she asked, "Are you sure it belongs to Mary?"

"We've checked the serial number," Dr. Davis said. "This is definitely Miss Putnam's missing laptop."

"I didn't take it."

"So, you are saying someone else planted it in your suitcase? Who would that be? Your roommate Miss Jin?"

"I don't know how it got in my bag, if that's where you found it."

"Is it possible you picked this up, perhaps accidentally, and took it to your room?"

Another trick question, Brenda thought. *Whether I say yes or no, I lose. Either way I'm screwed.*

She slumped in her chair. She was very tired.

But a moment later she straightened up. "What do you want me to say?"

"Miss Dickens," Dr. Davis asked, "did you take this laptop into your room at any time or for any reason? Please be careful and answer truthfully."

"No. I did not. I have never even touched this laptop."

"We have a witness," Mrs. Thompson said.

Shit. They've stacked the deck.

"You were seen, Miss Dickens," said Dr. Kramer. "Someone saw you take this laptop into your room two nights ago."

"Who?"

"Does it matter? You were seen."

Shit.

"So," said Kramer, "First, we have a stolen laptop, found hidden in your suitcase, in your room. Second, you have no innocent explanation for how that could have happened. Third, we have a witness who saw you take the laptop into your room. And fourth, you don't have an explanation for that either. You could have said you took it in for safekeeping, but by denying you took it, that means you haven't told the truth. There is only one logical conclusion we can reach. I'm sure you know what that is."

It's all over for me now, Brenda thought. *At least, maybe I can keep Amy out of this.*

Brenda was wrong to think that. Without her to watch my back, I wouldn't last long either. It was Putnam, of course, but I'd never be able to prove that, and without Brenda it would be that much easier to eliminate me.

I opened the door to Dr. Davis' office and walked in.

I don't even remember leaving the library, or walking down the hall to her office, but there I was.

Moreover, I was myself again, in my own body, seeing with my own eyes and hearing with my own ears.

Brenda was first to react.

"Amy, get out."

She said it softly, more like a prayer than a command. She sounded weary.

Kramer spoke next.

"We'll get to you next, Miss McDonald. Wait outside. You don't go barging into ..."

She made no attempt to keep the anger out of her voice.

"This is a private meeting, Amy," Dr. Davis told me. "You should not be here."

She seemed more sad than angry.

"Brenda didn't take the laptop," I said. "She doesn't steal."

Dr. Kramer's face flushed bright red.

For a moment, no one said anything.

Thompson asked me, "Who said anything about a stolen laptop?"

"It's obvious," I said. "Mary Putnam claimed her laptop was stolen. She spread rumors that we had taken it. I see her laptop on your desk and you've brought Brenda in here for an interrogation. What other conclusion could I come to?"

"Check your attitude, Miss McDonald," Dr. Kramer said.

"You're accusing an innocent person of a crime. I don't think I'm out of line."

"What makes you so sure she is innocent?"

There was an empty chair against the wall. I pulled it out next to Brenda and sat down.

"Brenda didn't steal the laptop," I said, "I did."

Like triplets joined together, our accusers sucked in their breath simultaneously.

Dr. Davis was the first to recover.

"You can't be serious," She said.

Brenda was next to speak. "This won't work, Amy. They've already decided I'm guilty. Don't get yourself involved. It won't help."

"I took the laptop," I announced again, "not Brenda. She's just trying to cover for me."

"We have evidence, Amy," Dr. Davis said. "And it implicates Miss Dickens, not you."

"I can prove it was me," I informed everyone. "You found the laptop in my burgundy suitcase, in Brenda's closet."

Kramer exclaimed, "*Your* suitcase?"

"Check the luggage tag. It has my name on it, not Brenda's. Her big suitcase is in my closet, but my small bag has been stored in hers since we got back from Christmas break."

"Amy." Brenda was holding my hand and squeezing it hard. "Please don't."

She still thought she could protect me. Still thought she could keep me out of it. I turned back to Dr. Davis.

"Eye-witnesses are always unreliable," I reminded her. "Yours is no different. The only way I could have known where you found the laptop is if I had put it there. You had to *tell* Brenda where you found it. You didn't have to tell me. I already knew. I'm the thief, not her."

Dr. Davis was just sitting there looking at us.

"Turn off the recording," she said.

"Mrs. Thompson, Dr. Kramer, leave me to talk to these girls in private, please."

Kramer started to argue, but a glare from Dr. Davis stopped her.

Mrs. Thompson and Dr. Kramer left the room. Kramer gave us a very dirty look as she passed.

When they were gone, Dr. Davis looked at us.

"I'm very disappointed in you," she said, "and, I admit, more than a little puzzled."

"I hope you understand," she continued, "that two confessions won't absolve you. It's not like we'll dismiss the charge because we don't know if just one of you is lying. We have a witness. We have the physical evidence. Found in your possession."

She pointed to the laptop.

"Maybe you think there is something noble about trying to protect a friend. But this is a deadly serious matter. It makes no sense to throw away your future to protect a so-called 'friend' whose actions have put you in this perilous position. Your whole lives are on the line, their promise about to be effectively ended. A true friend wouldn't do this to you or ask this of you."

"I don't have a lot of choice in this. On the one hand, you've both confessed. If you're somehow innocent, but lying to protect each other, lying is itself an honor code violation that merits expulsion. Especially lying in an official investigation. On the other hand if one of you is actually guilty and the other is lying to protect the guilty, then you both deserve expulsion, and obviously, if you're both in this together..."

Her eyes kept going slowly back and forth between Brenda and I.

"I beg you one last time. If the guilty party comes forward, I may be able to help the other. I can at least let the innocent party finish the term and transfer away quietly. Otherwise... Well, theft is a criminal matter. The police will have to become involved. I'll have to hand the whole thing over to them. I don't want to do that, that's the whole reason why I called Miss Dickens down here first. But if we can't resolve this privately, unofficially, then I will have no choice."

Brenda and I were still holding hands.

"I'm sorry, Dr. Davis," Brenda said, "but we can see that you've already made your decision. And apparently, so have we."

Dr. Davis was very quiet. She glanced out the window at a bright red cardinal singing in the dogwood tree outside and listened to that for a moment before turning back to us.

"I have to call the police, then." Her voice was very soft and low.

Brenda and I didn't even glance at each other. There was no need to. We were on the same wavelength now.

Dr. Davis hit her intercom. "Rosemarie," she said, "Please ask Mrs. Thompson and Dr. Kramer to come back in."

They must have been standing by the door because it opened immediately and they rushed in.

"Mrs. Thompson," Dr. Davis said, "Take these girls to conference room 'C' to wait."

To us, she added, "I'll call your guardian first."

The little conference room was just big enough for four chairs and a small table. The room was otherwise bare except for a framed painting of the campus. It was a beautiful painting, showing the campus in Fall, with all the trees in their Autumn colors.

Brenda frowned at me. She didn't say anything, but she was reproaching me for interfering. *There was no need for both of us to burn,* she was thinking. *No need at all.*

"We just have to start over," I said. "We knew there'd be setbacks. This is a big one, but..."

There was no need to say anything else.

I hate that Putnam is going to get away with this, we both thought together. *And by now, the whole school knows the story.*

52. CHANGES
AMY

We sat in that little room for hours, it seemed.

We didn't talk much.

And we didn't cry, although we took turns perched on the edge of tears.

I would feel my chest tighten and my breath come short, and be just about to burst out sobbing, and then I'd look at Brenda and catch myself. I could tell Brenda was going through the same routine. She'd start to cry, but I'd reach out and put my hand on her shoulder and she'd pull back from the edge herself. We must have gone through this a half-dozen times.

Finally, Mrs. Thompson returned and escorted us back. There were a number of girls in the hallway and we had to do the perp walk from the conference room to the office. Dozens of eyes, all accusing and hateful; and angry that we weren't showing enough shame to suit them.

I saw Abby Parris standing outside Kramer's office. She was the only one smiling.

The usual suspects were there in Dr. Davis's office; Davis herself, Dr. Kramer, Mrs. Thompson and Brenda and me. I had expected to see the cops, but they hadn't shown up yet.

"I haven't been able to reach your guardian, yet," Dr. Davis stated. "She is in surgery at present. I've left an urgent message, but haven't heard back. She is listed as the primary emergency contact for both of you, but if I don't hear back soon, I'll call your parents directly."

She shook her head.

"Do you know how they'll take this news? You've hurt them the most, I suspect."

"What a mess this is."

The door flew open and Cleo stepped in.

Dr. Davis nearly shouted: "Doesn't anyone in this school understand what a closed door means?"

Mrs. Thompson stood up and Kramer said, "Miss Smith, whatever it is you want, this is not the time!"

"I apologize," Cleo said, "but I'm here to prevent a gross miscarriage of justice. There has been a mistake."

"You have no place here!" Dr. Kramer was shouting. "Are you here to confess too?"

Cleo stayed calm. She had business cards and handed one to me, one to Brenda, and one to Dr. Davis.

"My Attorneys." she said. "Their law firm has significant resources, and they have agreed to represent the girls, pro-bono, as a favor to me, if it becomes necessary."

While we tried to swallow this information, Cleo added, "But I don't think it *will* become necessary."

"These girls have already confessed!"

"There is physical evidence and a witness, Miss Smith," Dr. Davis added. "A lawyer is a good idea if the police decide to prosecute, but I'm afraid expulsion is a foregone conclusion."

"And if new evidence proves that your existing evidence has been falsified, and that your witness is lying?"

"Do you think you have such evidence?"

"No, I do not."

"Then..."

"But," Cleo added, "You do."

"The security tapes, or, security hard drives, I suppose. I imagine it's all digital. Your evidence is there."

"I am also a witness. But I didn't see everything. I don't ask you to take my word. I only saw and know enough to point you to the exact time and place on your security camera footage where you should look. I can also tell you what to look for and what I think you will find."

"It was the night of the dance," Cleo said. "I didn't attend the dance, I stayed behind. Mary Putnam didn't attend either; she also stayed behind. Around eight o'clock, I saw someone who looked like Mary Putnam carrying what looked like a laptop upstairs toward Brenda and Amy's rooms. This is *after* she reported hers missing. Check the footage. If you don't, then you risk making a huge and regrettable mistake."

"I know I'm only a sixteen year old girl," Cleo said, "but my parents ran a security company, and before they were killed, I learned a few things. I suggest that after you view it yourselves, you show this footage to your witness first. Inform her that you know Amy and Brenda are innocent and remind her that perjury is a criminal matter. After your witness recants, then confront Mary."

Dr. Kramer looked embarrassed but she didn't say anything.

"We know how to conduct an investigation," Mrs. Thompson said.

Tactfully, Cleo, Brenda and I said nothing in response to that.

"Sunday night," Cleo said, "Eight o'clock or a few minutes before."

"These girls have already confessed," Kramer said.

Dr. Davis waved her silent.

"Mrs. Thompson," she asked, "Please go check the footage. We'll wait here."

Thompson left quickly. Kramer started to follow, but sat back down instead.

"What do you expect us to see on those tapes, Miss Smith?" She asked.

"As I said, if you actually have coverage of the timeframe, you will see Mary Putnam outside Brenda's room with a laptop. Maybe, if it is as I suspect, you might see more. Also, the rumor is that Abby Parris is your witness. I don't think you will see her on the tapes at all, making her testimony suspect."

"We don't really know when the laptop was put in Miss Dickens' room," Kramer said. "Only the guilty party knows for sure. If the footage is missing or unclear, it could have been put there any time in the last week. Your own testimony may be suspect, Miss Smith."

"I said I *think* it was Mary I saw, I'm not saying it was definitely her, though I feel pretty confident it was. I will swear that the person I did see was neither Amy nor Brenda. I'm hoping the tapes will clarify things."

We all sat there in the room together in silence for nearly half an hour.

Then the desk phone rang.

Dr. Davis answered.

"What? Are you sure?" She continued to listen for a while, then said, "Can you stream it up here to me?"

She put the phone down, looking more confused than anything.

A few minutes later, Thompson came back, did something to Dr. Davis's computer and they watched the footage. Brenda and I stayed put, but Cleo stepped over behind the desk so she could watch.

All Brenda and I could see were the expressions on their faces. First, intense concentration and puzzlement, then mild surprise, and then shock as the color drained from all their faces. A couple of minutes later, the expressions on Mrs. Thompson and Dr. Davis appeared totally empty. Dr. Kramer's face showed only anger. But Cleo was grinning.

After a long pause, Dr. Davis spoke to Dr. Kramer.

"Henrietta, show this footage to Miss Parris and ask her if she can explain herself. Mrs. Thompson, please go with her. Then, invite Miss Putnam to talk to us in your office. Don't let the two of them see each other. You know what to do. Call me when you're ready."

Kramer and Thompson left.

She turned the screen around so Brenda and I could see it and clicked on the replay button.

It was a dark image of the stairs leading up to our floor. There was a date-time stamp in the lower right hand corner. The first person visible was Cleo, heading down the main stairs. Every ten seconds, the viewpoint would shift, from the stairwell, to the north end of the hall way, to the south end, where our rooms were. The viewpoints made a complete cycle every 10 seconds.

A couple of other girls, dressed for the dance, came out of one room and hustled down the stairs. Then, another girl, head down, snuck up the stairs. She paused at the top and glanced around. She headed straight down the hallway, slowly at first, then quickly. We couldn't quite see who it was or what she was holding, it might have been a book. When she reached the end of the hall, she knocked very softly on Brenda's door. A moment later she opened the door, and she turned. The laptop she'd been carrying revealed itself as the sweater wrapped around it slipped. The camera got a perfectly clear shot of the laptop, and of her face. Mary Putnam went into Brenda's room and shut the door. Less than a minute later, the door opened and she came out, wearing the sweater, but empty-handed. She took the emergency stairs at the end of the hall and disappeared.

Dr. Davis spoke to Cleo.

"Thank you, Miss Smith. I'm sure you know not to talk about any of this for now. Please, leave me alone again with these two ladies," she asked.

Cleo did not hesitate, but left, still smiling.

When Brenda and I were alone with her, she looked us in the eye, me first, then Brenda.

"I'm sorry," she said.

"What I don't understand, Amy, is how you knew where the laptop had been found."

"I guessed," I lied. "There really is no other place to hide anything in our rooms. The luggage in the closet is where I've hidden birthday and Christmas presents for the Jins. If you found anything the size of a laptop, it had to have been 'hidden' there."

Dr. Davis nodded.

"Obviously, this exonerates you both. I don't know how I'll ever be able to apologize enough."

"Dr. Davis," Brenda said, "Don't. It is as you said, you had a witness and you had evidence, and no reason to doubt either."

Davis frowned and shook her head.

"When I pushed to admit you to the Academy, the main reason was not your academic potential, though I thought highly of that. The main reason I pushed was that I thought I saw an unusual strength of character in both of you. If I had better faith in my ability to judge people; their honesty and their honor, that would have been sufficient reason to doubt the evidence."

"Ma'am," it was my turn to talk. "We're not angry with you. We hope you're not angry with us. We worked hard to get here. We did it together. Our successes have come mostly because we have worked together. Our failures have come when we we've not been a team."

"I don't think you two understood what was about to happen to you."

"Sure we did," I told her. "A one to three month juvie conviction, then repeat the tenth grade at Riverplace High back in St. Louis. We know what Riverplace is like. We've been there. Even if we managed to survive that again, we'd still be at least one, and maybe two years behind in high school. The pressures to drop out of school without graduating would have been... significant."

"You were willing to go to jail to try to protect your friend. Did you believe she was guilty?"

"Not for an instant," I said. "And before you ask, I know, I *know*, she never thought I was either. The only possibility was that it had been planted. No way for us to prove that though. It's just dumb luck that Cleo happened to see Mary."

The phone rang again and Dr. Davis answered it.

"Ok," she said. "I'll be right down."

After hanging up, she turned back to us.

"Don't leave this office yet, please. I've got sodas, juice and bottled water in the mini-fridge; please help yourselves. If you need to use the bathroom, use my private bath." She pointed to the door in the corner. "I don't want anyone to see you until we've wrapped this up. Relax. I'll try not to be too long."

I looked at the clock when she left. Brenda had been pulled in more than six hours ago. Brenda's eyes found the clock too. She was thinking the same thing as me.

"Time flies when you're having fun," she said.

53. LAST WEEKEND
BRENDA

We went to my room to see if they'd done any damage in the search.

The hallways were empty and I relaxed a bit. Every evening, everyone would gather in the cafeteria a little early to chat and relax. I had no doubt what they were gossiping about just then.

I was hungry, but had no desire to face anyone just yet.

Karen was in my room, with Xuěyàn. When I walked in, they both looked at me like they'd seen a ghost.

The Jins needed and deserved an explanation, but I was incredibly tired and only thought about taking a nap.

"Everything's ok," Amy said. She was right behind me, holding up her palms as if to calm a storm.

"Brenda was falsely accused of something, but she, *we* have been cleared. Nothing is going to happen to us, either of us. Everything is ok now."

The Jins looked uncertain and unconvinced but said nothing.

I sat down on the edge of my bed. The pillow looked soft and cool.

Amy sat next to me.

Karen cleared her throat. "Dr. Kramer and Mrs. Thompson searched the room. They took a laptop from the suitcase in the closet. They searched all my stuff too."

"Sorry," Amy said. "The laptop was Mary Putnam's. The security tapes showed her planting it in the room. She is being escorted off the campus."

I could see the tension drain from both of the Jins. They suddenly looked very tired too.

Then, Xuěyàn stood up, her whole little body shaking.

"She is a bitch-slut!" I'd never heard anything even remotely like that from Xuěyàn's mouth. She switched to Mandarin, speaking very fast and I couldn't follow even half of it.

"*Liar, thief-whore* ... something, something ... *enemy* ... something, something ... *I slap her lie-face!*"

She caught herself and stopped, but kept frowning.

Then, she came over to me, squeezed between me and Amy on the bed and put her arms around me and cried.

Amy let this go on for a while, but then said, "We should go to dinner."

"I'm definitely not hungry," I said.

Xuěyàn had stopped crying and stood up again. Amy stood up with her, and so did Karen. They were all looking down at me.

"Don't be afraid," Karen said.

"Karen's right," Amy added. "This is when we show everyone that we can't be bullied. It's time to be brave."

"I'm not that brave," I said.

"Yes," Amy told me, "you are."

We entered the dining hall together and all conversation died as if it had been switched off like a light. We sat at our usual table.

Our timing was nearly perfect. Drs. Davis and Kramer had arrived just before us and were standing at the podium side-by-side.

"I have a few announcements," Dr. Davis said.

"There have been rumors, and I am here to tell you what is true and what is false."

"Certain accusations were made against two of our students. However, during our investigation, conclusive *proof* came to light that disproves all allegations made against Miss Dickens and Miss McDonald and completely exonerates them both. Some earlier evidence had suggested otherwise, but new evidence has proven that the original evidence was *falsified*."

She paused to let the word *'falsified'* sink in before continuing.

"Also, Miss Mary Putnam and Miss Abigail Parris are leaving our school. This very hour. They will not be returning."

The silence in the room got deeper.

"I know there will be other rumors. For a variety of reasons, some legal, I cannot comment publicly on them. But I will say this: We have an honor code which we all agreed to live by. We take that code seriously. If anyone cannot abide by it, they will be encouraged *or compelled* to seek their success elsewhere."

"I also know it will take a while for you all to assimilate the shock of this news. Take your time. But let me reiterate: You should not attach any suspicion whatsoever to Miss Dickens or Miss McDonald. They have been *proven* blameless."

Dr. Davis looked over the whole room, seeming to meet the eyes of every individual girl. She focused on me last of all.

"Finally," she said, "I have changed the dessert menu for tonight. In addition to the apple pie a la mode, I made arrangements with the kitchen and we will also serve fresh-baked oatmeal raisin cookies."

Amy was smirking at that last announcement.

Dinner was fairly quiet, a lot of whispering, but a couple of girls came by afterward and patted me on the shoulder or just mouthed some friendly banalities. Others smiled and nodded at me. Most just ignored me, still not sure how they should act.

I was *really* exhausted when we got back upstairs.

"You've got that date tomorrow," Karen reminded us. "That should cheer you up."

Damn.

"I don't know...," I said.

I could see Amy thinking.

"Karen's right," she said, "We have to go. The guys expect us. Besides, going through with the date will probably be easier than trying to explain why we want to break it.

"Ok," I sighed. "We'll see how I feel in the morning."

I was in my pajamas when the door opened and Aunt Diane barged in, trembling with rage.

"Is there something wrong with your phone, Brenda Angela Dickens? Or have you forgotten how to use it?"

Amy and I had turned our phones off before dinner. We just wanted to be left alone.

"Answer me, young lady!"

"Uh, I ..."

"I had to hear about these accusations from your provost. After the fact! Don't you think you should have called me right away? Your mom is going crazy right now. Not to mention Amy's parents. What the hell is wrong with you, girl?"

"Uh, I ..."

I had never heard Aunt Diane raise her voice before. She'd never been angry at me before.

She turned to Karen and pointed at her.

"You! Jin! Karen!

Di bit her lip and softened her tone; she knew she had no reason to be mad at poor Karen.

"Karen. Will you please get Amy and bring her here? I'd like to talk to my charges alone, if you don't mind. Please."

Di paced back and forth in the small room and when Amy came in, Di gave her a repeat of what she'd already said to me. She continued to read us both the riot act.

I was sure the whole dorm could hear every word.

Eventually, she calmed down, or ran out of steam.

She plopped down on Karen's bed and just stared at us for a while.

"What you should have done," she said, quietly, "was call me as soon as you were accused or questioned. Do not, never ever, agree to any kind of interrogation without a parent or guardian present. I am your legal guardian here. This could have gone very bad for you, for both of you. It could have been bad for all of us."

"I'm not happy with how this school of yours handled things either. Your parents, and I, are seriously considering whether or not this is the proper place for you to be."

Amy and I both sat silent while she went on. She talked about maybe suing the school, suing Putnam or putting her in jail, suing Dr. Davis and Dr. Kramer and half the individual students. She talked about pulling us out and sending us to Bryn Mawr, or even back to Riverplace in St. Louis. But as she talked we figured out she wasn't completely serious.

Di just needed to vent.

Finally, she said, very gently, "What do you girls want to do? Do you want to stay here? Do you want to think about it?"

Amy let me answer.

"Aunt Di," I said, "We know you want the best for us. We know you love us."

At that point, Di blinked and started to tear up. But she didn't cry.

"Amy and I worked hard to get here," I continued. "And we didn't get here by being quitters, or by being afraid of hard work, or by running away from problems."

"It really is a good school. A lot of the other students stuck by us. Cleo Smith worked hard to find the proof of our innocence, and the Jins have kept faith with us. We'll be fine here. We want to stay. But we'll do whatever you tell us to do."

We all sat quiet for a long while.

Then Diane stood up and so did we.

She hugged us both very tight.

"Call your parents," She said. "Do it *now*. And keep your damn phones charged up and turned on. Call me first thing in the morning."

The next morning, over breakfast, Amy and I decided to keep our date. Amy was right about keeping it being easier than breaking it.

We called Di and reminded her of our plans. She was much calmer but made us promise to call her throughout the day with updates on how we were doing.

Ricky's sister pulled in around 10 am. She climbed out to give me and Amy a critical once over. She wore her hair in a different style, but cut short like me and without any of those stupid extensions. I liked her right away. We apparently passed her inspection because she had us all pile into the car. It was a little Toyota, and would be cramped.

"Amy," she said, "You ride in the back with the guys. Brenda can ride up front with me."

Apparently my interrogation wasn't finished yet.

Teresa seemed like a nice person. Her questions were polite and friendly, mostly asking about my family and school history. In some ways it was reminiscent of my first interview with Dr. Davis back in July.

She made sure we had her number programmed into all our phones, and turned us loose.

We walked around the mall for a while, it was pretty big. We wound up at the arcade, and it was huge, with games I'd never seen. We had an early lunch first, in the arcade's restaurant and as part of our lunch bought a kind of debit card for the games. It wasn't too expensive. We played various games for nearly two hours. Amy and I had insisted on going Dutch, but the guys didn't think that was right, so we compromised. We paid for our own lunch, but we let the guys buy the movie tickets afterwards.

I don't remember the movie.

And it really wasn't a spectacular date, but it was relaxing and pleasant, a good distraction, and the guys were great company.

Someone, maybe it was Casanova, said that men make love with their penis, but women make love with their ears. A guy who has something intelligent to say, and who knows how to listen to a girl, is certainly very attractive. Both our guys fit that bill perfectly.

After the movie, it was time for dinner, and while there were plenty of restaurants, lunch had been big, and the food court offered plenty of more modest choices, so we did that.

I sat across from Ricky while we ate.

"I like your new glasses," I told him.

"I know you didn't like the old ones. You never said anything."

"I didn't want to hurt your feelings."

"Brenda. I'm a man. Men don't have feelings. You should know that by now."

Teresa picked us up and delivered us back at the Academy before dark.

She pretended not to look when our guys kissed us goodbye. Bobby kissed Amy on the cheek, but Ricky kissed me on the lips.

It wasn't the most romantic date, but I still remember it as one of the very best.

Final exams were the next week.

Every day was a full day. Two exams every morning, followed by two review sessions in the afternoon to prepare us for the next morning's exams.

Wednesday morning we had the math exams, and I was surprised at how easy it seemed. Math had always required me to work hard to do well, but this time it seemed almost easy. The answers just popped into my head as if by magic. At lunch, I felt refreshed, and almost giddy. I remember thinking; *this must be how Amy feels after a math test.*

On Friday, they changed things up since there would be no review sessions. The morning exam was extra-long and dealt with world history, and after a very long lunch break, we had an American history exam. Both of those went well, and I have to give Cleo credit for that too. She had been preparing us for both all year.

Cleo always made history interesting. When we studied with her, she made it seem like we had lived through the actual times ourselves.

54. KANDAKE

We were in my penthouse overlooking the harbor. Azim was fixing me a light dinner before he left for the evening.

"Kandake," he asked me, "was it wise to interfere? To help those girls?"

"No, Azim," I replied, "I'm sure it wasn't. The wise thing would have been to let Brenda and Amy go their own way and let events take their natural course. But I get tired of being nothing but cautious."

He smiled at me. "They are good girls," he said.

I was sitting at the table with the book the girls had given me. Azim saw me with it.

He asked, "Was it because of the book?"

I hesitated. "The book may have been part of it. And I couldn't forget how they pushed me behind them to face the two thug-boys by themselves when we visited Poe's tomb, back in January."

Azim nodded his head at that. He'd thought it was funny that the girls thought I needed their protection, but their quick act had impressed him too.

"Mostly," I continued, "I helped them because I was weak and careless, as you say; even though they were certainly worthy and deserving. When they gave me this book, they reminded me of my love for Eratosthenes. Love is rare. I did not want to see those two have a bad end at such a tender age. Love should be protected whenever possible, even if there is some risk. And truly, there is very little risk to me."

"Was it not dangerous," he asked, "to fabricate that security video, just to clear those two girls?"

"I contracted the faked video out to India. Even as a rush job, it won't be traced back to me. And, the Putnam girl really *was* guilty, I just created the evidence to prove it. My cover is still good. Nobody suspects I am anything other than the teenage orphan girl I appear to be. I hacked the school's security system over a year and a half ago and I've bugged the whole school. So if something happens, I should know about it in plenty of time, just like I knew they had found the laptop Putnam planted."

"Amy and Brenda are both intelligent ladies," Azim commented. "They are young, but smart. And they are curious."

"I know they are. Try not to worry too much, Azim. I promise to be more careful around them next year."

"Forgive me, Kandake. But I do not believe you. I think you will spend *more* time with them next year, not less, and that is a danger. There is a mystery around Amy. And you are a curious woman yourself. You will want to solve that mystery. You may even be tempted to trust her with things best not told. *'There are some secrets that do not permit themselves to be revealed'*."

I just nodded my head. Azim was right. I would need to be very careful.

I lied to Amy. I lied to Brenda. I lied to everyone. But since my whole life was a lie, it was easy.

When I was younger, I was a believer in magic, like everyone else in those days. But as the years passed, I abandoned it in favor of science. Science was provable and demonstrably more powerful. Magic, if there was such thing, was mostly tricks and superstition. Even if there was anything true about real magic, it was weaker than science. Or so I'd come to believe.

I've seen a lot of "magic" over the years, but it's always been explainable. If not by me, than by others. There had been a few incidents, like that time in Madrid, that no one could explain, but a few incidents meant little or nothing. This stuff with Amy, though, seemed different.

Of all the people in the world, I shouldn't be rejecting the idea that something like magic might be something true.

55. COMMENCEMENT
AMY

Commencement was held the last week of May. The big ceremony was held outside, for the seniors, who wore cap and gown. All the other classes were required to attend. This, we were told, was so we could show our support for our graduating classmates, and to give us a glimpse of what to look forward to when it was our turn.

There were separate smaller receptions for each class afterwards, held in the various halls and rooms around campus. There were forty-four of us in the sophomore class and we were put in the small auditorium. My mom and dad and Miz Sally had all flown in for the event. With Aunt Di and Uncle Chuck, we were probably one of the biggest groups. Karen and Xuěyàn both had their parents, Cleo's guardian or guardians were no-shows, but Azim was by her side, as always.

Dr. Davis gave a very short speech. It was short because she had to run to give a similar speech to the freshmen.

"It has been an interesting year for the sophomore class," she said. "But in the end, every one of you has done well, and everyone here will be welcomed back as juniors next year."

"Everyone here..." she'd said, pointedly not mentioning the two who had left school prematurely. I reflected that if it hadn't been those two, it would have been me and Brenda who would have been gone, so the total number present at this little function would have been the same.

"You have accomplished much to be proud of," Dr. Davis continued, "and learned a great deal. Even I have learned a few things." She looked directly at me and Brenda for a moment.

"It has been a privilege to serve you this year in your learning effort. It has been a tough year, and next year will be even tougher, but I have no doubt whatsoever that you are all up to the challenge. And when you graduate as seniors in two years, you will be prepared to succeed anywhere. But for now, you've earned the right to celebrate. Congratulations, ladies. We'll see you in the fall."

We were called up in alphabetical order and handed our little certificates of completion.

To my surprise, Karen was salutatorian of the sophomore class. She won her standing like a stealth missile. She'd just kept working quietly, sure and steady in every subject. I may have gotten higher marks in math most times, but she was beating me in everything else. She didn't want to show her certificate, but when Brenda talked to her proud parents, they spilled the beans and boasted that their daughter's class standing was number two.

"Next year, you beat the Japanese girl," Karen's mom told her.

Tamiko had taken valedictorian honors. She had been even quieter than Karen. We didn't see much of her on campus because apparently she already had an internship of some kind at Mercy Hospital. She didn't get to give a speech because we were just sophomores, so I don't know that being valedictorian of the sophomore class really meant anything.

Xuěyàn placed eighth and seemed depressed about that. I reminded her that it was her first year at the toughest girl's school in a strange country, and her frown lightened just a tiny bit.

Brenda's class rank put her in tenth place, astonishing, given the ordeal she'd been put through. By some miracle, I came in thirteenth, which was even more astonishing.

There were a few refreshments in the room, but we pretty much ignored them. After doing all the introductions with all our families, we said our goodbyes. Many of the girls who had avoided us before went out of their way to introduce us to their families. I could only imagine what stories they would be telling when they got home. We lingered a bit with Cleo and the Jins. Brenda invited Cleo and Azim to dinner with us, but while she thanked Brenda, she declined.

Xuěyàn was heading back to China with her mom to visit her cousins for a month and invited us to join her, in China, but this time it was Brenda and I who had to decline. I could tell Brenda was sorely tempted, but neither of us had passports, and neither my folks nor Miz Sally would allow us to be apart from them during the summer. They had missed us too much. Not that we could have afforded the airfare anyway.

So we all went back to Chuck and Di's house for a nice home-cooked meal. For probably the first time, their big house was crowded. Me and Brenda wound up sleeping on the floor in the living room, reminiscent of childhood sleepovers at each other's homes. The next evening, after a tearful farewell from Aunt Di, we headed back home to St. Louis. It was a night flight and I had a window seat. Below us, the lights of the cities and towns were scattered across the landscape like fallen stars or like hundreds of campfires flickering in the dark.

I look back now with awe at how daring Brenda and I were back then.

Now that I have a home and family of my own, with my own problems and responsibilities, a career and a mortgage and an elderly parent to take care of, I wonder if, faced with a similar test today, I would still be as prepared to sacrifice myself for a friend.

It was all done out of simple friendship, but there really is nothing simple about it.

Every morning when I was little, I would watch my dad shave. Shaving was always the last act of his morning ritual. He would already be fully dressed, with his shoes freshly shined, a towel draped over his shoulders to protect his collar. I would sit on the edge of the bathtub and watch. At first, when I was very little, my legs wouldn't even reach the floor, they would just dangle while I balanced myself on the rim of the tub. We'd talk about what we thought our day was going to be like. He used an old-time straight razor and a shaving mug and brush that had once belonged to his own father. Watching him whip up the lather in the mug is one of my earliest memories.

The first time Brenda stayed over at our place she stood in the doorway, wide-eyed at the sight of the flashing blade, both fascinated and a little bit frightened. Harvey used an electric razor, so this was something new for her.

She asked, "Does it hurt?"

"Only if I make a mistake."

"There are two reasons why men shave," he told us as he applied the lather. "The first reason is that most of the women in our life don't like whiskers. Usually." He smiled before sliding the bright blade across his cheek. It made a soft scraping sound like a playing card dragged against sandpaper. "The other reason is to force us to look in the mirror every day. Men want to be able to see the face of someone they can respect, and not some... jerk. It's a reminder to us to do our best every day. As we go about our daily tasks, we know that if we do anything bad, the next morning we will be looking at the face of someone we do not want to see."

Brenda took all this in with a serious expression on her face, and nodded slowly when he was done.

Women spend at least as much time in front of the mirror, so the lesson should apply to us as much as it should for our men.

But in my experience, few of us take the lesson seriously, either men or women.

I don't know how much influence my dad's little speech had on me and Brenda.

It may be that we have more courage when we are younger because we don't fully understand the consequences of our actions. I really don't know if bravery and sacrifice are honest virtues or merely symptoms of childish folly.

And while I'm sure that trying to take the blame for each other was the right and decent thing, I'm absolutely certain it was not the smart thing.

And yet, despite all my doubts, I still feel proud.

I've made many mistakes in my life, but standing by my friend wasn't one of them.

Friendship, loyalty and honor may very well be delusions, but the feeling of warmth I get in my chest whenever I remember those days endures.

And at night, when I lay my head on my pillow and close my eyes to dream or to reminisce, I always smile.

The End

WITCH MAGIC: EXCERPT

The sequel to False Magic. Coming early 2012:

It wasn't at all chilly, maybe even a little bit warm, but the air seemed damp. I could see fine along the trail and through the trees. The jungle canopy prevented me from seeing the sky clearly, but it looked gray. Of course, at that early hour, it was hard to tell the color of the sky, even though the sun had to be up by now. There was certainly plenty of light.

Amy followed a few steps behind me, watching for snakes. I thought it was probably too early for them to be stirring, but I could have been wrong.

We could hear the occasional cries of howler monkeys. Their call sounded exactly like a rusty saw cutting through a wooden plank. It was nothing like I'd expected.

Our trail led to a little grassy clearing that led uphill. It looked like it might have been a road at one time in the fairly recent past. The forest surrounded us on both sides. Up ahead, at the far edge of the clearing, the trees were thinned out a bit and I could see a structure beyond them.

When we got past the final line of trees, there was a small plaza and we could see the pyramid rising above us.

It was bigger than I expected and the wooden stairs built up the side for the tourists were steep, but the steps looked to be in good shape, so Amy and I traded a glance at each other, then started to climb. The stairs were not continuous. Three times they stopped and we had to resume our climb on a different flight of stairs, and when I pulled myself up onto the top platform, my legs were a little unsteady. The last step was a big one, so I gave Amy a hand and pulled her up.

The view was genuinely spectacular.

As far as we could see, the jungle canopy stretched away. On top of the canopy, and sinking a little into it, was a layer of morning mist that we couldn't see at ground level. To the east, Temple III poked its roof-comb up out of the forest, and a little beyond that, we could see the tops of Temples I and II in the main plaza. The sun was just a hazy yellow blob low on the horizon.

The platform where we were was narrow. There was a small doorway into the temple itself. I always thought it was odd that the Mayans had put those fairly tiny rooms on top of their big pyramids. The sides of Temple IV's pyramid had not been cleared of its overgrowth, and that masked how high it was. I thought that was probably a good thing. If I could see the steep sides and the ground below, my fear of heights might have expressed itself. Amy was fine. She was exploring the small space, trying to see if she could climb higher. I went to the south edge, to see if there was another ladder, but there was a drop-off that made me pull back.

I returned to the main platform in time to see Amy slowly backing out of the temple doorway. From inside it, I heard a low sound like a soft rumble or a heavy purr. Amy stood to the side and held up her hand, signaling me to be still.

I had thought jaguars were not that big, but I was wrong. The Central American jaguar is the third-largest feline in the world according to the travel guide; only the African lion and the tiger are bigger. If that's true, then lions and tigers must be much bigger than I thought too. This jaguar's shoulder was almost level with my waist and even without the tail, he was close to six feet long. It seemed to take forever for him to emerge from the doorway. His tail twitched when he was entirely out. His length matched the width of the platform. There was no place for any of the three of us to go.

He turned in my direction and I stepped back with my right foot. I could go no farther unless I wanted to drop two hundred feet to the forest floor. He made a sound like a cough.

Amy was close enough to touch him. She didn't do that, but she made a shushing sound. His head whipped back to her. Maybe, I thought, if we both attacked with our walking sticks, he wouldn't expect that and would exercise the better part of valor and go back inside. I knew better than to try running down the steps. The jaguar could take those steps faster than we could, and running would only trigger his pursuit reflex. Amy made the shushing sound again and he lowered his head. His posture wasn't aggressive though. He didn't sink down on his haunches like a cat does before it jumps a mouse. He seemed to relax. He swung back to look at me. We stared at each other for what seemed like a very long time, then with a quick glance at Amy again, he glided down the stairs and disappeared without making a single sound.

Amy and I looked at each other.

"Did you do that?" I asked.

"I don't know. Maybe?"

"So, what? He was sleeping in the temple?"

"Yeah, we woke him up. He heard us climbing the stairs, but he didn't stir until I walked in on him. He wasn't hungry, he just wanted to be left alone."

"So," I asked, "you can talk to the animals now?"

STORY NOTES

The Plan: Amy and Brenda have a secret plan. It is secret (for now).

Ch.2: Cleo Candace (Candy) Smith (Kandake):

Cleo is reading the "Malleus Maleficarum" in the beginning of this story. The Malleus Maleficarum was a book written in the 1400's dedicated to the proposition that witchcraft was real, and that witches were usually women because women are hypersexual and naturally prone to evil and to having sex with Satan. It was used as a handbook to persecute witches. The author of this book was Heinrich Kramer.

Azim (an Arabic name meaning "protector") calls Cleo "Kandake", but as Azim uses the term, it is nothing more than a title of respect.

However, Cleo *is* older than she claims to be, and she has a secret of her own.

The Accusers:

The Salem Witch trials of 1692 featured the following individuals as accusers of the innocent:

Betty Parris, age 7, was one of the first accusers, along with her cousin, Abigail Williams.

Abigail Williams, age 14, was another one of the first accusers. First symptom was an apparent epileptic fit with Betty Parris.

Ann Putnam, age 12, was a very active accuser. She later asked publicly for forgiveness on August 25, 1706, the only one to do so.

Mary Warren, was both an accuser and an accused.

Any resemblance between the names of these historical figures and the names of the following characters in the novel is purely coincidental:

Mary Putnam - ringleader of the Putnam posse.

Abigail Parris - Right-hand co-conspirator of Mary Putnam.

Betty Williams - A naive follower of Abby Parris.

Ann Warren - Originally best friend of Mary Putnam, she is replaced by Abby Parris as Mary's best friend.

Ch.15: Women's Lacrosse:

Based on the traditional Native American sport, modern women's lacrosse was first played in 1890 at the St. Leonard's School in Scotland. It was re-introduced from there back to the United States at Bryn Mawr School in Baltimore in 1926 by Rosabelle Sinclair. The rules are different from the men's version, and the play is often faster. Women's lacrosse is sometimes called "the fastest sport on two feet" by its fans. The lacrosse stick is sometimes called simply, the "Crosse."

Ch.22: Harvey = Ralph Ellison:
Brenda's dad dresses up as a rabbit for Halloween, but tells Amy he is not the Easter Bunny, he is Ralph Ellison.

Explanation of this joke (which, in the book, only Harvey appreciates) goes like this:

Elwood P. Doud was a character in the movie "Harvey". Played by Jimmy Stewart, he was a grown man with a 6' 3.5" invisible rabbit named "Harvey" as his best friend. Jimmy Stewart won a Best Actor Oscar Nomination for his performance. The story won a Pulitzer Prize for Drama for the stage version.

Ralph Ellison was the African-American author, best known for his book entitled, "The Invisible Man." Winner of the National Book Award in 1953.

So: Harvey -> Invisible Rabbit -> Invisible Man -> Ralph Ellison.

Ch. 19: While watching the public beheading of a criminal, the Roman Emperor Caligula is said to have remarked: "Would that the Roman people had but one neck!" (Utinam populus Romanus unam cervicem haberet!). This is attributed to Caligula by Suetonius, Seneca and Cassius, but a few other writers ascribe this remark to Nero.

Ch. 21: The Princess Bride: When Inigo Montoya kills Count Rugen his last words to the Count are: "I want my father back you son of a bitch." - This line resonates strongly with Brenda.

Ch. 27: "...cut off the head of a live goose or duck, then re-attach the head and restore it.":
Cleo is making a reference to a story reported in the Westcar Papyrus where the Egyptian Magician Djedi performs this trick for the Pharaoh Khufu, who reigned 2589-2566 BC.

After the first visit to Wilson's, Cleo takes the girls to a French restaurant in the basement of the Latham Hotel in Georgetown. The restaurant is the Citronelle, considered by many to be one of the finest in the world.

Ch. 30: Mrs. Jin: Chinese women always keep their maiden name, while children take their father's surname. So, Xuěyàn's mom would have a different last name than her daughter. Brenda knows this, but Amy doesn't, hence Amy's minor "Mrs. Jin" mistake.

In old China, the reasoning for women keeping their maiden name was two-fold: As a mere woman, she would be unworthy to bear the illustrious name of her husband's family. That would have been an insult to his ancestors. Besides, changing her own name would have been an insult to *her* own ancestors. While many old customs remain, the position of women in modern China has radically improved.

Ch. 37: Resolution: "Thanks, Amy. You're number one with me, too."

"Dandy" Don Meredith (1938-2010), former Quarterback for the Dallas Cowboys and commentator for Monday Night Football alongside Howard Cosell and Frank Gifford. During one game, the camera focused on a fan who looked directly into the camera and extended his middle finger. The camera did not move away, and for once, Cosell was speechless. But without missing a beat, Meredith said, "He thinks they [his team] are number one in the nation."

ABOUT THE AUTHOR

Born a Scorpio, but now a Sagittarius, the author is skeptical of, but fascinated by, the paranormal.

I live on Earth, but "e pur si mouve", so I never know where I am!

I despise education, but love learning. I read a book once.

I have touched an elephant, ridden a camel, eaten a rat, been held hostage in the jungles of Guatemala and I may have heard the eastern colossus of Memnon sing. The world is too big for me to see it all, and that makes me sad.

I have known true love.

I am the proud owner of a beautiful Smith-Corona typewriter on which not a single work of fiction has been typed. I now pound away on a clickity-clackity-sounding modern computer keyboard, but sorely miss the soft music of mechanical hammers striking the paper-covered platen.

As a writer of fiction, I am a professional liar, but everything I say is true.

- J M Brown

Connect with Me Online:
Twitter: http://twitter.com/@falsemagic2k
Email: jmb@falsemagic.com
graMix Publishing: http://www.gramix.com
False Magic Website: http://www.FalseMagic.com

www.ingramcontent.com/pod-product-compliance
Lightning Source LLC
Chambersburg PA
CBHW050926120626
46552CB00001B/72